# A WOMAN'S PLACE

Printed in Australia
Cover design by Shawline Publishing Group Pty Ltd
Images in this book are copyright approved for Shawline Publishing Group Pty Ltd
Illustrations within this book are copyright approved for Shawline Publishing Group Pty Ltd

First Printing: March 2023
Shawline Publishing Group Pty Ltd
www.shawlinepublishing.com.au

Paperback ISBN 978-1-9228-5028-7
eBook ISBN 978-1-9228-5035-5

Distributed by Shawline Distribution and Lightningsource Global

 A catalogue record for this
work is available from the
National Library of Australia

More great Shawline titles can be found here:

New titles also available through Books@Home Pty Ltd.
Subscribe today - www.booksathome.com.au

# A WOMAN'S PLACE

## LAINIE JONES

*For the wonderful men in my life – this book is not about you.*

# AUTHOR'S NOTE

While actual historical events are referred to throughout this novel, *A Woman's Place* is a work of fiction. Barragunyah is a fictional place (and a fictional earth-spirit) with a made-up name. You will not find the towns of Lurradallan or Darrobine on any map of New South Wales.

# PROLOGUE

Moonlight followed her uneasily, silvering her naked skin and scattering diamonds on the python spiralling around her torso. She stepped into the clearing and the chattering of night-things fell silent as she began to dance, her broad feet making patterns in the moist grass. The trees sighed, watching and waiting until she left the moonlight and joined them in the shadows they held beneath their limbs.

Pain scored her flesh. Sorrow swam in her eyes.

And her anger roared through the night.

*I sang to show them the way. I eased their hunger with the fruits of my body and gave them riches beyond their dreams, but it was not enough.*

*It was never enough.*

*They swept over me like a river in flood, stealing and murdering, raping and destroying, changing my stories to fit their own, wrapping their dirty secrets in lies and laughter, and songs from far off lands.*

*Their hard-footed creatures cut deep my skin, marking me as property of the pale ones, though fire and flood, drought and mud, told them countless times that I belong to none.*

*They crossed boundaries they were too blind to see. They ignored those they exiled and starved. They spared not a thought for the anguish they left behind.*

*I gave them my body, but they demanded my soul.*

*No more.*

*I shall reclaim what is mine and their children, and their children's children, will reap the bitter harvest.*

# JULIA

A niggling unease hits me the minute my brother drives off in our hire car, a prickle of anxiety that makes no sense because I'm actually glad he's leaving. 'Of course I won't need the car,' I'd told him. 'You'll be back before I notice you're gone.' But as I watch the red Jeep vanish in a cloud of dust, reality hits home; I am now alone at the back end of nowhere, without transport or electricity.

We'd come to Barragunyah to scatter our grandmother's ashes on the earth she loved, and to sort through her things before putting the property on the market. We'd allowed ourselves only a week and I had hoped to use this rare time together to talk about Gran, to reflect on her life and what she meant to us. But Peter has no patience for sentimentality; for him it's all about the money.

It was money that triggered his sudden departure. One phone call from his business partner about some unexpected financial crisis and he was packing his bag. It was if he'd been looking for an excuse to leave, and I wondered if Barragunyah had been up to her old tricks again. I said nothing, of course; some questions are best avoided.

Following him outside as he headed for the car, I suggested he phone the airport first, to check if a pilot was available. He shot me a scathing look, so I let it pass. He might be used to dashing around the country in chartered planes, but if he intended to call from the car, he'd clearly forgotten about all the random black spots around here. His problem, though, not mine.

Peter and I have never really got along. Because he was faster, stronger, and smarter than me when he was nine and I was three, he thinks his superiority is set in stone. In his eyes, my PhD in History runs a poor second to his Bachelor of Commerce degree; after all, commerce deals with the institutions that run the planet. History is just old news.

Like Gran's life.

We'd set aside our differences while we made the funeral arrangements, but our tenuous cordiality came undone when the will was read. Gran had left Barragunyah to me and her financial investments to Peter — which was fine by both of us until the solicitor explained that nursing costs and falling interest rates had whittled away most of her money. Unsurprisingly, Peter demanded a half-share of the property. I knew why Gran wanted Barragunyah to be mine, but it was hard to explain without sounding crazy, so after a half-hearted protest I agreed to the split. To be honest, at the back of my mind was the hope that sharing might offload some of the guilt I felt about selling a property that's been in the family for five generations.

But I should have known Peter's involvement meant Peter's agenda—which was to junk everything and get rid of the place as soon as possible. We'd sniped at each other over one thing or another from the moment we arrived at Barragunyah. It had not been fun.

But now he's gone and I'm blissfully alone. *Totally alone,* a voice in my head whispers, sending a shiver through my bones. I rub my arms, tell myself I'm being ridiculous, and go inside to put the kettle on. While I wait for it to boil, I give Peter's long to-do list a glance before tossing it in the wastebasket beside the stove. I have my own ideas about what to *prioritise,* but all I want right now is to sit on the veranda and enjoy the late afternoon peace, as Gran and

I had done so often in happier days.

I sit on the steps with the old rose-patterned china teapot beside me, sipping from Gran's favourite bone china cup until the sun vanishes behind the distant hills and a damp, swirling mist creeps in. When the chill gets the better of me, I go inside to light the fire. Without Peter around, the silence is so deep I can hear the hiss of the flames and the sharp, popping sounds of the wood as it catches. In the distance, the lugubrious howl of a dingo reminds me of all the empty space between Barragunyah and its nearest neighbour and I feel a rush of gratitude for the fire, not only for its warmth against the chill that seeps beneath the doors and through cracks in the old weatherboards, but for its cheerful light.

The electricity was disconnected a few years ago, so the fire and candles are all the light I have. I watch the shadows dance among the cobwebs on the high ceilings and try to imagine what the house was like when my ancestors lived here. Did the rooms buzz with visitors, ring with the laughter of children? My memory gropes for Gran's stories about those early days and I realise that most of her tales were of farming — of the Black Angus cattle she loved, of work dogs and horses and fencing and planting, as if the house itself was an insubstantial thing superimposed upon the land.

It was a large property back then. Over the years, for one reason or another, parcels of land were sold to neighbouring farms; and while barely a hundred acres now, the homestead is still quite isolated. Apart from the property agent who checks on things once a year, Peter and I were probably the first to drive down the corrugated, potholed track in years.

When we called in to see the agent after collecting our hire car at Lurradallan Airport, he'd warned us Barragunyah was run down. Even so, I was totally unprepared for the air of abandonment and melancholy that overlay everything — the fences with rotting posts and rusted barbed wire, the brown and barren paddocks, the wooded gullies, where I used to ride my pony, choked with weeds and pocked with rabbit holes. The house, once a grand country homestead, brought me to tears when I saw its weatherboards bare of paint, and unsightly patches of rust on the iron roof. Even the lovingly tended garden I remembered was an overgrown wilderness. I was devastated to see the place so neglected. Peter was just angry Gran hadn't sold sooner, when it would have fetched a better price.

As if anything to do with Barragunyah could be that simple.

It was the agent who'd reminded us there was no electricity. He also told us the nights had been extremely cold and suggested we buy heavy-duty sleeping bags when we picked up supplies in Darrobine. In the end, we bought more than we'd intended; the sleeping bags, a couple of torches with long-life batteries, an impressive range of food that didn't need refrigerating, and a ridiculous number of candles.

The candles were Peter's idea. He'd only stayed at Barragunyah a few times as a kid, but said he still remembered how the absolute darkness of the countryside used to spook him. I hid a smile, wondering if it was the dark that had unnerved him or something else.

Barragunyah can be mean if she doesn't like you.

The house has an old Aga, a wood-fired combustion stove, but we didn't know if there'd be any firewood, so we also bought a small portable cooker and some cans of gas. As it turned out, the woodshed was well-stocked and the Aga had sprung to life with little persuasion, cooking our meals, warming the house, and heating the water as effortlessly as it had done for years. The thing about wood-burning stoves, though, is that you have to remember to feed them — and I haven't. While I've been sitting on the veranda steps thinking about Gran, I've let the fire go out.

I should fetch more wood from the shed, but I can't be bothered. There'll be enough hot water for a shower, and a can of chicken soup heated on the gas ring will do for dinner. While the soup is warming in a saucepan, I grab a torch and wander down the veranda to the storeroom where an old tin trunk had caught my eye the previous day.

When I open the door, memories I'd bottled-up while Peter was here leap at me from every corner. It's full of junk now, but this little room neatly tacked on to the main house was once my schoolroom. The light from my torch falls on the scarred wood of my old desk and I run my fingers over it, leaving trails in the dust and disturbing a daddy longlegs. In times gone by, my mother and grandmother had sat at the same desk, no doubt as eager as I was to be finished with lessons and out in the sunshine. Now the room is cold, and bleak with neglect, and my memories seem unreliable and off-kilter. Ignoring the despondency creeping into my thoughts, I focus on the tin trunk I came for.

It's larger than I thought — far too heavy to carry — so I poke around until I come across some hessian sacks. With a bit of manoeuvring, I get one sack under the trunk, drag it along the veranda, through the French doors, and into the living room. Now I'm ready for a quiet evening sifting through Gran's memorabilia and wallowing in nostalgia.

I set my empty soup bowl on the floor beside me and begin unpacking the trunk. I haven't got far when a sudden drop in temperature reminds me that while the open fire looks cosy, it doesn't warm the house like the Aga. Torn between satisfying my curiosity while I slowly freeze to death, or facing the bitter night outside to fetch more wood, I choose a third, easier option. Leaving everything on the floor, I have a quick shower and go to bed.

This cold weather doesn't fit my memories of Barragunyah.

When I think about my childhood here it's always summer, the grass golden-brown and crunchy underfoot, the heat shimmering above the paddocks like a mirage, and everything moving slowly as if through thick honey. I remember the nights especially, alive with the sounds of frogs and insects, a black velvet sky dusted with stars.

Now, snuggling into the fleece lining of my sleeping bag on the bed that was mine all those years ago, I gaze through the window. There is not a star to be seen.

I wake just after dawn to the sound of rain thundering on the iron roof. In the faint light, I can see water dripping from the stained ceiling and the sheen of a puddle spreading across the floorboards. I drag myself reluctantly from the warmth of the sleeping bag and go searching for a mop and something to catch the drips.

The fierceness of the downpour surprises me. Summer storms were common when I lived here, but weren't the winters usually dry? A childhood memory stirs and I see myself on my pony beside Gran, both of us in oilskins, noses red with cold, faces glistening from the icy rain as we watch the rising creek forewarning a winter flood. Anything out of the ordinary was exciting to me then, but now the prospect of being flooded in makes me uneasy. Which is absurd. It's only a storm.

I'm putting a bucket under the drips in the bedroom when I remember the things I'd left on the floor last night. I rush to the living room, fearing the worst, but thankfully all the other rooms are leak-free except for a tiny stream cascading down the brick wall behind the Aga in the kitchen. The overflow seems to escape through gaps in the stone floor of the hearth, so I leave well alone and return to the bedroom to get dressed.

I need a hot drink after my efforts and the little gas cooker does its magic again, saving me a trip to the woodshed in the pouring rain. I make a pot of tea and take a mug of the steaming brew to the window seat. Tossing the dusty cushions onto the floor, I settle on the smooth, silky-oak boards and rest my eyes on the watery world outside.

I've always loved rainy days and I sit there, daydreaming, enjoying the freedom of setting my own agenda, until my stomach growls, demanding breakfast. As I empty a can of baked beans into a saucepan and set it on the gas ring, I tell myself I can't keep doing this – I'll have to fetch wood for the Aga the minute the rain stops. Apart from wasting gas, the last thing I want is to run out of hot water for the shower.

After I've washed my plate and cup, I turn my attention to the tin trunk I'd been unpacking last night. It's filled with relics – photo albums going back years, letters, old birthday cards, some childish drawings, Christmas decorations I remember making myself from gumnuts and she-oak cones. There's even a bundle of baby clothes carefully wrapped in tissue paper. I fondle the soft pink wool of a tiny matinee jacket, wondering if Gran had knitted it for my mother.

Tears sting my eyes as I try to imagine Mum as a baby. She should be here with me now, offering motherly direction, some woman-to-woman advice about my future while we amble through the past. But she's never been around when I need her. Picking through the trunk, I pull out a likely photo album and flip through its pages. And there she is, staring out at me with that challenging expression I'd found so bewildering as a child.

My mother, Annie the rebel.

Beneath the photo is a date, December 1961, which makes her eighteen. I stare at the image, wondering, not for the first time, how we could be so different. I'd inherited her height and slim build, but my eyes were hazel instead of green, my curly hair an ordinary dark brown. Annie's thick coppery hair had gone to Peter, along with her confrontational temperament and stubborn sense of righteousness.

I was the difficult child, the sulky one, the kid who'd rather hide in a corner with a book than talk to people. At least, that's how Mum saw me. As a child, I sensed her disappointment in me, but it took me years to work out how I'd failed her. I close the album, glad that Peter isn't around to see my tears.

Reaching deeper into the trunk, I fish out an old cloth-covered notebook, a shabby brownish thing that might once have been red. When I open it and see the name on the inside page, my historian's heart skips a beat: Alice Larson, my great-great-grandmother, the first woman to live at Barragunyah. I flick through the yellowed pages and realise it's a diary of her early years here.

I've unearthed a pot of gold.

# ALICE



*September 13, 1889. It is hard to believe this beautiful house is my new home. Even harder to grasp is that I have three native servants to help me manage it. In view of my previous situation, I would find this comical if the dark women were not so daunting. They seldom speak, and their eyes will not meet mine, but I feel them watching me, judging me against some standard of their own. I sense they find me wanting.*

Alice peered through the open kitchen door to where the older woman – Bessie – was chopping mutton for the stew. Not for the first time, Alice wondered what her native name was, although it hardly mattered as John would never allow her to speak it. Bessie, Rosie, Mary, her husband had said when he presented them to her, and that was that. Young Rosie was scrubbing the floor in the parlour, but the third, Mary, a tall, sinuous creature with strange pale eyes that made Alice's skin prickle, could be anywhere. She seemed to come and go as she pleased, a freedom Alice had not been permitted when she was in service.

Now, as John kept reminding her, she was no longer a servant but the lady of a substantial house, her only tasks to keep her own servants in line and please her husband. Having dreamed of such a life since she was a child, Alice should have been the happiest woman in New South Wales. Why, then, was she still riddled with discontent?

Born in the dank Midlands of England, Alice watched the daily struggles of her mother and dared to imagine a different life for herself. At the parish school, her enthusiasm for learning nourished her dreams for a few happy years, before ending abruptly at age nine when she was sent to work in the mill with her mother and sisters.

Ten hours a day, six days a week, for two back-breaking years, Alice crawled beneath the looms scavenging for loose cotton, fearing at any moment she'd be crushed in the machinery like other child workers before her. At eleven she progressed to the looms, enduring three more years amid the thump and clatter of shuttles and treadles before she decided she'd had enough. There had to be more to life than slaving in the mill until she married.

There were ructions in the family when she quit, but she'd expected that. 'I'll get another job and you'll still get my wages,' she said to placate her mother. 'But I'll not put up with that noise and stink another day.'

Her sisters laughed when her new job as a lowly scullery maid saw her working fourteen-hour days. Alice shrugged off their scorn; her new position had prospects that mill work didn't, and she was determined to be noticed.

By the time she was eighteen, Alice was parlourmaid in a grand London house and well on her way to becoming a lady's maid. But although her life had changed for the better, a restlessness she didn't have words to explain gnawed like a rat in the cellar of her mind. As a child, she'd pictured herself becoming a lady, but London soon cured her of that foolishness; either you were born to it or you weren't. Yet something, perhaps the mulishness of which her mother accused her, told her she could do better than serving the lucky few who *were* born to it. All she had to do, she thought, was be ready when that something better turned up.

So Alice eavesdropped shamelessly on her employers' conversations, absorbing new ideas, latching onto new words, listening carefully to their pronunciation. In the silence of her thoughts she practised what she heard, imagining her broad Midlands burr taking on an upper-class tone but not daring to speak that way aloud for fear the other maids would laugh. Long after they were snoring, she burned her pilfered candles late into the night, reading books she covertly borrowed from the master's library, noting ideas that were new to her, copying interesting passages into cheap exercise books. Learning was the key to everything, she thought. Finding a door the key would open was another kettle of fish altogether.

Alice was serving the soup when she overheard the conversation that would change her life.

'A reckless idea, Freddie,' the master was saying. 'What good can come of it?'

'Come now, James, look what the antipodes did for cousin Henry,' Frederick Enright replied. 'You yourself said he was a dreamer who'd not amount to anything, but in just ten years, he's back home with a sizable fortune.'

'Henry had no wife to consider. You are proposing to take my sister to the far ends of the earth, and you want my blessing?' Alice's master shook his head. 'And quite frankly, Freddie, I cannot see you as a miner.'

'I have no intention of taking Jane to the goldfields, James.' Enright dabbed a linen napkin to his mouth. 'It's wool that interests me. In the early years of the colony, a chap named Macarthur did very well out of Spanish Merinos – I plan to do the same.'

'Sheep, eh? You will need land...'

'Indeed. And as Crown land in New South Wales is only twenty shillings an acre, I can afford to purchase a large holding.'

'Large holding or not, you are expecting a lot from Jane,' Alice's mistress said. 'I would not care to go to that wild place.'

Jane Enright nodded. 'Nor will our servants. They have refused outright to come with us.' She pursed her lips and glanced at her husband. 'But Freddie knows I'll not leave until I find suitable replacements.'

Alice, on her way to fetch the second course, paused at the doorway.

Enright sighed. 'Damned if I know why they stopped transportation; a decade ago we'd have had our pick of convicts.'

'Are you waiting for something, Alice?' Her mistress stared at her coldly.

'No, ma'am.' Alice bobbed a curtsey and hurried through the door. Leaving it slightly ajar, she paused on the other side, straining her ears.

Enright's deep voice sounded weary. 'Still, as I keep telling Jane, there's bound to be trained darkies available.'

'And I'll say it again, Frederick, I'll not deal with savages.' Alice could picture Mrs Enright's lip curling. 'At least, not without good English servants to keep them in line.'

Alice heard a murmur of agreement, then the mistress said, 'You could threaten to dismiss your servants without a character; they'll step up.'

'Tried threats, tried promises,' Enright said. 'Cowards won't set foot on a ship.'

Mrs Enright's voice was firm. 'Nevertheless, Frederick, I will not go without a maid and a cook at the very least.'

Below stairs, the kitchen was in the usual hubbub as they prepared to serve the next course, but Alice barely noticed. Wild thoughts buzzed in her head like flies around a midden as she attended to her duties. A place where dreamers prospered, where lives changed. And Mrs Enright needed servants. It was as if that hidden door had opened with no effort on her part.

Alice sat on a high-backed wicker chair in the shade of the veranda, thinking about how much her life had changed. It was hard enough to believe she had travelled over thirteen thousand miles to the far side of the world, let alone that she was now mistress of a large house with servants of her own.

Although not as grand as the London mansion of her former employers, her new house was beautiful in a way that suited the sprawling countryside she now called home. She loved the wide shady verandas that protected it from the hot sun, the spacious rooms with their polished wooden floors and ornate ceilings, the French doors that opened onto the verandas, the twin window seats in the parlour where she often whiled away the hours with a book. Yet for all its elegance, the large house, with its six bedrooms waiting to be filled with John's sons, sometimes seemed more of a burden than a blessing. As for the land, that was too huge to comprehend. Ten thousand acres, John boasted, but the number meant less to her than the disturbing fact that there was not another house in sight.

When John first told her about his property, he said he had named it Oakdale, after a farm in Surrey where he'd worked as a child. Then suddenly and inexplicably, he had changed it. Alice frowned, remembering her blunder the night he announced the new name.

John had been at the cabinet, his back to her as he poured his pre-dinner whiskey. 'I've renamed the place,' he said without preamble. 'It's to be called Barragunyah now.'

'Barragunyah.' The word rolled pleasingly off Alice's tongue.

'I like it, John. It suits this land much better than Oakdale. What does it mean?'

'Means nothing. It's just a name.'

She had failed to notice his defensive tone. 'But it's a native word, isn't it? What do they say it means?'

'Why would I give a tinker's curse what the blasted natives say?'

John promptly dropped the subject, leaving Alice disconcerted. She knew now that he loathed the native gibberish, but at the time, still trying to find her way around John's moods, she'd been baffled. Yet since that night, with an uneasy certainty she could not have explained, Alice had come to believe John had no say in the name at all. Some inner sense told her Barragunyah was an ancient word, rooted in the land and steeped in time, an unchangeable word that was much more than a name or a place. She kept this fancy to herself.

Alice's thoughts drifted to her early days in this strange, topsy-turvy country. She had hated it at first, hated the oppressive heat, the upended seasons, the dull colours of the land, the brazen blue of a sky so vast it frightened her to look at it. It hadn't helped that Jane Enright, secure in the knowledge Alice had nowhere else to go, treated her more like a slave than a servant. Alice's only pleasure in the years she worked for the Enrights had been those few precious hours on Sunday afternoons with Billy, the old native stockman who taught her to ride.

As she'd grown more sure of herself on the quiet pony he had chosen for her, Billy taught her about the terrain as they rode, showing her where to look for water in country as brown and dry as an autumn leaf, pointing out rock-falls that indicated instability and dry river-beds that would become roaring torrents after rain, teaching her how to tell good, productive earth from that which was useless for farming. Slowly but surely, she lost her fear of the new land and began to love it.

Those pleasant and instructive afternoons had ended the day the

Enrights arrived home early from the social gathering they attended after church. Jane Enright had nearly had a seizure when she saw Alice sitting astride the horse with her skirts askew, cantering up the dusty track to the yards. Recalling the look on her face, Alice chuckled, although the aftermath had not been funny. Forbidden to ride, or to speak to Billy, she was forced to spend her Sundays with the Enrights, a further curtailment of freedom she found hard to bear.

She had been in the colony four years by then and was no longer sure what she'd hoped for when she left England. Out here, in the back of beyond at the bottom of the world, it seemed the only paths open to her were no different from those she had left behind – marry or remain in service for the rest of her life. The latter prospect was disheartening, the former increasingly unlikely once she turned twenty-five. Although her dark hair had lost none of its lustre and her waist remained slim, she knew quite well that her marriage prospects grew dimmer with each passing year.

Alice was serving tea and fruit cake in the church hall the first time she saw John Larson. It was impossible not to notice the flurry of excitement that rippled through the gathering when he arrived, the whispered speculations about his age, wealth, and marriageability. Alice had quickly lost interest in the gossip – whatever his age, if he was wealthy, some eager mother looking to marry off her daughter would soon commandeer him.

A month later, she was again setting out the afternoon tea when he sauntered over to the table. 'Pretty lass like you can do better than waiting on that lot,' he said, jerking his chin towards the chattering women. His moustache twitched as he smiled at her.

Alice smiled back. How could she help it? He was tall and handsome, with a neat beard and thick brown hair. Only the lines around his eyes and a slight paunch beneath his waistcoat showed he was past his youth.

'And how might I do better, sir?' It was a frivolous question, a social nicety of the kind she often heard but never had the chance to practice.

'Marry me and you'll not skivvy for any of 'em again.'

Alice gaped at him, speechless at his audacity. He was joking, of course, but that was no excuse. Smiling stiffly, she handed him a cup of tea.

He put it down. 'I'm not teasing you, lass.' He took her hand. 'Come with me.'

She should have refused. And she might have if she hadn't noticed Jane Enright glaring at her from across the room. A smidgen of her old defiance awakened, and she allowed him to lead her outside to the scruffy patch of grass the church ladies called a lawn. A large native fig tree stood in the centre of the fenced enclosure, throwing deep shadows in the afternoon sun. He drew her beneath its spreading branches.

'Alice, you know my name, and I've made it my business to know yours, so I'll dispense with the formalities. I'm forty-eight years old, and I've made my pile. All I need now is a wife.'

Sure he was mocking her, Alice lifted her chin. 'I believe the Enright's eldest daughter is considering prospects.'

He snorted contemptuously. 'I've no interest in the gentry and their offspring. Unlike Enright, I earned my fortune and I want a woman with a background like my own. A woman who will give me sturdy sons, not spineless milksops.'

Perhaps she should have walked away right then, Alice thought later. Instead, she had listened, half-dazzled, as John's story unfolded like a bolt of bright cloth.

Born in Surrey in 1840, he had toiled alongside his tenant-farmer father from the age of eight. At seventeen, seeing no future in slaving for others, he worked his passage to Australia and headed for the goldfields. Unlike many who couldn't adapt to the tough conditions, John thrived. By the time he was thirty, hard work and good luck had made him a wealthy man. With his fortune settled, he ventured north to see what else the country offered.

'I had nought particular in mind,' he told Alice. 'But when I saw sugarcane plantations springing up all along the Queensland coast, I knew I'd found another goldmine.'

'So you bought a plantation?' Intrigued by a story so different to her own, Alice smiled encouragingly.

'I did not. I went into shipping.' He laughed and held up a hand, forestalling her questions. 'You see, it was clear to me that the most successful growers used Kanakas…' His moustache twitched at her puzzled expression. 'South Sea Islanders, lassie. Big lads, who'll work twice as hard as a white man for half the pay – so I hired ships and imported 'em. I'd brought in thousands before the missionaries started bangin' on about blackbirding and slavery. When I saw the way things were heading, I got out of the game and came south again.'

He spread his hands and smiled. 'And here I am. I've ten thousand acres stocked with cattle and sheep. I've hired builders – real builders, not the bush carpenters they use around here – to build me a grand house, and I've ordered quality furnishings from Sydney Town. So, you see my dear, I speak the truth – all I need is a wife to share my good fortune.'

Alice walked to the veranda's edge and leaned on the railing, staring out across the wide, empty land, her eyes resting on the faint emerald tints that overlay winter's dun with a promise of spring.

Once John had convinced her he was sincere, his bluntness had seemed merely honest. And didn't his proposal fit her dreams? To be mistress of her own home, to be free to plan her own life, to share her ideas with a man who had similar aspirations. Wasn't that what she had always wanted?

Their marriage in the little church was attended only by the Enrights, with Alice's former mistress struggling to conceal her disapproval and resentment. Afterwards, they'd set off in a well-sprung cart for John's property and its newly completed house. For most of the long trip, Alice had prattled about her dreams and how she looked forward to helping create something worthwhile for their future.

She frowned, knowing now how her words must have blown past him with less impact than the breeze stirring the dust in the tracks of their buggy. John had no interest in her dreams at all. Her duty was to fulfil his dreams by providing him with healthy sons.

Alice ran a finger inside the high lace collar of her white blouse. Not for the first time, she wished that clothing for the lady she was now supposed to be was not so uncomfortable. In this heat, she would feel more at ease in a servant's simple loose frock and pinafore than in her long sweeping skirt with its abundance of petticoats and tightly corseted waist. But John insisted she dress stylishly to reflect his status in the community and gave her a generous allowance to do so. That she rarely saw anyone but him seemed to have escaped his notice.

*January 1, 1890. John and I have been married fifteen months and I know little more about him than what he told me when he introduced himself at the hall. He is often away, but never tells me where he is going or when he will be back. When he is here, the only thing on his mind is to produce an heir. So, today being not only the first day of the New Year, but of a new decade, I will stop deceiving myself and face facts: I have all I dreamed of as a child and more — yet in truth, I am no different from my mother and grandmother and all women before me. My body is for breeding, my purpose, to serve my husband.*

# JULIA

I mark my place in Alice's journal and wander out to the veranda to stretch my legs. Rubbing my arms against the chill, I stare through the rain at the drenched landscape and try to imagine myself in her place all those years ago. How isolated she must have felt, constrained not only by distance but by the restrictions placed on all women back then. And judging by what she'd written in her journal, her husband's attitude didn't make things any easier. Which was pretty typical of men in those days.

That last thought pulls me up. *Those days?* Who am I kidding? My miserable forays into romance proved men these days weren't much different.

Okay, I'm being unfair. It's true the only two men with whom I've been seriously involved both expected me to rearrange my life and career to suit them, but that's probably because I play down my own ambitions. At least, unlike great-great-grandfather John, neither of my lovers were keen on starting a dynasty.

Quite the opposite.

My hand drifts instinctively to my stomach as I think about Alice's shattered dreams and sigh for my own. I'm glad Peter hasn't guessed my secret. The last thing I need is my brother interfering with my unborn child's future. Because he would. When I think about it, brother Peter, ancestor John, and ex-lover Stuart have a lot in common. And there it is. Stuart's name has slipped past my guard and all the angst I'd suppressed comes rushing back.

A longing for Gran, with her comforting hugs and hard-earned wisdom, engulfs me. What would she say? I wonder. What advice would she give me? As if in answer, I can almost hear her voice whispering through the rain… *Wait. Think things through…*

Sudden tears sting my eyes when I realise her final act on earth ensured I did just that. I'd put off telling Stuart I was pregnant until after the funeral, then prevaricated again when I came to Barragunyah without telling him. As for thinking things through – the longer I delay, the more certain I am that I don't want him involved in raising my child.

During the drive from Darrobine, as Peter and I sank into an awkward silence, my thoughts had turned to how I would manage this unexpected change in my life. If I gave up teaching at the university, could I survive on sessional work? I'd earn less, but working online from home would make things easier. On the other hand, I could keep my position and put the baby in day-care, but having been brought up by a mother who was never around when I needed her, that's not a pattern I want to repeat.

But keeping Stuart out of the picture is another issue altogether. I'm not sure I have the right to do that. Am I being selfish? Or stupid? Sometimes I feel so conflicted it's as if my brain is splitting. Maybe it's grief. Or hormones. Whatever the reason, it's messing with my head. I want to think about Alice, not me. About the past, not the future.

Like most women of that era, marriage meant Alice had even less control over her life than before. I want to know if her story changed after her child was born. Did John reward her for being a dutiful wife and giving him an heir?

The rain continues to pelt down, a cold wind driving it under the eaves of the veranda. I haven't forgotten that I need to stock up on firewood, but I'll get drenched if I go now. Reason enough to go back inside and learn more about my great-great-grandmother.

# ALICE

*May 28, 1890. I had a queer exchange with Mary this morning, which I will write as plain as I can. As we passed in the hallway, she stopped and pointed to my stomach. 'Missus go away now,' she said in her broken English. At the same time, a different voice, whispering inside my head, said, 'Barragunyah will reject your boy child.'*

*Mary rarely speaks, so her blunt direction to 'go away' was odd. As for the other, I decided I had imagined it. I asked Mary what she meant, and she stared at me insolently, saying nothing, while the voice in my head (I had not imagined it) spoke as if Barragunyah was a living creature intent on harming my baby.*

*I thought Mary was playing some native trick on me and I was about to chastise her when she looked at me with those strange eyes and my breath seemed to stop. I would believe when Barragunyah rid herself—herself!—of the boss man, said the voice in my head. Then she calmly walked away, leaving me quite shaken. How did she even know I was with child when I have only recently suspected it myself?*

*It was only later, when I recalled the voice had said the baby was a boy, that I realised it was superstitious nonsense. Back home, I had an aunt who swore she could tell a child's sex by dangling a ring over the stomach of the expectant mother. She was wrong as often as right. If I had remembered that at the time, Mary would not have fooled me so easily.*

Alice, now certain she was with child, found her joy clouded with anxiety. Mary's warning, absurd though it was, emphasised Barragunyah's isolation and her lack of female support. Alice's mother had birthed eight children with little trouble, but she'd had experienced women close by to help. Alice had only her servants, and however knowledgeable the native women might be, John would never allow them to attend to the birth of his child. She would have to persuade him she needed extra help.

She approached the subject before dinner one evening, after the first whiskey had mellowed his mood and before the third made him cantankerous.

'John, I would like to go to Darrobine,' she said tentatively. 'I think we should make inquiries about engaging a midwife, and perhaps a nursemaid.'

He smiled – a rare occurrence these days. 'You're sure then, lass?'

Alice returned his smile. 'I believe I'm over two months gone.'

'That's grand news, Alice!' For a moment, she thought he was going to embrace her, but he turned away and reached for the decanter. 'You can come with me at the end of the month when I fetch supplies.'

Alice had hoped to go sooner, but she was not surprised – a trip to Darrobine was not taken on a whim. In fine weather, it took a full day, in the stormy season, when the track could become a treacherous bog, it was next to impossible. She would have to be patient.

Being alone didn't usually worry Alice, but she resented the isolation forced upon her at Barragunyah. She hoped that once the child was born, John would encourage visitors or allow her a horse and buggy of her own so she could call on neighbouring properties, as he did during his frequent absences.

Or at least that is what she assumed he did. In truth, she had no idea where he went or how he spent his time. Even when he was home, now that his goal to produce an heir was all but accomplished, Alice seldom saw him except at the evening meal where he drank too much, ignored her attempts at conversation, and carped about unreliable stockmen – the native ones who refused to work on Barragunyah, and the white ones who scarpered without notice.

Defeated by his monologues, Alice would sit in silence until he lurched to his feet and headed for the den, a port decanter clutched in his hand. For a time, she wondered if he had tired of her and was keeping a mistress, but as his moods grew more bizarre, she suspected it was something about Barragunyah that unsettled him.

She knew it made no sense, yet a nameless unease that slipped unguarded into his ranting, and his wary expression when he looked out over his pastures, suggested a man who saw menace behind every tree. Alice found his attitude puzzling. The property did not belong to her, but she had come to love it with a passion that surprised her.

Her attachment began in a small way with a vegetable garden she created to pass the time during John's absences. She enjoyed the hard work and, when the seeds she'd ordered from the produce store at Darrobine flourished beyond her expectations, she extended the area to include shrubs, fruit trees, and whatever flowering specimens the store could provide. Her upbringing in the bleak industrial Midlands had given her no preconceived ideas about reproducing an English garden, so she learned by trial and error which plants preferred the areas shaded by the house and which enjoyed full sun. As the garden expanded, she took daily walks to collect wildflowers, saving the seeds and pencilling notes in a special journal about the soil and conditions in which they grew. Like the cuttings she took from native trees and shrubs, and the lilies and ferns she dug from the banks of the creek, some died and some thrived, but bit by bit, the garden prospered and grew larger.

The area of land she covered on her foraging expeditions also grew larger when she rode. Unsure if John would permit it, she chose not to tell him, reasoning that as he was away so often, he would probably never know. Wearing her oldest skirt and blouse, a wide-brimmed sunbonnet that tied beneath her chin, and her sturdiest boots, she went to the yards one morning and ordered the current stable-hand to saddle the quietest horse.

She rode warily that first day, not venturing too far from the house, but found unexpected delights in trickling streams and shadowy glades she had not known existed. As her riding confidence returned, she cantered farther afield, always remembering Billy's advice to take notice of the lie of the land, its markers, and special features. Gradually, as Barragunyah took shape in her mind, her love for the place grew stronger.

One day she came across a native campsite beside a creek. The dark people looked at her suspiciously as she rode in, glancing away when she smiled at them and calling out in their own tongue. Five children of various ages scampered from the water's edge and ran to hide behind their mothers. About to dismount, Alice hesitated. She raised her hand tentatively in greeting, but the women refused to acknowledge her. Had she overstepped some hidden boundary, breached some nameless protocol? Whatever the case, she was clearly unwelcome. Disappointed, Alice reined the horse's head around and headed back the way she had come. It was only when she thought about it later she realised she had seen no men in the camp. Would that have made a difference to her reception? Perhaps the women felt vulnerable without their male protectors present. She dearly wanted to learn more about the silent people who inhabited this land, but who could she ask? Certainly not John, who never had a good word to say about them.

Alice's one regret about the child she carried was that it put an end to her riding, curtailing the solitary pleasure she enjoyed while exploring the countryside. Yet in the quiet darkness of her bedroom, when the slow beating of her heart merged with the never-ending night-sounds, she felt a deep connection to the land seeping into her bones. She longed to share this bonding with someone, but if she mentioned it to John, he would think her a fool. Bessie and Rosie would look at her with startled eyes and turn away as they always did when she tried to engage them in conversation rather than simply giving orders. As for Mary... Well, somehow Alice could find neither reason nor courage to converse with Mary.

*July 13, 1890. I woke with a start last night to find Mary in my room. I could just make out her shape in the moonlight shining through the curtains, silvering her eyes and giving them an uncanny cast. She was muttering something – I caught the words 'white death' and feared for my life, but I remained calm and asked what she wanted. Her silver eyes flashed, and she became still. As ridiculous as it seems when I write it, I felt as if my whole future rested on Mary's acceptance of my place in her world. We stared at each other in silence for a while, then the whispering in my head began. John was lost, the voice said, but I might yet save my son. Then she melted back into the shadows, leaving me trembling and wakeful for what remained of the night.*

*I rose at dawn, in need of a cup of tea, to discover my servants were absent, their chores neglected. Fetching wood to light the stove myself, I wondered if they had gone walkabout as John had warned me they might. As I pondered the meaning of this strange expression, I realised how little I know of their lives. They are my servants, but I do not know where they live, whether they have husbands or children, or even their real names.*

*Later, as I scooped flour from the sack to make bread, I recalled John telling me that one of our neighbours had poisoned his natives' flour ration. My breath caught in my throat and I wondered if that was what Mary meant by 'white death'. I know John hates the natives, but surely he would not deliberately harm them.*

Alice had not realised how on edge she was until John returned that evening, looking grubby and dishevelled. She watched warily as he went straight to the cabinet where he kept the spirits and poured himself a whiskey.

'You look tired, John,' she ventured. 'You are working too hard.'

He grunted and flung himself into his armchair. 'What else can I do? Good men won't stay on this godforsaken place.'

She seized the opportunity. 'My women have gone too. I've not seen a glimpse of them all day. Do you suppose they've all gone walkabout?'

He did not meet her eyes, but that was not unusual. 'No, lass, it were a pestilence—or so Jackson says. Wiped out the whole camp. We spent the day burying 'em—have to do it fast in this heat.'

Alice sank into a chair. 'Dead? All of them? Dear God! What sort of pestilence?'

'Who knows? Don't much matter now.'

'So, Mary was right…'

John glanced at her sharply. 'Right about what?'

'Oh, nothing – she just – she may have known they were ill.' Alice blinked back tears. 'I should pay my respects. Will you take me to their graves tomorrow?'

'For God's sake, woman! Why?'

'They were my friends, John.' And suddenly, too late, Alice wished it were true.

'Friends? They're bloody natives!'

'They were all the company I had. You are never here.'

He looked at her, understanding dawning slowly on his face. 'I'm sorry, Alice, I didn't think... I will make it up to you.' His face hardened. 'No native will ever set foot in this house again.'

'That's not what I...'

'Hush, Alice.' John reached out and took her hand. 'We'll go to town tomorrow, engage a midwife, a nurse, and any other servants you want. Honest white women who'll be proper companions for you in my absence. Would you like that?'

'Of course, but...'

'Pack what you need tonight. We'll leave at first light.' He gently touched her face, then turned and left the room, whiskey bottle in hand.

Alice stared after him, her thoughts racing. Did her husband know more than he was saying about the natives' deaths? Did he have anything to do with it? She seemed to recall Jackson was the man he'd told her about, the one who had poisoned his own natives. But John would never do that! He was a taciturn man, often unreasonably angry, but he was no murderer. She shivered, rubbing her arms, wishing she had not thought that ugly word. A pestilence, he said, and she must take him at his word.

To do otherwise would be to admit the father of her child was a monster.

They set out just after dawn. John was typically silent until they crossed the property's outer boundary when he became more talkative, pointing out features of the landscape he thought Alice might find interesting and recounting news about various neighbours. She wondered at his changed mood but said nothing, content to enjoy the journey and make the most of his more congenial company. But at the back of her mind, the horror of her servants' deaths persisted, and Mary's strange warning echoed through her thoughts. *John was lost, but her son might yet be saved.* What did she mean? Was it a threat? A curse? Reminding herself Mary had also insisted the baby was a boy, Alice pulled herself up sharply. She would not give in to superstitious nonsense!

It was just on dusk when they arrived at the small town of Darrobine. Alice's clothes were overlaid with a fine coating of grit and her eyes stung from the glare of the sun, yet despite her occasional dark thoughts, it had been the most enjoyable day she had spent since she stopped riding. Her heart leapt to see people strolling the wide main street and clustering under shop awnings to chat. And as John pointed out the new wooden building containing the School of Arts and the library, the wide veranda that had been added to the courthouse, and the produce store that supplied her seeds and plants, she noticed how graciously he smiled at passers-by, dipping his broad-brimmed hat to ladies and lifting his hand in a nonchalant salute to men who returned the courtesy. *This* was the man she had married, not that morose fellow at Barragunyah.

He reined in the tired horses outside the hotel, leapt lightly to the ground and lifted Alice down with a tenderness that touched her. A boy scurried from a lane at the side of the building and John tossed him a coin.

'We'll be staying a night or two. See you rub the horses down before you feed and water 'em.'

He turned to Alice, offering his arm. 'Come m'dear, let's get you settled before I go.'

'Oh? Where are you off to?'

He smiled indulgently. 'To see my agent about hiring you some serving women.'

'It is getting late, John. Shouldn't we wait until tomorrow?'

'Sooner's best. Lord knows how long it'll take to find 'em. I'll meet you in the hotel dining room at seven o'clock.'

Alice nodded, allowing herself to be led meekly up the steps of the hotel. She hoped to have some say in the servants they chose, but tomorrow would be soon enough to insist.

John returned smelling of whiskey but in an expansive mood. 'Well, that went better than I expected,' he said, striding into the dining room and settling in the chair opposite Alice. He rested his elbows on the starched linen cloth spread over the table. 'I've some business to attend to tomorrow so you can spend the day as you please. I noticed a new haberdasher's in the main street that might tempt you.'

Alice smiled. 'I shall look forward to a day in town but...' She hesitated, choosing her words carefully. 'I would like to talk to your agent myself about the new serving women.'

John's moustache twitched as he returned her smile. 'No need, m'dear,' he said, clearly pleased with himself. 'It's all settled. I've got you three fine lasses, just as you asked.'

'I see.' So she was to have no say in choosing her servants, after all. How foolish of her to assume otherwise. 'Is it too much to expect that one of them is a midwife?'

'Two have experience in birthing and caring for infants. The other's a slip of a girl but comes with a good character. You'll have all the help you need when your time comes.'

Darkness trembled at the edge of Alice's vision. *Barragunyah does not want your son.* The words were so clear Mary might have been standing in front of her. And suddenly she knew that any birthing experience her new servants had would be useless at Barragunyah. She should have suggested she move to town before the child was born.

'Are you not pleased?' John was watching her closely.

She forced a smile. 'Of course. I just expected it would take more time. When will they arrive?'

'Mrs Davis and the girl will come next week with the produce merchant when he makes a delivery. The housekeeper, Mrs Macalister, will return with us. You'll like her, Alice. She comes with an excellent recommendation from a Lady Donaldson in Scotland.'

'She's married then? What of her husband?'

'Mrs Macalister is a widow. Mrs Davis comes with a husband, a shiftless chap by all accounts, but I had to take him on to get her. Still, I can always use an extra man and he may stay put with a wife to anchor him.'

'And the girl?'

'Didn't catch her name. Sarah something. About fourteen. You can train her up.'

Alice spent her day of leisure in a turmoil of mixed emotions. It was pleasant to stroll along with time to spare, nodding at strangers, peering into the new shops that lined the main street, choosing fabrics, threads, and linen from the haberdashers, having lunch with John at a cosy tearoom, and dinner later at the hotel. If not for Mary's warning, the day would have been perfect, but the moment she let her guard down there it was, worming through her thoughts like a grub in a tomato.

The following morning Alice emerged from the hotel to find the cart loaded and Mrs Macalister standing beside it, her belongings in the back among sacks of flour, sugar, and oats. The new housekeeper was a daunting sight. Almost as tall and broad as John, she had a round freckled face and frizzy ginger hair pulled into a bun that sat on her nape. Alice stared at her uneasily. She will try to intimidate me, she thought, as John introduced them. I cannot allow that. There will be battles.

Then the woman smiled. The creases around her lively blue eyes suggested she smiled a lot. 'I'm not one for formality,' she said in a deep Scottish brogue. 'Call me Mac. Macalister's such a great gobful.'

Alice's apprehension vanished. She returned the smile. 'Well, Mac, I hope you'll be happy at Barragunyah.'

If the journey towards home was any indication, Mac would be happy anywhere. Her animated conversation and astute questions about the surrounding countryside made the morning pass quickly, and Alice enjoyed her company immensely. At the same time, she couldn't help wondering about the truth of Mac's experience as a housekeeper. She showed none of the deference of a woman accustomed to service, speaking and acting as if she believed herself their equal.

Perhaps she knows I was the Enrights' servant, Alice thought. That would explain her familiarity, but John would be angry if it continued. She was surprised he hadn't already reminded the housekeeper of her place. As far as he was concerned, their past was behind them and he expected everyone, Enrights and servants alike, to treat his wife with the respect due to the mistress of a substantial property.

Yet for the first part of the journey, John also seemed to enjoy the woman's company, pointing out features of interest as he had done for Alice on the outward trip. But when they stopped at midday to boil the billy and eat the lunch the hotel had packed for them, Alice sensed a change in his mood. He filled his pannikin with tea, took a leg of fowl from the basket and moved apart, his back to the women and his eyes fixed broodingly on the horizon. Alice watched him warily, abbreviating her responses to Mac's questions in an attempt to silence her.

Mac took the hint, her eyes narrowing as she absorbed the tension.

It did not occur to her it might be because she herself had forgotten her place. She had worked in many menial positions, but that made her no less of a person – she was her own woman and would enlighten the Larsons about her background if it suited her. But like her mother and grandmother before her, Maggie Macalister had the *sight,* though she hardly needed it to recognise that the mistress was afraid of upsetting her husband. But the real problem, Mac observed, the one that lay like a knife between the two of them, was that the husband was afraid of returning home.

They travelled in silence for most of the afternoon. It wasn't until they reached the fence marking Barragunyah's boundary that John spoke. 'Big storm brewing,' he said, reaching down to open the gate. 'It'll hit hard before we're home.'

Alice did not think the lightning flickering on the horizon looked very threatening. 'The clouds seem too far off,' she said unthinkingly.

He shot her a dark look. 'And what would you know, woman?'

Alice flushed and said nothing. With all his concerns for propriety, how dare John humiliate her in front of the new housekeeper?

But the housekeeper was not concerned with Alice's embarrassment. She didn't need to look at the sky to know that he was right – a storm was indeed brewing. She had sensed it the moment he opened the gate. Maybe a rainstorm.

Maybe some other kind.

The clouds were roiling blue-black towers by the time they reached the last gate. Thunder reverberated across the plains and intermittent lightning speared the ground.

John's mood was grim. 'Barely a mile to home, but I doubt we'll arrive unscathed.'

As he looped the reins over his arm and reached down to open the gate, the sky split with a mighty crack. The horses screamed and bolted, throwing John from the cart. Alice made a grab for the reins, but they were tangled around John's arm, his weight dragging the horses' heads around, aggravating their distress. The near horse kicked back and Alice heard John cry out, then the wheels hit a rock, the cart overturned, and everything went black.

When Alice came to, rain was cascading from a night sky, and Mac was shaking her. 'We've got to get you out of this storm, lass. Can ye stand?'

Alice blinked water from her eyes. 'Where's John?'

'Trapped beneath the cart. I've freed the horses, but I canna lift the cart alone. We need to get help.'

'Of course.' Alice attempted to stand but fell back, gasping, as pain shot from her ankle to her thigh.

Mac put an arm around her waist and hauled her to her feet. 'Lean on me,' she said. 'It'll hurt, lassie, but it canna be helped. Ye must show me the way to the house.'

Allowing Mac to support most of her weight, Alice looked around for a familiar landmark. But the horses had bolted from the track, and although she knew Barragunyah's shape well enough in the daylight, in the darkness, with her head spinning, the pain in her ankle shrieking, and rain blurring her vision, she did not know where they were. Panic crept in as she tried to orient herself. Why couldn't she think straight?

A dark figure loomed out of the rain.

Alice's breath caught. 'Mary? I thought you were…' She bit her lip, dashed the rain from her eyes. 'No matter, we must get help for Mr Larson. Can you show us the way home?'

Mary looked dispassionately at the upturned cart, then gestured to them to follow her.

'Don't let her out of your sight, Mac,' Alice said, clinging to the Scotswoman's arm.

Mac glanced at Alice curiously, then followed the shadowy form into the night.

Alice hobbled to the bedroom to check on John. Two days had passed since the accident and still he had not regained consciousness. The housekeeper looked up as she entered.

'Thank you, Mac. I'll sit with him now. Is there any change?'

Mac hesitated. Change there was, but not one Alice would care to hear – her husband would be dead by morning. A wonder he had lasted this long with his head all but caved in. 'Prepare y'self for the worst, m' dear,' she said gently.

'The doctor should be here by tomorrow, surely…?'

'He's beyond the help of any doctor, hinny.'

Alice looked at her husband. Beneath the muslin bandages that swathed John's head, his face was grey. His breathing, which had been harsh and laboured yesterday, was now barely perceptible in the rise and fall of his chest. She shivered. 'Mary told me Barragunyah would get rid of him.'

'Mary?' Mac's eyes narrowed. 'She who led us home the night o' the storm?'

Alice nodded. 'That's not her real name, of course…' She trailed off, refocusing her thoughts. 'I cannot allow my child to be born here.'

'Mary warned you about the bairn too?'

'Yes. You may think I'm foolish but…'

'Nay, hinny. If one such as Mary gives warning, it'd be awful foolish to ignore her.'

The terms of John's will ensured Alice would live comfortably, although the greater part of his fortune, including Barragunyah, was to remain in trust until his son attained his majority.

'And if the child is a girl?' Alice asked the executor.

'In that case, I am to administer her fortune for her until she marries.' Douglas Granger allowed himself a self-satisfied smile.

Alice swallowed her irritation. 'What is to happen to Barragunyah in the meantime? I don't wish to raise my child there – it's too isolated.'

Granger nodded. 'Perfectly understandable, Mrs Larson. You can well afford to purchase a house in Darrobine – or in Sydney Town if you prefer. As for Barragunyah, I shall find a good man to manage the property.'

Alice wondered how long his *good man* would remain there. Would reliable men stay now that John was no longer there to bully them? Or was it Barragunyah that drove them off? She dismissed the thought – to mention that perplexing issue would serve no purpose.

'I had my fill of cities as a girl,' Alice said. 'I'll buy a place here, in Darrobine.' *And I'll still be too far from home,* she added silently.

She and Mac had been staying at a boarding house in town since John's funeral, and it surprised Alice to discover she was homesick for Barragunyah. It was not only the house and garden she missed but the space, the solid earth beneath her feet, the brooding, animated silence of the night – and something else – something that defied words and reason but felt as if a piece of herself had been lost. One night, she woke in tears, confused and frustrated.

'I had the strangest dream,' she told Mac the next morning. 'Mary was in it, insisting I return to Barragunyah. But each time I did, she sent me away. I could not please her.'

Mac raised her bushy eyebrows. 'In the dream, did ye have the bairn with ye?'

'I don't think so...' Alice paused, frowning. 'There was mud – mud everywhere. It didn't look like Barragunyah, yet it had to be because Mary was there. She was trying to show me something she kept pointing to…' Alice looked at Mac in horror. 'The baby! It was drowning in all that mud and there was nothing I could do. What does it mean, Mac? Is she telling me I'll lose my child?'

'A strange dream indeed.' Mac looked at at her uneasily. 'Its meaning is hidden from me, hinny, but all the same, when the bairn is born, I would keep away from Barragunyah.'

*December 31, 1890. I have a son! George John Larson was born two days ago at my new cottage in Darrobine. My dear friend Mac delivered him safely and is caring for us both. I am so glad to have her with me. Sarah, the little maid John engaged before his accident, has also joined us. Mrs Davis did not work out, but Mac has found another woman, so I have nothing to do but nurse my son and take pleasure in his existence. I should still be in mourning, but the only thing that troubles me is being cut off from Barragunyah. I would return in an instant if not for Mary's warning. Everything she told me, and all that followed, has convinced me George should not live there. Yet I know, with a certainty that baffles me, I will go back one day. How that will come about remains to be seen.*

# JULIA

I close Alice's journal and place it beside me on the window seat. Reading about Barragunyah's early years has kept me riveted for most of the day and I can't help wondering why I haven't heard these stories before. I suppose, if Alice's descendants suspected John had played a part in the massacre of the Indigenous people, they would keep that to themselves. But I would have thought tales of the enigmatic *Mary* would be told and retold, growing more dramatic over the years rather than fading into oblivion.

I also wonder why I know so little about my great-grandfather, George. I remember Gran telling me he died in World War One, before she was born, but did he ever live at Barragunyah – or did Mary's *curse* keep him away? Maybe Alice's next journal will fill in these gaps.

I'm about to fossick through the tin trunk again when I look out of the window and see that light is rapidly fading from the grey, sodden sky. I've been waiting for a break in the weather, but the rain hasn't let up all day. Unless I get that firewood now, I am in for a cold night and an icy shower.

I get stiffly to my feet and do a few stretches when my body reminds me that sitting all day is not what it's made for. I put on my waterproof parka and head for the laundry where Gran's gumboots sit upside down on an old shoe rack. Luckily they're still usable as my sneakers would never survive the mud that now lies between me and the woodshed. I give the boots a couple of hard knocks on the veranda rail and check for spiders before slipping them on over my thick socks. Pulling up my hood, I stride out to face the rain.

Remembering how quickly the logs burned to ashes the previous night, I make several trips, stacking the wood according to size in a collection of sturdy baskets set aside for the purpose on the back veranda. This takes me quite a while and, by the time I drag a couple of baskets inside, my jeans are soaked through, my hands are red and raw, and my face is frozen. And the rain is bucketing down harder than ever.

As I set the fire in the Aga, I scan the headlines of old newspapers stacked in a box beside the stove. The ones on top are from the early 1970s and show a markedly different country to the one I've been reading about all day. Patrick White has won the Nobel Prize for literature, the Whitlam Government is transforming the nation, the Sydney Opera House has just opened. It's fun browsing through these snippets of history without Peter accusing me of slacking, but the minute I think this, I'm wondering why he hasn't texted me.

I've switched off my mobile to save the battery, but I check twice a day to see if Peter's messaged me about when he'll be back. He hasn't, so I switch off again quickly, ignoring all the other texts, which are mostly from Stuart. Knowing my brother, he'll probably turn up without warning, then complain about how little clearing and sorting I've done while he's been gone. And to be fair, he wouldn't be wrong. Tomorrow, I promise myself, I'll get stuck into the real work and won't even open the trunk.

But tonight is mine.

I empty a can of tomato soup into a saucepan and set it on the stove. While the soup simmers, I light a fire in the open hearth in the living room and settle on the floor with a bottle of mineral water, a jar of olives, and the second of Alice's journals. Flipping through the pages before I begin reading, I can see from the dates these jottings are less frequent and not as detailed as those in the first journal, sometimes months passing without a comment. Perhaps, as a new mother, she'd been too busy to record her thoughts regularly. I will have to use my imagination and read between the lines to fill in the gaps.

# ALICE

*February 6, 1898. George is so excited about starting boarding school in Sydney that I have to hide my dread at the prospect of his departure. I know he cannot further his education in Darrobine but the thought of this house without him is unbearable.*

*I am not the only one who will miss my boy. Mac's misery is written all over her dear face as she irons his new school uniforms, Dulcie has baked him so many treats he will be unable to take them all on the train, and Sarah has packed and repacked his favourite books and treasures several times as she tries to cram as much as possible into his portmanteau. In contrast, I sit here idle, brooding on my loss and the loneliness I face when I return from Sydney without him. How will I fill in six long months until I see him again? How will I fill in the next ten years as this pattern repeats itself again and again, as I know it must?*

The silence of the house and garden without George was even worse than Alice had imagined. For two weeks, she walked around in a daze, regaining some semblance of normality only when a brief letter arrived from Sydney. She read it to herself and wept because he seemed so happy. Did he miss her at all? She read it aloud to Mac and Dulcie and Sarah, carried the scrawled note in her pocket, reread it a dozen times a day until it was limp and grubby.

'This won't do, hinny,' Mac said on the Monday of the third week. 'Ye must pull y'self together.'

Alice sighed. 'I know. It's just that life is so empty without him.'

'You've a property fifty miles away, going to rack and ruin if that smarmy lawyer is telling it straight. If ye took that in hand, it would pass the time.'

'Go back to Barragunyah?'

'Aye. Why not? There's nought to stop ye now Geordie's at school.'

'What's the point? Most of the stock was sold after that last fool manager left.'

'So restock it. I can help ye there.'

'You?' Alice looked at Mac curiously.

'I wasn't always a housekeeper, hinny.' Mac winked. 'If the truth be told, I never was a housekeeper at all until I came to you.'

'But your reference – from Lady whatshername.'

'Wrote it m'self.' Mac chuckled at Alice's expression. 'Maybe it's time I told ye something of my secret past.'

Maggie Macalister, she told Alice, was born Margaret Donaldson, the daughter of a wealthy Scottish landholder in Aberdeenshire. The only girl in a family of eight children, Margaret followed her brothers around from the time she could walk, learning of animal husbandry and crop rotation, taking part in hunts, and joining in her brother's escapades. At sixteen, the life she loved was ripped from under her feet when she was married off to the eldest son of an impoverished earl.

'I had no say in the matter,' Mac said. 'I was no beauty, but I had a good dowry, and he would inherit a title. It was as simple as that. And who knows – if the wee weasel had treated me with some respect, it might have worked.'

'What happened?' Alice asked, fascinated.

'My bonny gentleman turned out to be a feckless gambler. After paying off his debts one time too many, his father decided a stint in the antipodes would cure him and booked passage for us to New South Wales. But instead of buying land with the portion his father had given him from my dowry, he took us straight to the goldfields, staked a claim he was too lazy to work, and set about gambling away the lot. It wasn't long before all he had left was his gold fob watch and a wife he'd never cared for. Naturally, it was me he decided to sell.'

'Sell? You mean…?'

'Aye.'

Alice's eyes widened. 'What did you do?'

'Clobbered him and his crony with an iron pan, pocketed the fob watch and the money he'd been paid for me, and took off on the crony's horse.'

'Good lord! Then what?'

'I pawned the watch and bought m'self work clothes and boots. Sold the horse and took a Cobb and Co coach as far from the goldfields as I could get. Changed m' name. Took whatever work suited m' fancy. Farmhand, cook, shopkeeper, nurse, teacher – I've done it all. If anyone started sniffing around or asking questions, I moved on.'

'Mac, that's a terrible way to live!'

'Nay, 'twas grand, that gypsy life. I've seen some fine country these past thirty years, learned a few tricks, met some good people – and some bad uns.' Mac paused. 'I've got set in m' ways since I met you, hinny, but I can take off again if you'd prefer not to have me around now ye know m' background.'

'Don't you dare! What would I do without you?' Alice gazed at her friend with open admiration. 'I always knew there was more to you than you let on.' She grinned. 'So, my lady farmer, what must we do to get Barragunyah productive again?'

Two weeks later, Alice arrived for her appointment with Douglas Granger. Once seated in the familiar overstuffed leather chair in his office, she ignored formalities and got to the point.

'Mr Granger, now my son is at boarding school I intend to return to Barragunyah. I will need to restock it, so I will need money – I think two thousand pounds to begin with.'

'Dear lady, that's quite impossible.' Granger stroked his beard. 'I haven't even appointed a new manager since the last one left.'

'No need. I shall manage it myself.'

He smiled and leaned back in his chair. 'My dear Mrs Larson, it takes a man of experience to run a property as large as Barragunyah. It is certainly no task for a woman.'

Alice's smile matched his. 'You have appointed nine such experienced men in seven years, Mr Granger, and Barragunyah is now producing no income at all. I do not see how I could do worse.'

He sat upright and gaped at her. 'My dear Mrs... You don't think that I... After all, there has been a depression. Shearers' strikes. Drought. Things are difficult for everyone.'

'I know that. I'm not blaming you or your managers, Mr Granger. I'm simply stating a fact – I could not do worse. I believe I could do better. Given the present state of affairs you've just mentioned, you will agree there is nothing to lose by allowing me to try.'

The lawyer cleared his throat and changed tack. 'I seem to recall you saying the place was too isolated.'

'Yes, for bringing up a child. That no longer applies. Now, about that two thousand pounds?'

'Mrs Larson, you must be aware the current depression has affected sheep farmers most particularly. Oversupply to Britain and Europe has seen the price of wool decline to barely sevenpence a pound. Until we are fully out of the economic woods, so speak, I do not think sheep are a wise investment.'

'I quite agree. I do not intend to run sheep, Mr Granger. I plan to import a bull and some fine Scottish cows and begin the district's first Black Angus stud.'

Three years later, Alice and Mac sat astride their horses, admiring the new calves. 'Eleven heifers and eight bull calves so far,' Mac said. 'A grand start for the new century.'

'It is indeed.' Alice smiled. 'When the other cows have calved, we'll need to fence off more paddocks.'

'Aye. That team working on the Enright property must be nearly finished. If we engage them now, they'd have it done in a month.'

Alice nodded. 'And be away before anything upsets them.'

'Will yon lawyer cover the cost?'

'Probably not. Despite the evidence, Mr Granger still expects us to fail.' Alice looked at her friend. 'Actually, I'm thinking of selling the cottage in town. The money from that will pay for fencing and the other improvements we've been talking about. We can take rooms at the hotel for the few weeks George is back in Darrobine.'

'He's almost eleven now – ye don't want to try him here again?'

Alice sighed. 'I don't think so. You saw what he was like last time.'

The success of their Angus breeding program, and Alice's delight in living at Barragunyah again, had convinced her she had misunderstood Mary's warning. When she thought about it rationally, the notion that Barragunyah would harm her son seemed ludicrous. So last year she'd decided George could spend his school holidays on the property.

George had hated the place, his endless complaints making his visit a misery for all of them. There was nothing to see and nowhere to go. It was too cold to swim in the river and too hot to ride. The house was draughty. There were no other boys to play with. The fireplace smoked. His bed was lumpy. Alice put up with his grumbling for three days before they headed to town, where George's characteristically sunny disposition had returned.

For Alice, it was a grim reminder of the way John's mood had lightened as they left Barragunyah, only to darken again on that final homeward trip. It seemed Mary's curse – or whatever it was – still functioned. The antipathy men seemed to feel for the place had been her initial concern when Mac suggested they restock the farm.

'It will be hard to find men to work here,' Alice had pointed out. 'For some reason, they don't stay long. It used to drive John to despair.'

'But ye can ride, can't ye, hinny?'

'Yes, but…'

'As can I. And young Sarah too, I'll warrant, since she grew up on a farm.'

'You're suggesting we work it ourselves?'

'Aye. Why not? Black Angus are hardy, quiet beasts, they'll not need much care. And you'll be starting small – between us we can easily oversee two or three paddocks.'

Mac had been right as usual, and the imported animals had thrived with little effort on their part. Now, heifers that had arrived as calves were dropping their offspring alongside their mothers' newborns, and last year's young males were growing into muscled bulls that would bring a good price as stud animals. In a year or two they would have a substantial herd. Alice smiled, wondering what the gossips would say when the Barragunyah women sold their first breeders.

Her only regret was George's indifference to all they were doing on the property. If the next decade passed as quickly as the one just gone, he would inherit Barragunyah with no appreciation of its potential. Her heart ached to think he might sell the place, but each passing year made it increasingly obvious that her son preferred city life.

*19th October, 1900.*

*Dear Mother,*

*Even at Barragunyah you will have heard of the Federation celebrations planned for early next year. Think of it, Mother, the Commonwealth of Australia! Sir says only a fool would miss an opportunity to be there on the day, and as I am quite sure you don't want your son to look a fool, I'm hoping you'll let me spend the Christmas holidays in Sydney with Andrew Bardwell and his parents. After Federation Day they are going to Lake Illawarra, where they have a cottage near the beach. Andrew says it is loads of fun, swimming, fishing, prawning and such, and I'm invited! I know it means I will miss Christmas but we can make it up next year. Please say yes!*

*Love, George*

*PS Please write back quickly.*

*PPS Love to Mac and Dulcie and Sarah.*

Alice read George's letter over and over, wanting to refuse him and knowing she couldn't. She understood his excitement, but he seemed to have forgotten that she would not only miss spending Christmas with him but also his eleventh birthday. Was there a way around it?

*6th November, 1900*

*Dear George,*

*News of Federation Day has indeed managed to reach us, so I have decided to come to Sydney and enjoy the celebrations with you. I met Andrew and his parents at your awards night two years ago and look forward to seeing them again.*

*Unfortunately, the pre-Christmas trains are booked out, but I shall arrive in time for your birthday. Mr Granger has secured us rooms in a good hotel for the duration of my visit. I will leave it to you to decide whether you spend the remainder of the school holidays with your friend or return with me on 4th January*

*As always,*

*Your loving Mother*

George's next missive was a hastily scrawled note.

> *Dearest Mother,*
>
> *I am glad you are coming to Sydney. I look forward to seeing you, but if you don't mind, I will spend the rest of my holiday with Andrew and the Bardwells.*
>
> *Love, George*

Alice minded very much. But what could she do?

***January 4, 1901.*** *I am writing this on the train after leaving Sydney this morning. The Federation celebrations were certainly impressive, but only George's excitement made the day bearable for me. At times I would have given anything to hear cows bellowing rather than the booming guns, prayers, speeches, and songs that marked the event. Now, with only the clatter of wheels to keep me company, I will jot down what I remember of the day.*

> *We left the hotel early…*

George bounded down the hotel steps. 'Hurry, Mother! I don't want to miss a thing!'

Alice quickened her pace, ignoring a faint headache courtesy of rowdy New Year's Eve revellers and a violent thunderstorm which had kept her awake most of the night. She looked up warily at the overcast sky, hoping another storm wouldn't dampen today's festivities.

George, now taller than his mother by several inches, was striding ahead, looking very grown up in a new suit with a waistcoat and long trousers. Looking at him, Alice wondered again at how quickly the years had flown. Her son's easy manner and confident grin seemed a far cry from the wide-eyed child she had taken to the Sydney boarding school four years ago. Alice was proud of the young man he was becoming, but she was also painfully aware that her son wasn't just growing up, he was growing away from her. He turned, smiling, waiting for her to catch up, and she pushed the thought away, determined to enjoy this special day with him.

The street was already swarming with people and Alice was alarmed to see armed soldiers stationed at intervals along the kerb. 'I hope they're not expecting to use those things,' she said, eyeing the bayonetted rifles.

George laughed. 'Really, Mother, they're just part of the show.' He looked around to get his bearings. 'This is where the tram stops. I hope we don't have long to wait.'

Overhearing him, a passing man shook his head. 'You'll wait all day, sonny. Trams aren't running.' He nodded to Alice. 'They sayin' it's too dangerous, Missus, what with everyone spillin' out on the roads.'

She looked at him in dismay. 'But the day's barely begun.'

He shrugged. 'You won't get a cab for love nor money, neither. It's shank's pony I'm afraid.' Tipping his hat, he disappeared into the crowd.

'That's a poor start to the day,' Alice said, frowning. 'Perhaps we should return to the hotel and ask the manager to hire us a carriage.'

From the look on George's face, she might have proposed eating spiders. 'But we'll miss the parade! Martin Place isn't far – we can walk.'

'Well, if you're sure… But don't you dare lose me in this crowd!'

George grinned and tucked her hand into his elbow. 'I won't let you out of my sight.' He looked around with enthusiasm. 'Can you believe how many have turned out? Everyone in New South Wales must be here! Have you ever heard such a clamour?'

'No, never,' Alice agreed fervently.

Despite a cloudy sky, the day was turning warm and Alice, unaccustomed to wearing a corset, began to perspire. George, oblivious to her discomfort, forged through the crowds, chattering happily. 'Andrew says they've hired an upstairs room in George

Street so we can see everything. Fancy me having a street with my name on it, Mother! Andrew's only got a cathedral.'

Alice jerked back as someone trod on her skirt. A moment later, her hat was knocked askew. 'George, please slow down or I'll arrive looking like something the cat dragged in.'

George threw her a cursory glance. 'You look all right. Anyway, we're nearly... See, there's Andrew across the road!'

His friend was waiting in the alcove of an imposing sandstone building. He greeted Alice politely before pointing to a narrow staircase half-hidden behind a heavy wooden door. 'Our room's up there.' He grinned at George. 'Mother's arranged a sort of picnic. Wait till you see the cake!' The boys bounded ahead, Alice following more slowly, smoothing her jacket and setting her hat to rights as best she could.

Later, sitting on the train with a pencil poised over her journal, Alice attempted to sift through the kaleidoscope of images that flitted through her mind. The stirring music of the marching bands, the clip-clop of hooves announcing the mounted police and the Lancers, the long stream of trade unionists carrying banners demanding an eight-hour working day. She jotted down the trades she could remember: shearers, miners, painters, dock-workers, stone-masons, chandlers, iron-workers, butchers, bakers, barrel-makers...

Her pencil paused  her friends wouldn't be interested in a list, they'd want to hear about the Highlanders in kilts, Indians wearing bright turbans, Maoris on big-boned horses, and those societies with outlandish names like Oddfellows and Druids, and so many troopers it seemed as if all the Imperial Forces must have been there.

She smiled, remembering how the boys had hung over the windowsill cheering the fire brigade, brass helmets gleaming in the sun as they marched alongside horse-drawn engines. The boys' enthusiasm had dimmed though, as a long procession of religious leaders, members of parliament, university scholars, press representatives, and foreign leaders strode down the street below them. Her own attention had also wandered until George grabbed her arm.

'Look, Mother, there's Edmund Barton, the Prime Minister!'

'And his ministers with him,' added Stanley Bardwell. 'Just think, boys, those men will lead the new Commonwealth of Australia!'

Alice's feet were aching and her mind numb by the time the Governor-General came into sight. Then it was over, and Stanley Bardwell was hurrying them down the stairs and into the carriage waiting to take them to Centennial Park for the formal ceremony.

As they alighted from the carriage, Elizabeth Bardwell surveyed the surging hordes in dismay. 'Oh, my dear, I didn't expect this. Where do we sit?'

Her husband pointed to a large rotunda some distance away. 'That's the new Federation Pavilion; there'll be seating there, but we'd best hurry.'

They pushed through the crush only to find wooden barriers guarding the seats. 'Invited guests only,' an official snapped.

Bardwell looked at three similar enclosures nearby. 'In there, then?'

The man shook his head. 'Reserved for the press, the military, and school children.'

As they walked away, disappointed, Elizabeth lowered her voice, 'Why don't you boys slip in there with the other children? I'm sure nobody would object.'

'Mother!' Andrew rolled his eyes. 'You'll have us singing in the choir next!'

Bardwell looked around, bemused. 'I'm sorry, I didn't know it would be like this.'

'We don't need to sit, we just need to see.' George said, with the carelessness of a boy wearing comfortable shoes. He pointed. 'What about over there on that bit of a rise?'

Bardwell nodded glumly. 'Probably as good as we'll get.'

It proved to be a good vantage point, but other spectators clearly thought the same and by the time the opening prayers began, they were well and truly hemmed in.

'Can you ladies see?' Bardwell asked.

'Well enough,' said Elizabeth. 'Mrs Larson?'

'I can manage. The boys might do better if they climbed that tree over there.'

George studied the big Moreton Bay Fig. 'You up for it, Bardwell?'

Andrew looked inquiringly at his father, who nodded. Andrew grinned at George. 'Race you,' he said.

Elizabeth Bardwell raised her eyebrows in alarm as the boys pushed through the crowds towards the tree. 'Oh dear, not too high,' she said.

Alice glanced at her; had her suggestion been unwelcome? But all boys climbed, didn't they? She gave a mental shrug and shifted her attention to the Pavilion where the ceremony was underway. This was what Mac and the others would want to hear about when she got home. But in the endless stream of hymns and prayers and speeches that followed, she found her thoughts drifting to Barragunyah – they would need to import a new bull soon, clear and fence more paddocks… The final notes of the choir died away and Alice shook herself out of her reverie in time to hear Australia proclaimed a Commonwealth.

Relieved, she turned and waved at George perched comfortably in the fig tree, but his focus was still on the rotunda. She turned back. 'Is there more?' she asked the Bardwells.

'Lord Hopetoun is about to swear in the new government,' Stanley Bardwell whispered.

As man after man was presented to the Governor-General, Alice's thoughts drifted again until a twenty-one-gun salute jolted her back to witness the hoisting of the flag and Lord Hopetoun reading a message of congratulations from the Queen. Then the choir sang the anthem and the official ceremony was over.

George climbed from his perch and ran to Alice, grinning. 'Wasn't that grand, Mother! What shall we do now?'

'I thought we'd go back to the hotel for lunch.' Alice smiled at the Bardwells. 'I hope you'll join us as my guest. I'd like to return your hospitality.'

George looked at her, aghast. 'Mother, we can't go back yet! There are entertainments all over the city!'

'I think your mother is tired, George,' said Elizabeth Bardwell gently. 'I know I am.' She looked at Alice. 'Might I suggest Stanley take the boys to see some sights? I plan to rest before I change for dinner and tonight's concert. We have tickets for you and George if you'd like to come, then afterwards we can watch the fireworks.'

Alice hesitated. She had hoped to spend more time alone with George, but seeing his eager face, she knew it was not to be. 'That's kind of you. We'd be delighted.'

# JULIA

I put down Alice's journal and peer through the window at the rain, picturing the Federation celebrations; the streets lined with grand archways and colourful bunting, a stirring band leading the parade past all those cheering people. Knowing that two of my ancestors had been there has somehow brought that long ago day into the present and I can almost hear the clatter of horse-drawn cabs, the rattle of steam trams, almost feel the excitement. The letters I found tucked inside the journal are more poignant, a touching insight into how Alice's relationship with her son had changed as he grew up.

I get up to put another log on the fire, then check my watch and change my mind. It is already past midnight and tomorrow I want to get an early start on Gran's things. I don't regret the way I've spent my time while Peter's been in Melbourne, but if I make some inroads into the sorting, it will prevent grumbling when he gets back.

First, if the Aga has done its job, a hot shower. The faithful old stove has certainly made the house a lot warmer, so I add more wood to the embers and close the vent, hoping it will burn slowly until morning.

In the bathroom I stand for ages under the steaming water. When I was a kid, showers at Barragunyah were strictly timed, but now, with all the tanks overflowing, abundant hot water is a luxury to be enjoyed. Afterwards, I sit for a while before the dying fire, drying my hair and thinking about Alice until my eyelids droop and I head off to bed.

I dream of Mary and wake with a sense of urgency. I don't know how I know it's her, as she has neither face nor form, but dreams have their own certainties even though the details fade the minute I open my eyes. She wants me to do something, but I have no idea what it is. I'm lying in bed, trying to make sense of the hazy fragments, when I notice the drip from the ceiling has become a steady stream. I sit up and see the bucket I'd placed beneath it is almost full. Braving the bleak, chilly morning, I open one of the French doors, dash across the veranda and empty the water over the railing. In between the house and the woodshed, small lakes are spreading across the mud and my thoughts leap to the rutted track down which Peter will soon be driving. I don't think he knows how easy it is to get bogged.

I go back inside and switch on my mobile. Still no messages. The least he could do is keep me in the loop – for all I know, he could still be in Melbourne. Annoyed, I send a text to warn him about the road, switch off my phone again and toss it on the table. There is nothing more I can do until he contacts me.

I add kindling to the embers in the Aga's firebox and watch the fire blaze into life. Feeling absurdly pleased that I've kept it going through the night, I fill the kettle, place it on the hotplate, then return to the bedroom to get dressed.

Toast cooked on the hotplate of a slow combustion stove smells and tastes different from bread cooked in a toaster. Memories of all the breakfasts I've enjoyed with Gran waft through the room like aromatic ghosts, making me long for some homemade marmalade with the tart, chunky bits I'd loved as a kid. Drowning my reminiscences in a second cup of tea, I head for Gran's bedroom.

It is nearly midday by the time I've sorted through her personal items and I'm an emotional wreck. Gran bought good quality clothes made to last and wouldn't dream of throwing something out simply because it had gone out of fashion. Many of the dresses, skirts and blouses hanging in her wardrobe are so familiar I can picture the time and place she wore them. A green print dress brings back memories of my first trip to Darrobine. The divided skirt she wore with the soft leather riding boots I coveted reminds me of the times we'd ridden along the fence lines together, checking for breaks. I'd been upset when I found those boots all cracked and mouldy on the veranda, but what finally brings me undone this morning is the smart navy coat and hat I helped her choose for my mother's memorial service. I stare at the unworn outfit with a sort of horror, reliving all the anger and grief and confusion that had brought me so low at the time. I toss the garments onto the double bed and when I've finished crying, I glare red-eyed at the mountain I've made of her clothes.

I have to be ruthless.

I grab one of the black garbage bags we bought and fill it haphazardly, reasoning that if I don't look closely, I won't be plagued by memories. Soon I have the bed cleared and several large plastic bags stacked in the hallway.

My face in the long central mirror of the cedar wardrobe looks back at me miserably as I open each of its three doors for a final check. Hanging space, shelves and drawers gape at me blankly. I'm about to turn away when I glance up and see a cardboard shoebox in the back corner of the top shelf.

Climbing onto a chair, I take down the box and remove the lid. My heart skips a beat; the box is filled with handwritten letters. I carry it to the kitchen where the kettle is hissing on the stove. I make another pot of tea and while it brews, I briefly check my mobile. Nothing. Is Peter deliberately avoiding me? I don't bother leaving a message.

I sit at the table and randomly fish a letter from the box, holding my breath as I unfold the single page. It is dated 1910 and signed by George. If I keep finding treasures like this, I don't care if my brother never returns. I settle back with the letter, trying to picture Alice reading it all those years ago…

# ALICE

*The University of Sydney*
*Camperdown Campus,*
*22nd November, 1910.*
*Dearest Mother,*

*It meant the world to me to have you and Mac at my graduation ceremony. I am pleased that you both enjoyed the somewhat sober dinner afterwards (as you can imagine, the party became more rowdy once parents left). I am sorry I couldn't return with you on the train, but it would have been disastrous to miss the interview I mentioned. And yes, before you begin wondering, I have been offered the position as a legal clerk with Anderson and Chamberlain. I begin in January, which means I will need to leave Darrobine right after my birthday. I know you were keen for me to stay longer but needs must. At least we will spend Christmas together this year.*

*As for the matter of my father's will, now I am about to attain my majority, please tell Mr Granger to arrange an appointment for mid-December. Speaking of which, Andrew's parents gave him an automobile when he turned twenty-one. It really is tremendous fun! Do you think Father might have left me enough to purchase one?*

*Looking forward to seeing you soon,*
*Fondest love,*

*George*

Alice dashed away her tears as she heard Mac come in. She was being foolish. Her son was a lawyer now and she was proud of him.

'Bad news?' Mac jabbed her chin toward the letter in Alice's hand.

Alice forced a smile. 'Good news, in fact. George has secured the position he wanted with that Sydney legal firm, and he'll be home for Christmas. What more could I ask?'

'That he'd come home for good, I expect. But that's never goin' to happen, hinny.'

'I know. I kept hoping he'd choose to begin his career in Darrobine or Lurradallan, where I could see him more often, but I knew I was deluding myself. I have to accept that Sydney is his home now.'

'Aye, a city boy through and through, that one.'

'A boy no longer. Where have the years gone, Mac? In just a few weeks, my baby will be twenty-one.' She shook her head and smiled. 'At least his letter solved one problem. Remember we were wondering how we could make his coming of age special? Now I know just the thing!'

'And what might that be?'

'I'm going to get him an automobile.'

Mac raised her eyebrows. 'Good Lord! And I thought we were deciding between roast lamb or beef.'

'Well, that too. But he said he'd like an automobile.'

'Did he now? I doubt you'll find one of those contraptions in Darrobine. Or Lurradallan either, for that matter.'

'I suppose you're right.' Alice frowned. 'Douglas Granger might know where I can get one. I'll ask him next week when we go to town. I need to make an appointment for George about John's will.'

'Ah, that.' Mac pursed her lips. 'I still don't see why ye won't come out and ask Geordie his plans for Barragunyah and offer to manage the place. Even old Granger can't say ye haven't done a good job.'

'It has to be George's decision, Mac. From his point of view, it would make sense to sell Barragunyah and use the proceeds to buy a house in Sydney.' She looked at Mac miserably. 'I didn't tell you this, but at his graduation dinner he put it to me – somewhat vaguely, I admit – that I might enjoy living with him in the city.'

'I see.' Mac's eyes narrowed. 'And would ye?'

'No. It would be wonderful to see George every day, but Barragunyah is more than my home, it's my life. I cannot imagine what I'll do if he sells it.'

Douglas Granger's beard was white now, and his waistcoats somewhat wider, but his self-satisfied smirk, Alice thought, had not changed a jot. When she'd made the appointment for George a few weeks ago, Granger had been dismissive, making it clear that now her son was old enough to make his own decisions, her views were no longer of interest. As for her question regarding automobiles, she may as well have saved her breath – there were none to be found this side of the range, Granger told her, and in his opinion a good thing too. So, it was back to lamb or beef for George's birthday, and some money if she could discover what the things cost.

Now, as she introduced her six-foot tall son to the solicitor and noticed that Granger had to look up to meet his eye, she sensed George would not be as easily manipulated as she had feared.

Bestowing a superficial smile on Alice, Granger shook hands with George and gestured toward his private office. 'We'll talk in there, young man,' he said. 'Your mother will be comfortable here. I'll tell Miss Perry to bring her a cup of tea while we discuss business.'

'Thank you, sir, but I'd prefer that my mother join us.'

Granger raised his unruly white eyebrows. 'We have a lot of facts and figures to go over – I wouldn't want to bore the little lady.'

George turned to Alice and winked. 'You clearly don't know my mother as well as you think, sir, if you imagine a few numbers will daunt her.' He crooked his elbow and offered his arm to Alice. 'Come, Mother, I'm sure you'll be as interested as I am to see how

Mr Granger has managed Father's estate these past two decades.'

'Yes, indeed.' Ignoring the exasperation clearly evident on Granger's face, Alice placed a gloved hand on her son's arm, and they entered the inner sanctum together.

If Alice was surprised at the size of John's legacy, George was astounded. 'It seems I'll have more than enough for an automobile,' he said, grinning. 'Thank you, Mr Granger. You've done very well by me.'

'Of course, dear boy. And we have yet to address the question of Barragunyah. As you intend to live in Sydney, may I assume you'll sell it?'

'I certainly want to be rid of it, I've never liked the place.' He glanced at Alice. 'Sorry, Mother, I expect I've made that rather obvious over the years.'

Alice nodded but could not speak. His words were like a spear through her heart.

Granger smiled complacently. 'I'll put the word out at once. The market for a property like yours is excellent at present. Its sale will increase your fortune substantially.'

'I haven't been clear; I want to be rid of the place, but I have no intention of selling,' George grinned. 'What I want you to do, Mr Granger, is make the deeds over to my mother.'

Alice's head jerked up, seeing her own astonishment reflected in Granger's face.

'I'd… My goodness, no… I'd strongly advise against that, young man,' Granger stammered. 'Barragunyah is worth a lot of money. And… Well… the fact is, women cannot legally own property.'

'With respect, sir, you're a little behind the times,' George said. 'The Married Women's Property Act was legislated in New South Wales in 1879.'

'Oh, yes that… Well, of course, but the fact is, a property like yours… It… it requires a strong man at the helm.'

George chuckled and reached for Alice's hand. She stared at him, suddenly realising he was enjoying this.

'Mr Granger, my mother has been at Barragunyah's helm since I was a child. It is she who has made it what it is, she who deserves the credit and the rewards.' He paused and turned to Alice. 'I'm sorry, Mother, how rude of me. I haven't even asked if this is what you want...'

Alice looked at her son, at his laughing brown eyes, his handsome face, not trusting herself to speak for the lump in her throat. She nodded, then found her voice. 'Of course, I would like to remain at Barragunyah and manage it, but to give it to me is no small thing,' she gulped. 'You must be sure, George.'

'Never surer of anything in my life,' he said, squeezing her hand. 'Let's have those deeds, Mr Granger, and get the thing done so my mother and I can celebrate.'

# JULIA

I'm smiling as I put the letter aside, thinking how right it was that Barragunyah became Alice's property – a woman's place, with quite different connotations than the term usually means. It had been a place of women ever since.

My smile fades when I remember I will be the one to end that long tradition. I've already ignored Gran's wishes by promising Peter half of the proceeds, but even if he wasn't involved, I'd have to sell the place. As these thoughts flit through my mind, I feel suddenly uneasy, that same prickling of anxiety I had when Peter left. It's as if I've set in motion something I can't control, something too big to comprehend. Which makes no sense at all. I push my misgivings aside and reach for another letter.

This one is dated 1918 and addressed to my great-grandmother Ellen…

# ELLEN

*12th July, 1918.*

*My Darling Ellen,*

*Forgive me for not writing earlier but I have been shuttled around all over the place, not knowing from one day to the next where I would land. Thankfully, I am now back where I belong, with my own battalion.*

*Fritz's shelling continues, and the men are in low spirits after another winter in the trenches. The tales they tell bring back memories of my own stint in the winter of 1916; freezing water up to my knees, sleeping in mud, rats the size of cats. Did I ever tell you about the time my eyelids froze shut? Even now, in what passes for summer in this part of the world, the mud is ever present, and the rats continue to thrive.*

*But enough of that, I would rather think of you. Your letter dated May 28 arrived yesterday. I am sorry that you lost your position at the hospital. I know you expected it, but I thought Matron might find a compromise, as I know she thinks highly of you. Dismissing a dedicated nurse simply because she has married makes little sense to me in this time of need. As one of your many wounded soldiers, I can confidently say it was you, rather than the doctors, who saved my life after Bullecourt.*

*My dearest love, I cannot believe how lucky I am that you agreed to marry me. I am sorry my orders made our wedding such a rushed affair, but we shall make up for it after the war when I take you to Australia. You will love Sydney, but I want you to see Barragunyah too, my mother's property in the country. I have written to tell her we are married (I would give anything to see her face when she learns I have a wife). Dear wife, I wonder if you know how proud I feel when I write that word? I wonder how you feel to be Mrs Larson?*

*I must leave it there for now, sweetheart. New briefings have just come through and I need to pass on the news to the men. Know that you are always in my thoughts and in my heart. One final word: Should I fail to return, please go to my mother at Barragunyah. She will take care of you. Of course, we both know old Fritz could not keep me from you in a million years, but just in case. You have the address.*

*My fondest love,*

*George*

Ellen folded the letter and slipped it into her apron pocket. The other letter, the official one from the War Office, lay open on the table where it had sat for three days. She was surprised they had sent it to her instead of George's mother – they'd been married only four months and she knew the paperwork took time to go through the proper channels. Her widow's pension hadn't even come through yet; she didn't know how she would have managed without the allowance George had set up for her. She smiled; he'd laugh when she told him, no doubt reminding her of how she had argued against it.

'You can use the allowance or not, sweetheart,' he'd said. 'It's up to you, but I'll feel better knowing the money is there if you need it.'

Her legs seemed to fold beneath her. She pulled out a chair and sat down heavily. George wouldn't laugh. George would never laugh again. She stared at the letter on the table, not seeing it, but sorely aware of the vast changes those cold, official words meant for her future. For their child's future. The child she hadn't had the chance to tell George about.

Ellen's hand went instinctively to her stomach. A drop of water landed on her wrist, and she looked up, puzzled. It was several minutes before she realised she was crying. Angry at herself, she brushed away the tears. Crying wouldn't help. In her time at the hospital she had seen enough death, enough weeping widows, to know that only those with families to support them could afford to fall apart. Women like her, with neither family nor friends to call on, just had to get on with it.

George had been puzzled at first by her solitary nature. 'The other nurses look up to you,' he said. 'They'd be delighted to call you their friend.'

She had shrugged and looked away. 'I don't have the knack for friendship. It's not that I don't like them, it's just that unless we're talking about work, I really don't have anything to say to them.'

It was only when she told George about her childhood that he'd understood. Given his own privileged upbringing, she'd expected him to think less of her, but instead, he had wrapped his arms around her in an almighty hug. 'Poor old chook,' he'd whispered. 'Now you've got me.'

She looked around the large, pleasantly furnished room. It was a more expensive flat than she would have chosen, and George had to pay six month's rent in advance to secure it. Ellen had been appalled at his extravagance, but he'd insisted he could afford it. 'I'll not have my wife living in some squalid London dump while I'm away at the Front,' he'd said, his expression so horrified it made her laugh. But that was five months ago. When the lease was up, she'd have to find somewhere else to live. Worse, if her widow's pension didn't come through soon, and George's allowance had to stretch to food as well as rent, she'd be lucky to afford one of those dingy dumps he despised. She knew he would hate the thought of his child growing up in such a place, but what choice did she have?

Ellen folded her arms on the table and stared at the typed letter. Maybe it was a mistake. Maybe he was missing in action. It wouldn't be the first time the bureaucrats got things mixed up. He couldn't be dead. Not George. He was too full of life.

The first time she'd seen him he was fresh off a hospital ship, his shoulder full of shrapnel and two bullets in his leg. Even then, half delirious with pain, he'd made a joke and paid her a cheeky compliment.

His recovery had been slow, with some challenging setbacks. Ellen was sure it was his love of life and laughter, and the way he liked to spread it around, that had pulled him through. She had never met anyone quite like him. Once he had reached the stage of 'walking wounded' she'd often find him out of bounds, forsaking the officer's wards to chat with the wounded Tommies and Diggers. Nobody else could cheer up the boys like George. He did a good job on the female hospital staff too; her fellow nurses, the VADs, and even Matron, had all succumbed to his easy-going charm. Ellen smiled again, thinking of how any one of them would have been delighted to walk out with Lieutenant George Larson. But it was her he had asked, making sure he did everything by the book so she wouldn't find herself in trouble with her superiors – a patient flirting light-heartedly with a nurse was acceptable, courting was not. Like the rest of the nursing staff, she had seen him head off to the convalescent hospital with mixed feelings, glad he was well enough to move on, but knowing the wards would be gloomier without his cheerful presence. Then she had come off duty one night and found him – still on crutches – waiting for her.

He had invited her to dinner at one of London's finest establishments and she'd said yes immediately. But when he ordered champagne, and she saw the prices on the menu, she felt uncomfortable. 'It's awfully expensive. Far too much to spend on a nurse you hardly know.'

His clear brown eyes held the hint of a smile as he peered at her over the menu. 'But not nearly enough to spend on the girl I'm going to marry.'

That was just before Christmas 1917. He'd rented the flat as soon as he was discharged from the convalescent hospital in February and by March they were married. Until his orders to return to the Front arrived in May, Ellen enjoyed the happiest weeks of her life.

But now it was over.

Ellen took the letter from her apron pocket and read it again… *should I fail to return, please go to my mother at Barragunyah; she will take care of you.*

How could she turn to a woman she didn't know? A woman on the other side of the world who, given the haphazard nature of mail services in wartime, might not even know yet that her son was married. A somewhat daunting woman too, if George's tales of her running a cattle-breeding property were anything to go by. Ellen could just imagine the welcome she would get, turning up on the doorstep of a woman like that with a baby in tow. Yet what else was she to do? George seldom spoke of money, but he was from a wealthy family and would hate his child to grow up in poverty. His own father had died before he was born but had left his wife and son well provided for. George would want no less for his own child. She read the words again. *You have the address.*

*Barragunyah.* A strange name. His mother adored the place, George had told her, although he had never lived there himself, much preferring Sydney, where he had gone to school and university.

Ellen sighed and got to her feet to fetch pen and ink. She would write to Mrs Larson and see if she replied. But as she sat down again with a sheet of George's fine notepaper in front of her, an unpleasant thought intruded. Did his mother even know George was dead?

# JULIA

Time is galloping on and leaving me behind. Staring at my watery reflection in the darkened window, I wonder if my own life will pass as quickly. It seems as if I barely finished reading about George as a schoolboy at the Federation celebrations with his mother, before I learn he has finished university and launched a career in law. Today I find him wounded in battle, married to an English nurse, fathering a child, and dying on the Western Front. What happened in between? Why do I know so little about my great-grandfather?

Putting the box of letters aside for the time being, I return to Alice's journals, hoping to find some answers there…

# ALICE

*July 15, 1918. I had the dream again. The one that has haunted me since John died. At first it was the same as it always is – Mary trying to tell me something, then my horror when I realise I've lost my baby in a sea of mud – but this time the dream continued... It was night and the sky was alight with fireworks, reminding me of the Federation celebrations. Yet this was no celebration; it was a scene from hell. In dazzling flashes of light, I saw not just my baby, but countless babies, all holding out their tiny arms as the mud swallowed them. I knew I would never find George amid all that chaos and I woke in panic.*

Alice clawed the sheet from her face. It's a dream, just a dream, she told herself, trying to still her racing heart. It was nothing, it meant nothing. A cup of hot milk would lay it to rest.

She sat up, reaching for her dressing gown, and saw someone standing at the foot of her bed. She could barely make out the shape in the faint moonlight filtering through the window, but she knew who it was.

'Mary! You startled me.' Alice stared through the gloom. It had been years since she'd last seen her, yet she seemed unchanged, as if the heavy hand of time that had lined her own face had no effect on Mary. 'I was dreaming about you.' She paused, frowning as she remembered how the dream had shifted.

She shivered and pulled her dressing gown around her shoulders. 'Did I call your name? I think I may have. I'm all right now. It was just a dream...'

As her eyes adjusted to the darkness, Alice saw Mary held something in her arms. She couldn't quite make out what it was, but the way she held it so tenderly, close to her breast, it had to be a baby.

Her heart skipped a beat. 'What have you got there, Mary?'

The moonlight brightened, bathing the room in an eerie glow. Alice caught a glimpse of a pale, naked body, blue eyes, a gummy smile. A little girl. She reached for her...

'Is somethin' wrong, hinny? I heard ye call out.'

Mac stood at the doorway, her face planes of light and shade in the glow of a candle, her sleep-mussed white hair an unruly halo.

Alice looked at her, confused. 'Mary brought a... Did you see Mary?'

Mac came in and sat on the edge of the bed, placing the candleholder on the bedside table. 'Nae, hinny. Was she here? I thought ye might have had that bad dream again.'

'I did, but it was different this time. Oh, Mac, I think...'

Alice pursed her lips, afraid of the words she might say. She was shivering. Mac took a quilt from where it hung over the brass rail at the foot of the bed and placed it around her shoulders.

'Out with it, hinny. Best to tell a dream out loud before ye forget.'

'I hardly know what to make of it, Mac. I don't know why...' Then, suddenly, with a certainty that made her gasp, she did know. 'Dear God, Mac. George is dead.'

Mac frowned. 'Mary told ye this?'

'No. But he is. I just know. Mary was showing me... She was... There was something different... I've forgotten what... I only remember the mud.' Alice's voice was suddenly flat and heavy. 'I've always assumed the place in my dream was Barragunyah, because

Mary was there. I was wrong. It was a place I've never seen, nor ever want to. A hellish place.' She stared at Mac, her eyes dark with grief. 'Babies drowning in mud. That's what I saw. So many babies I could barely comprehend. George was one of them. I knew he was lost. Knew I'd never find him.'

'Things may not be so dark, hinny. Can ye not recall what Mary told ye? It might put things in a better light.'

When Alice shook her head, Mac lumbered to her feet. 'If we leave at first light, we can get to Darrobine before the post office closes and send off a telegram to the war office. Or mayhap we can make use o' their new-fangled telephone to make some inquiries. I'll rouse Dulcie to get us somethin' to eat and tell Sarah to harness the horses.'

Alice did not see her friend's troubled expression as she left the room.

*August 25, 1918. Today I received a letter from George saying he has married a girl in London. I would feel happier for him and his Ellen if the news were not so old. The letter was dated March 21st and who knows what has happened since? My fears for him are such that his marriage to some British nurse I have never met seems insignificant in comparison.*

*September 12, 1918. The War Office has confirmed what I already knew. George is dead. There is no body, but nor is there any doubt. Like so many other young Australian men, he was swallowed by mud on the battlefields of Europe.*

# JULIA

I mark my place in Alice's journal with George's letter to Ellen and put it aside. I feel leaden and dislocated as I get up and walk to the window. The rain is relentless. All four tanks are overflowing, adding to the sea of mud between the house and the woodshed. *Sea of mud.* I try to imagine the battlefields of France, lacerated by trenches, shell-shattered, churned by millions of marching feet into a quagmire that swallows young men.

It is beyond me.

The Great War, they called it, the war to end all wars, but all it did was ensure that men became more efficient killers for the next one and all the others that followed. And while men stuffed up the world, women like Alice and Ellen had their future hollowed out until all that was left were broken dreams. It was bloody depressing.

Suddenly angry at men in general, my rage turns to Peter. Why hasn't he responded to any of my texts? Is he so caught up in his money-centred world that he can't message me an ETA? Has he given any thought to the fact that until he returns with the car, I can't recharge my mobile?

I glance at my watch. I've missed lunch, but I'm not hungry. I shove more wood in the Aga, fill the kettle, stick it on the hotplate. Then I put on my parka and Gran's boots and trudge through the mud and rain to fetch more wood. By the time I've refilled the baskets, my bad mood has evaporated, and the kettle is bubbling cheerily. I make a fresh pot of tea and reach again for the box of letters.

# ELLEN

*Barragunyah,*
*January, 1919.*
*Dear Ellen,*

*Please forgive me for not replying earlier. I think you will understand, as nobody else could, that my grief for George laid me so low that when I received your letter, I failed to fully understand your situation. Now I have recovered somewhat, I realise that George's child, my grandchild whom I dearly wish to meet, will have been born since you wrote. I hope all went well and that you and the baby are in good health.*

*Although we have never met, you are my daughter-in-law so I hope you will not take offence at the enclosed bank cheque. Until George's estate is settled, you may use the money in whatever way you choose. However, you would make an old woman very happy if you would consider spending some of it on a passage to Australia and stay with me at Barragunyah for a while. Although the dangers of war are now over, I know I am asking a lot of a young mother to travel so great a distance with an infant, so I hasten to add that I will gladly send additional funds for your mother or sister, or anyone else you might wish to accompany you. (I'm afraid George told me nothing about your family, so I am making assumptions.)*

*I understand if you choose not to come, and will travel to London myself as soon as possible. All I ask is that you consider a visit and write to me with your answer at your earliest convenience.*

*My very warmest regards to you and my grandchild,*
*Sincerely,*
*Alice Larson*

Ellen had just finished feeding Georgina when the postman pushed the letter through the slot in the door. She glanced at it in dismay as she buttoned her dress and sat the baby up to burp her. It had to be another bill, but what for this time? What hadn't she allowed for? There were only a few shillings in her purse and nothing at all in her bank account until her pension was paid next week. Lifting the baby to her shoulder, she went over and picked up the letter. Her breath caught in her throat when she saw the Australian stamp. The postmark was dated three months earlier.

It had been September before she finally found the courage to write to George's mother and she had been on tenterhooks ever since, wondering how news of an expected grandchild had been received amid the horror and grief of George's death. From the little George had told her, Mrs Larson was a formidable woman; strong, independent and, of course, wealthy. Would she think Ellen had married George for his money? Would she think she was using the baby to play upon her sympathies to garner financial support? Ellen was not ashamed of her background, but she knew only too well that the moneyed class did not willingly allow their sons to marry the likes of her. She and George had had that conversation several times, but he'd always dismissed her concerns.

'My parents weren't always well off,' he had said, laughing. 'Mother will tell you that herself when you meet her.'

But Ellen knew the self-made ones were often the worst when it came to arranging suitable marriages for their offspring. With money came the desire for a title, or at least a respectable lineage to establish the family's place in society. Her own mother had discovered that the hard way.

Rose Moran was the daughter of a Midlands mill owner who

had made a fortune in textiles before marrying into local gentry. Indulged by her ambitious father, Rose received an education more suited to boys than to girls, a matter that caused her mother some anxiety. Fortunately, when she made her debut at seventeen, in the London season of 1893, Rose's shy manner had concealed her intelligence and she had attracted proposals from several young men with appropriate titles and connections. Rose refused them all.

Impatient with their stubborn daughter, her parents demanded an explanation and Rose admitted her affections lay with Angus, a young foreman at her father's cotton mill. With their blessing, she told her parents reticently, they hoped to marry in spring. Her father sacked Angus immediately and forbade Rose to see him again. When they risked his wrath and eloped, he cut his daughter out of his will and never spoke to her again, nor allowed his wife to contact her.

Rose and Angus had been married four years, and Ellen had just turned three, when Angus died in a carriage accident as he walked home from the tavern where he worked. For the next seventeen years, Rose was driven by one desire – to educate her daughter and instil in her a sense of independence. She took in sewing to support them, working by candlelight late into the night and rising at dawn in all weathers to deliver her pieces to the factories. Riddled with consumption by the age of thirty-eight, Rose died on the same fateful day in 1914 that Archduke Ferdinand and his Duchess were assassinated. The royal deaths made headlines and ignited the Great War. Rose's death was marked only by her daughter.

Yes, Ellen knew all too well what happened when money married a nobody, for the repercussions of her mother's ill-starred love had determined the course of her own life. She had never been to school, working from the age of four alongside Rose and reciting the alphabet and times-tables as she learned to sew. Rose taught her to read from discarded newspapers, to tally by calculating the payments they would receive for their work, showing her how each penny had to be accounted for. A quick and intelligent child, with a seriousness and determination that belied her age, Ellen's education was broader than any she would have got at a parish school, but with no opportunity to make friends, she lacked social skills. Later, despite her nursing competence, she felt awkward and insecure around her co-workers and avoided socialising with them. Only George had brought out the lighter side of her nature. And George was gone.

Steeling herself, she settled the baby in the dresser drawer that served as a crib and opened the letter. It consisted of a single page, but as she unfolded it, another piece of paper fluttered to the floor. She picked it up, then sat down in a hurry. A bank cheque for five hundred pounds – a small fortune! She felt suddenly sick. Was George's mother trying to buy her off?

Ellen felt only marginally better when she read the letter. *George's child, my grandchild* – as if eliminating all trace of the superfluous mother – and yet… *you are my daughter-in-law… I hope you will not take offence… use the money in whatever way you choose…*

Her own letter to George's mother had been an agony to write, made all the harder because she knew so little about her. Had this letter been similarly difficult for her unknown mother-in-law on the other side of the world?

What to make of her offer? That was the problem. *Go to my mother at Barragunyah,* George had said, and there was certainly nothing to hold her in London. Yet it was a long way to travel alone with a baby, especially with Spanish Influenza so pervasive. The war might be over, but if you could believe the newspapers, the disease was killing more people than the guns had. More than 2000 people a week were dying from its ravages in Britain alone.

Ellen had never been a worrier – as a nurse, she was accustomed to dealing efficiently with problems as they arose – but now she had

Georgina, she worried about everything; money, the rising cost of food and rent, her lack of family support. If she caught the flu, what would happen to her baby? How would she cope if Georgina caught it? She could not afford doctors or expensive medicines. And that was the crux of it, she thought, her mind following a well-worn trail. George would want his daughter to have the best of everything, but even if she took in washing to supplement her pension, or sewing as her mother had, Ellen would be able to provide only the most basic living.

She read the letter again. *All I ask is that you consider a visit and write with your answer at your earliest convenience… Alice Larson.* Ellen had not even known her name was Alice. At least she wasn't asking her to stay forever, just to visit. George had intended them to live in Sydney so if it didn't work out, if she hated Barragunyah, or if she didn't get along with her mother-in-law, maybe she could get work in the city as a live-in nanny. Surely it wouldn't be hard to find a wealthy family who would allow her to care for Georgina alongside their own children.

Of course, there was still the flu. But it had been raging for months now and she could as easily catch it here, shopping for a loaf of bread in London, as on a ship or in some foreign port along the way. There was even a chance it had not yet affected Australia, a country George had described as warm and sunny. Ellen went to the desk for pen and paper. For Georgina's sake, she would have to take the risk.

# JULIA

After a restless night, I wake with my head filled with images of mud and lost babies and dark prophets of doom, as if Alice's nightmares have infiltrated my consciousness. It doesn't help that the rain is still drumming on the iron roof. It's a sound I usually love, even when nature overdoes it as it has these past few days, but the possibility of being trapped here by a flood gives the sound an ominous dimension. I lie in bed, grateful for the warmth of my sleeping bag, trying to imagine Ellen travelling all that way with a baby when the deadly Spanish flu was rampant. Would I have been as brave?

It is still dark. Hoping a hot drink will send me back to sleep until daylight, I get up, add more wood to the stove, and heat some long-life milk in a saucepan. As I sit at the kitchen table drinking warm Milo by the wan light of a single candle, I admit I'm actually quite worried about Peter. I am past being annoyed. I think something has happened to him. I'll call his company after breakfast and send a prayer to the phone god for my depleted battery to last while I press all the infuriating buttons that are apparently necessary before speaking to a human at his workplace.

I am just getting back into bed when I hear footsteps, soft and stealthy, on the veranda outside my room. Peter? No, why would he be so furtive? I flick on a torch, but even as I shine the light outside, I know I am being ridiculous – Barragunyah is at least twenty kilometres from the main road, so nobody is going to arrive without me hearing a car. Telling myself it's only my imagination, that I'd hear nothing as subtle as footsteps in the pelting rain, I nevertheless lie awake picturing all sorts of horrors until dawn shows its feeble light and I finally drift into an uneasy sleep.

Now, as I wait in the morning gloom for office hours so I can make my call, I try to distract myself with some old photographs I found with the letters. But as I gaze at George and Ellen on their wedding day, I cannot shake the eerie feeling that I am being watched.

# ALICE

As she waited on the wind-swept wharf, Alice pulled the sepia photograph from her purse and studied it for the umpteenth time. It took an act of will to force her gaze away from her heart-achingly handsome son in his uniform to fix Ellen's features in her mind. The girl was a beauty, no doubt about it, fair hair pulled back in a loose knot on her neck, a fine straight nose, large dark eyes with a serious expression. It had been taken on their wedding day and she was simply dressed in a dark skirt and white blouse with a high lace collar. George had enclosed the photograph with the letter he'd written to tell her he was married. What a shock that had been! Alice hadn't known whether to laugh or cry. It didn't seem right – her only son marrying a girl she had never met.

Alice glanced around at the small crowd gathered with her on the wharf. Strangers all of them, just as Ellen was a stranger. Tucking the photograph back in her purse, she was hit by a wave of loneliness, that same feeling of alienation from everything and everyone that had overwhelmed her for months after George was torn from her. But she could not succumb to that again, not here, not now, when she was about to meet George's wife and child. It's these awful masks, she told herself. It was hard not to feel alienated when people were forced by law to cover their faces with gauze pads that made everyone look somehow less than human.

She had arrived in Sydney nine days earlier to meet her daughter-in-law and granddaughter when they disembarked from the *Orsova*, only to learn that all the passengers were in quarantine at North Head. She had panicked, thinking the worst, until she was told it was standard procedure to combat the spreading of Spanish Influenza.

She had known about the pandemic – who didn't? – but secluded at Barragunyah, her mind split between Ellen's arrival and the spring calving, the seriousness of the disease had scarcely registered. It was only when the stationmaster at Lurradallan had been reluctant to sell her a train ticket she realised she should have paid more attention.

'Sorry, Missus, there's restrictions on long distance travel,' he told her. 'Because of that flu, yer know? People dropping like flies in the cities, they say. You wouldn't get me goin' down there, not for love nor money.'

Alice had been taken aback but would not be put off. Noting his name on a plaque at the ticket office, she put on what she hoped was a winning smile and tried again. 'Mr Saunders, my son's widow arrives in Sydney from England in a few days and won't know a soul. It's essential I am there to greet her.'

'Essential, eh? Well, they make allowances for essential business. You'll need a doctor's certificate, though.'

'I'm sure I can arrange that. I'll need one first class ticket to Sydney and two for the return journey.'

'No first-class carriages since the war, Missus. It's potluck for everyone these days.'

'I see.' Alice sighed. She'd been hoping some degree of comfort and privacy would make the trip to Barragunyah less daunting for an English girl unused to such long distances. 'Very well then. One ticket down, two back.'

'Tell you what, Missus, I'll let you have the ticket down – essential business, as you say – but gettin' back's a different kettle o' fish. You have to sort that out at the other end.'

He'd been right about that, Alice mused now. Ellen and the baby would have medical certificates from the doctor at the quarantine station to say they weren't infected, but unless they left the same day, they'd face further restrictions. She herself would be examined at Central Station before they boarded the train, and heaven help her if she had a sniffle or a temperature.

Alice had originally planned to stay in Sydney a few days, to introduce Ellen to George's solicitor and show her around the city, but that would have to wait now. Which wasn't so bad as it turned out; with everything centred around the need to prevent contagion, the city had little to recommend it. People were forbidden to go to libraries, theatres, and even church, and only a few diners at a time were allowed in restaurants. Sydney people, who she remembered as friendly and outgoing on her previous visits, now seemed dour and intimidating – hardly surprising when they were made to wear masks and were constantly being told where they couldn't go and what they couldn't do. There was certainly none of the exuberance she had seen on Federation Day, or the patriotic excitement when the troops had sailed off to war.

She shivered, aware that it was the stirring of memories rather than the breeze, which sent a chill through to her bones. It was early spring, and the harbour sparkled in the sunshine, not unlike that shining day she had seen George for the last time. The laughing faces of those young men, and the enthusiasm of the crowds who had waved them off, seemed an abomination now. Like the war itself.

A ferry sped across the blue water, kicking up white foam as it headed for the wharf. A murmur spread through the waiting crowd and Alice's heart gave a little skip. She was more nervous than she'd expected. What would two strangers talk about? *You'll love her, Mother*, George had written, and under different circumstances, with him there to introduce them and smooth away any awkwardness, she was sure she would have. But her initial reaction when she'd read his letter had been irritation. Surely, they might have waited until she could be with her son on his wedding day? They should have married at Barragunyah or in Sydney, not London, so far away from everyone who knew and loved George.

A harsh sob escaped Alice's lips. From the corner of her eye, she saw people glancing at her. That wouldn't do at all. Pull yourself together, she told herself sternly. But it was hard, knowing that if she'd had her way, if they had waited to marry, she would not now have a daughter-in-law and a granddaughter.

Georgina. The name brought a smile to Alice's lips. That alone had warmed her heart towards her son's widow. Alice had forgotten the exact date of her birth but knew that, like her father, she was a December child, which would make her around nine months old. What would she look like? Would she have George's brown eyes and dark hair, his wide smile?

The ferry slowed and pulled into the wharf. A deckhand leapt ashore and whipped a heavy rope around the mooring bollard, allowing the vessel to align with the dock before securing it. A gangplank was thrown across the gap.

Alice's anxiety increased. How would she look to this stranger she was now related to by marriage? Would the new outfit she'd purchased at David Jones make the right impression? Alice had little interest in clothes beyond decency and practicality, but for this special occasion, she'd allowed the shop assistant to advise her. The navy-blue jacket and narrow skirt that skimmed her ankles were comfortable enough, but the silly shoes with their raised heels, instep buckles, and long pointed toes were not. As for the hat, its narrow brim was barely enough to shade her face.

The passengers began to disembark. Alice straightened her posture. It's too late now to worry about how you look, she told herself firmly.

# ELLEN

Ellen hung back, clutching Georgina tightly as the other passengers surged eagerly from the ferry. Straightening the wide lace collar of her brown dress, she turned her attention to her daughter, checking for the tenth time that there were no food stains on the little knitted jacket. I'm as jumpy as a cat, she thought wryly. Am I afraid my mother-in-law will eat me? She peered through the salt-dusted windows at the masked people on the wharf. A few of the *Orsova* passengers had complained when officials at the quarantine station told them masks had to be worn in public, but most were so relieved to be released from their hated place of detention they would have agreed to anything.

Ellen did not share their relief. Although the accommodation at the station was rough and the food poor, she had been impressed by the efficiency of the nursing staff and entranced by the beauty of the setting. When permitted, she had walked the sea-sprayed cliffs carrying little Gina, pointing out gulls and the large birds that an orderly had told her were sea-eagles. However, she was aware that much of her pleasure stemmed from postponing the meeting with George's mother, and she'd used the time to rehearse what she would say. But those rambling conversations in her mind had failed to find the words she sought and niggling fears of being rejected, or browbeaten into surrendering Georgina, gnawed at her confidence with no less intensity than the day they had left London.

She looked up as she stepped onto the gangplank and realised that not everyone was wearing a mask. A slim, well-dressed woman of middle years was watching her closely, her face uncovered, the gauze fluttering in her gloved hand. She smiled and Ellen's breath caught when she saw her eyes crinkling at the corners just as George's had.

She pulled off her own mask and returned the smile. 'Look, Gina, there's your grandmother.'

A whistle blew and the train shuddered, emitting a hiss of steam and clouds of smoke. Carriages jerked into motion as the great wheels began to move. A smell of soot wafted through the open window.

Alice stood up to shut it. 'Do you mind? The smoke makes my eyes water.'

Ellen shook her head. 'Not at all. It's better for Gina if it's closed.'

The baby lay asleep beside her, bolstered by a folded shawl on the leather seat. The seat opposite had been flipped over and the large family group occupying the two facing seats were chattering loudly. Despite the narrow space left to them, Ellen was glad of the privacy.

'We have a long journey ahead of us,' Alice said. 'It would have been preferable to have our own compartment but the war, and now this flu...' She spread her hands helplessly.

Ellen nodded towards a group of men swaying in the aisle. 'We're lucky to have a seat at all, I think. To have this one to ourselves seems a luxury. I saw some people looking at the space beside us, but I think the baby put them off.'

The train was crowded with an assortment of passengers, both seated and standing in the aisles. Some men had sleeves or trouser legs folded over the stumps of missing limbs, and Ellen felt a familiar pang as she thought of George. She glanced at her mother-in-law. She would miss him too, although Ellen couldn't imagine they would ever find the words to speak of their shared loss.

The baby stirred in her sleep and Alice smiled indulgently. 'It's been a tiring day for her. I'm sorry it was so rushed. I intended to show you around Sydney but as I explained…'

'I'm sure I'll see the city properly when the influenza has passed.' Ellen hesitated. 'George thought we would live there, you know.'

Alice nodded. 'Yes. He has a lovely house at Rose Bay overlooking the harbour. It's yours now, of course, but I hope you will like Barragunyah enough to stay a while.'

Ellen stared at her, bewildered. 'Mine? But I don't expect… I mean… George's house is yours now, surely?'

'You are his wife and his next of kin, my dear. His solicitor will need to iron out the details as I don't believe my son got around to changing his will when you married.' She leaned closer, pitching her voice low against the rattle of the train. 'I don't know if George told you, but he is,' she paused, '*was* quite well off. You are a wealthy woman.'

'No.' Ellen's mouth tightened. 'No, thank you, Mrs Larson. I would be grateful for an allowance for Gina, but I want nothing else.'

'Then you will have to give it away, *Mrs Larson*, for it is yours whether you want it or not.'

'But…' Ellen frowned. 'I didn't marry George for his money, no matter what you may think.'

'Now why would I think that?' Alice sighed. 'Ellen, I'm sure you'll agree that these past few hours have been a strain on both of us. But we have at least ten more hours before we reach Lurradallan, and unless we use the time to get to know one another without hiding behind trite civilities, it is going to be an unbearable journey.'

Ellen's eyes widened. George had said his mother could be blunt-spoken—but she was right, it had been awkward. Yet it would be worse once she knew about her daughter-in-law's impoverished background and lack of formal education. She took a deep breath. It was probably best to get the unpalatable truth out of the way.

If necessary, she could leave the train at the next stop and catch another one back to Sydney. 'What do you want to know?'

'To begin with, I'd like to know why you're afraid of me.'

'I see.' Ellen lifted her chin, straightened her back. 'Very well. I'm afraid you will want to take Georgina from me. I know what wealth and power can do to arrange such things. But I tell you now, I will never allow it.'

'Good. I would think less of you if you did.' Alice smiled sadly. 'Of course, I want Georgina – she reminds me so much of George at that age – but I want her mother too. I would never try to separate you.'

Alice held up her hand as Ellen went to speak.

'As for wealth, I would like to know why you feel threatened by it – I'm sure there's a story behind your antipathy – but first let me make something clear. Yes, I am a rich woman, but you are richer by far. You need have no more fears on that account.'

'I cannot take that in.' Ellen shook her head. 'Whatever the case, I want you to know that is not why I married George. Please believe that.'

'Oh, I believe you.' Alice chuckled. 'But while we are on the subject and getting to know each other, I think I should tell you I married George's father for his money.'

Ellen looked stunned. Alice laughed again, then relented.

'It was a mutual agreement. John wanted a wife to provide him with sons and I was tired of domestic service.'

'You were a domestic servant? But I thought… I'm sure I remember George saying his parents each made their own fortunes.'

'That's right. But I made mine after John died.'

'I see. You invested your husband's money?'

'Not at all. John left everything in trust for George. I got a generous allowance, but that was all. When George went to boarding school, Barragunyah was worth almost nothing, but with the help of my friend Mac, I turned it into a profitable farm. When George came of age and inherited, he gave the deeds of the property to me.'

Ellen felt as if the world had slanted, setting everything askew. Her own life was shifting even as they spoke. George's mother was nothing like the woman she had imagined. She stared at Alice, who had removed her stylish hat and placed it on the seat. Her thick dark hair, swept up into a bun on top of her head, was threaded with grey, her face etched with fine lines. The deep blue eyes, surrounded by crinkles like George's, were watching her intently.

'If we are going to be blunt, Alice, may I ask you a question?'

'So, you can say my name after all?' Alice smiled. 'Of course, go ahead.'

'Why didn't George live with you at Barragunyah?'

It was Alice's turn to feel uncomfortable. Of all the questions the girl could have asked, why did she have to choose that one? She wanted to get to know her daughter-in-law, not frighten her off.

She sighed. 'George didn't like it there. Most males don't.'

'But his father…'

'Hated it. Although his pride prevented him from being fully aware of it. You see, Barragunyah is a woman's place.'

Ellen frowned. 'I don't understand.'

'It's not something you *can* understand. It's something you *know* because…' Alice sighed again. 'First, I'll have to tell you about Mary.'

# JULIA

When I finally get through to Peter's secretary, she is so distracted it takes a while to make it clear who I am and why I'm calling.

'Oh, my god,' she says at last. 'Just a sec, I'll put you through to one of the partners.'

More waiting, while I stare anxiously at the scarily low battery level on my phone. *Don't you dare die yet,* I plead.

The gruff voice in my ear makes me jump. 'Matt Scarborough here. Where the hell's Peter? He should have been here days ago! The board's in an uproar!'

My stomach does an unpleasant flip. 'He didn't turn up? But he left two, no, three days ago.' I realise I've lost track of time. 'What I mean is, he left as soon as you called.'

Deathly silence on the other end, then: 'He said he'd charter a plane. Do you know which company he used?'

'Sorry, I've no idea.' I clear my throat. 'Actually, I haven't heard from him since he left, and I was hoping…'

The faceless voice sounds angry. 'He might have had an accident. Did you think of that? Why the hell haven't you checked?'

'Because I haven't got…'

My phone dies.

I place it on the kitchen table and whisper my excuses to the empty room. 'Because I haven't got a car. Because it hasn't stopped raining since Peter left and the causeways will be flooded. Because even if I had a car that could make it across the causeways, the road is probably impassable.'

I sink into a chair and plonk my elbows on the table, resting my head in my hands. What has happened to my brother? His partner, or whoever it was I spoke to, is right. I have to assume that Peter's car has broken down, or he's had an accident. The question is, where? If he broke down on the main road, a passing driver would have given him a lift. Likewise, if he had an accident on the main road, someone would have called the police or an ambulance. And if he'd been badly hurt – I won't allow myself to think beyond that – he had ID with him, so it's a fair bet his partners would know by now.

But they didn't. Which means he is probably stranded somewhere on Barragunyah's private road and has been there, in God knows what state of hurt, for several cold, wet days. But again, where? The track from the house to the main road is a good twenty kilometres and Peter could be anywhere along that winding ribbon of slippery black-soil mud.

'And another thing,' I say to the invisible partner in Melbourne, 'I'm all alone, eighty kilometres from the nearest town, and my phone just died. Any suggestions on what I should do about that?'

A random thought intrudes, and my mind skips to a whole new problem. I leap to my feet and begin rustling through the various bags and boxes we stashed in the kitchen cupboards. I spread everything out on the table and make some rough calculations. We bought enough to feed the two of us for a week, and I haven't eaten much since Pete left. If I'm careful, I might have enough food to last about three weeks. Maybe.

By the time night closes in I'm wrecked, although I've done nothing but mooch from room to room all day like a lost dog. Tomorrow I'll face the rain and mud to look for Peter, but today, with its nasty little surprises, has been a write-off. Too agitated to read Alice's journals or sift through old letters, I've been poking around the place haphazardly, as if I'll find answers to questions I haven't yet asked.

It's a big house, something that didn't really register with me when I lived here. Back then, all that mattered to me was the feeling of belonging I got from being here, the sense of security that came from knowing I was loved and valued. And being young and city bred, I was more interested in the exciting world beyond the garden fence.

There are six bedrooms – which seems excessive until I remember all those strapping sons John expected Alice to provide – and two smaller rooms that I think were servants' quarters. The big eat-in kitchen, with the Aga and a scrubbed pine table scarred by the years, is the heart of the home, but there is also a formal dining room with handsome rosewood furniture that currently wears a coat of mould. In the cosy sitting room, the sofas on which I once loved to sprawl with a book, are threadbare and damp-smelling, but the leather chesterfields in the big living room have weathered the years well, as have the pair of leather armchairs in the room Gran called her office, and which I imagine was once John's den. The bathroom and laundry, added in Ellen's time I think, to replace the outside toilet and washroom, are built seamlessly into a corner of the wide wrap-around veranda alongside the schoolroom.

With its high, ornate ceilings, timber floors and elegantly carved fretwork, it is easy to see that the house must once have been beautiful – I certainly remember it that way. Now it just seems sad. Or is that a reflection of my current mood? I attempt to revive my spirits by picturing Alice and Ellen living here with baby Gina…

# ALICE

Looking back, Alice thought Barragunyah's homestead hadn't really come to life until Ellen and Georgina arrived. As her granddaughter crawled on the polished floors, took her first tentative steps, clattered down the hallway in her mother's shoes, and rode her dinky on the veranda, the house lost its ponderous aura. There was more noise, more light, more activity, more people. All those empty bedrooms that John had hoped would contain his sons were now filled with women of varying ages – Mac and herself, Ellen, Gina and Lizzie, her governess, Dulcie and Sarah.

And if Gina was the lively spirit of the house, its steady heart was Ellen. Her quiet presence, thoughtful observations and self-deprecating wit brought serenity to the hustle and bustle of daily life, while her brisk efficiency and nursing skills were invaluable whenever anyone – human or animal – was sick or injured.

In the early years after her daughter-in-law came to Barragunyah, Alice had lived in dread that Ellen would leave and take little Gina with her. Her fears had heightened when she agreed to accompany Ellen to Sydney to inspect George's mansion at Rose Bay. Alice could see the young woman was impressed with the beautiful house, its view of the harbour, and the gracious tree-lined street in which it stood among similarly imposing homes. George's solicitor had rented it to a wealthy businessman, but the lease would soon expire and Ellen needed to decide what to do with it.

Alice tried hard not to impose her own hopes. 'I believe it's a good area,' she said cautiously. 'You'd meet respectable people, have a social life. Gina could go to the best schools.'

'Yes, I can imagine.' Ellen folded her arms, clasping her elbows in her hands as she looked out over the water. 'Would you live here?'

'Well, no. I know George loved it, but Barragunyah is the only place for me.'

Ellen looked at her seriously. 'Alice, I want to ask you something and I want you to answer me truthfully. Please don't try to spare my feelings.'

'Very well.'

'Do you find Gina and me too much of a disruption?' She held up her hand. 'No, let me finish. Before we came, you had peace and privacy at Barragunyah. You must miss that.'

'Not a bit. I love having you there. But I understand why you would find it dull, why you would want to mix socially with people your own age.'

Ellen flashed one of her rare smiles. 'You must know by now that I'm uncomfortable around people my age. I have no desire to socialise.'

'But you're still young.' Alice hesitated before she voiced her most niggling fear. 'You may wish to remarry and you're unlikely to meet anyone suitable if you're secluded at Barragunyah.'

'I was widowed at the same age as you were. You didn't remarry.'

Startled, Alice raised her eyebrows. She had never thought of herself from that perspective. 'It was enough for me that I had my son. I've explained that John and I didn't marry for love. You and George, I think, were very much in love.'

Ellen nodded, her gaze still on the harbour. 'Yes, we were. But I'm not a person who loves easily and I don't expect to feel that way again. Like you, I have my child and that is enough.'

'Gina's education must affect your decision. She'll soon be five and it's too far to travel to school each day from Barragunyah. You could buy a house in Darrobine, as I did, but I suspect that might not appeal to you.'

'Alice, Georgina isn't George. She's happy at Barragunyah and there's no evidence that Barragunyah isn't happy to have her there. If you're able to bear the added disruption, I thought I might employ a tutor, a governess.'

Alice's heart leapt. 'Are you saying you will stay? You won't move to Sydney?'

'If you'll have us.'

'Oh, my dear, I can think of nothing I'd like better.'

Alice rubbed her aching hip as she limped up the front steps onto the veranda – at sixty-seven, she was starting to feel her age. If not for Ellen and Gina, she thought, Barragunyah would be deteriorating as surely as the women who ran it.

Mac was seventy-eight, with failing eyesight and a heart condition she referred to offhandedly as a dicky ticker. Dulcie was sixty-three, and though she rarely complained, the constant ache of her arthritic joints made her short-tempered. She still ran the kitchen with her old efficiency, but the milking and egg collecting, along with the care of her two beloved milking cows and a flock of hens, had been taken over by Gina. Sarah, the youngest of them at fifty, had never fully recovered from a bout of pneumonia last winter and could barely summon the strength to do the laundry, let alone the other chores she once attacked with vigour.

Ellen had been a blessing from the beginning, gradually and unobtrusively taking over the management of the household, smoothing the bumps of day-to-day living and transforming the homestead. Tentatively at first, then with growing confidence as her efforts were appreciated, she replaced dusty velvet drapes with cotton or lace. She cleaned, painted, and re-papered, rearranged furniture, oiled timber floors until they glowed. Her style and energy had turned a gracious but gloomy house into a beautiful, comfortable home.

Alice, accustomed to the old ways, was astonished at the things Ellen thought of to add to their comfort. When she said she was getting the house wired for electricity, Alice was sure she was wasting her money. How on earth could they get power way out here? She'd asked. A wind-powered generator, Ellen said, just wait and see. And when it was up and running, they'd all been as excited as eight-year-old Gina, who'd raced from room to room, tugging on cords to light the oddly shaped glass bulbs dangling from the ceiling. A month later, when an electric refrigerator arrived to replace the old kerosene one, Dulcie had cried.

In 1928, the year Gina turned ten, Ellen paid for telegraph poles and wiring all the way from the main road to Barragunyah. The reason for this extravagance, Ellen explained, was to contact the doctor if anyone was seriously ill or injured. As it turned out, they could also telephone ahead to place orders with the produce store, the haberdasher, and the grocer, confirming the supply of the items they needed and giving them more time to enjoy their monthly trips to Darrobine.

Alice had worried that Ellen spent so much on Barragunyah, but since that black day in 1929, when some American foolishness upset the world's finances and instigated what people now called the Great Depression, the property suddenly seemed a better investment than stocks and bonds which could become worthless overnight.

Even so, both she and Ellen had lost a great deal of money in those difficult years, and they were not alone – the Depression had affected most people one way or another. Like most farms, Barragunyah had struggled to survive, but it was worse in the cities. As businesses failed and jobs were lost, men took to the roads, tramping through the countryside with their meagre possessions in swags on their backs, desperate for paid work but willing to settle for a meal or a handout of flour and tobacco. Alice and Mac offered odd jobs to the few who ventured down Barragunyah's track, but they never stayed long, always restlessly seeking something better.

Alice lowered herself into a cane chair on the veranda, unconsciously still rubbing her hip as she considered Gina's proposal. Those awful years were now behind them, but how could anyone be sure it wouldn't happen again? Gina, with the energy and optimism of youth, had no doubts at all and had been badgering her for months to fence off more pastures.

'We need those extra paddocks, Grandmother,' she'd said again over dinner last night. 'Then, if market prices are down, we can wait until things pick up before we sell.'

Alice smiled, remembering. 'I'll think about it,' she'd said. 'Fencing's not cheap. I'll want to go over the books first.' They both knew she'd agree eventually. The girl loved the Angus herd with a passion that equalled Mac's, and her ideas, although not always fully thought through, usually made sense in the long run.

At fourteen, Gina was a lively bundle of energy, more at home on the back of a horse than in the classroom Ellen had had built onto one end of the veranda. Not that she wasn't smart as a whip – Gina had no trouble getting through the lessons Lizzie gave her – she simply preferred being outside.

Alice stood up carefully, leaning on the veranda railing to gaze across the garden, past the fence to the lush paddocks, remembering that once she had stood in this very spot, thinking about how lonely she was. She could not have imagined then what happiness was in store for her. Sorrow too, of course; she would never get over losing George. But she knew now that everything was part of a pattern that was often hidden while time wove the threads of experience into the fabric of life. Then one day, there it was – strands from the past looping through the present to reveal the shape of the future.

Life was full of surprises.

# JULIA

I am buffeted by an icy wind as I slog along the slippery road in Gran's gumboots. I've fallen twice already and between my parka and the boots my jeans are soaked and covered in mud. The second fall jarred my wrist and frightened me with images of lying in the rain with a broken leg until I died of exposure or starvation. My imagination is running riot, but it has good cause considering that nobody knows where I am.

I'd taken leave from work when Gran died and although I'd told a couple of colleagues I was going to get her house ready for sale, I didn't mention where it was. I don't think Peter told anyone either; the man I spoke to in his office certainly didn't know, and the last person my brother would tell is his ex-wife. In hindsight, our lack of communication seems rash, but location hardly matters when you can be reached on your mobile no matter where you are.

Unless you have no way of recharging the damned thing.

In a corner of my mind is the vague hope that now Peter's business partners know he is missing, they'll try to track him down. More likely, judging by the obvious chaos in his office, they'll put it into the too-hard basket and assume his uncaring sister has been spurred into action. But speculation is pointless; I have to deal with the situation as it is.

I stagger over a ridge and peer through the rain at the first of the three causeways that intersect the track from Barragunyah to the main road. The creek bed had been dry when we'd arrived, but now the concrete crossing is hidden beneath a roaring torrent. People have died trying to cross swollen creeks like that, but what choice do I have? Slipping and sliding to the water's edge, I stare at it helplessly. How deep is it? Will I be able to resist the force of the water and make it across?

A big old eucalypt on the creek's bank has dropped several branches, so I grab one and strip away the twigs. Now I have a stout staff to steady me and probe the depth. Trying to ignore the Emergency Services mantra drilled into every Australian brain – *if it's flooded, forget it* – I tell myself that if I tread cautiously, I'll be okay.

Three steps and I'm gone. I flounder for a moment, trying to regain my footing, but the makeshift staff is whipped from my hand and the rushing water tumbles me about like a rag doll. As the weight of my sodden parka begins to drag me under, I instinctively yell for help and my mouth fills with water. Then my head smashes against something hard and darkness takes me.

When I open my eyes, Mary is bending over me, urging me to my feet. I'm so frozen I'm not sure I can move, but there's no question of disobeying her. I sit up cautiously and roll onto my hands and knees, slipping in the mud, before finally pushing myself upright. The swollen creek laps at my bare feet; I've lost Gran's boots. There's no sign of the track or the big eucalypt, so I assume I've been washed downstream, although it's impossible to guess how far. The water seems to be half a metre higher, raging like rapids over the creek's rocky embankments. There's no way I could have escaped that without help.

*Move!* Mary's command slips between my scattered thoughts, and she shoves me hard. I take one wobbly step and I'm down in the mud again. She pulls me roughly to my feet, slips an arm around my waist and half lifts, half drags me across the ground. Even through the layers of my waterlogged parka, I can feel the heat of her large, strong body against mine. After a while, I find my balance and our pace quickens.

'How did you know?' I ask her. 'How did you find me?'

She doesn't reply. Doesn't even look at me, and I realise that I'm of less consequence to her than a displaced animal. I try to explain, to justify my foolhardy behaviour.

'I was looking for Peter,' I say inanely. 'My brother. I think he's had an accident.'

She looks at me then. Her eyes are the colour of sunlit water and for a moment, I feel I am drowning again. She doesn't speak. She doesn't have to. In the deep pools of her eyes, I see the red Jeep skid on the gravel and overturn. I see Peter hurtle through the shattered windscreen. I see the blood on his face, the ungainly angle of his neck. The world closes in on me again.

# ELLEN

Ellen woke with a start, the dream so vivid she was surprised to find herself in bed instead of on the banks of the creek. She rolled over, reached for her slippers and robe, and padded down the hallway towards the bathroom at the end of the veranda.

The night was overcast with no sign of the stars that, earlier, had glittered like ice crystals across the great expanse of sky. She opened the bathroom door quietly, closed it behind her and fumbled for the cord to switch on the electric light. She frowned, momentarily puzzled, then, as if her hands knew more than she did, reached for the candle and matches that someone had placed on a shelf. A soft glow lit the room. Ellen went over to the new claw-foot bath and turned the tap, smiling as she recalled everyone's excitement the day the plumber finished installing it and the inside toilet. Like all the tradesmen she hired to work at Barragunyah, he'd completed the job in record time, eager to be paid and away. She was always fascinated at how unease gradually overtook men when they worked on the place, yet despite their haste to depart, not one had ever tried to cheat her or leave a job unfinished.

She put her hand under the tap to check the temperature and adjusted the cold water slightly – it would not do to scald her patient. She looked up as Mary carried the unconscious woman into the room and lowered her to the floor. Ellen nodded. There was no need for words; she knew what she had to do.

'I had a peculiar dream last night,' Ellen said. She reached for the jug of cream and poured a generous helping onto her porridge. 'Two dreams actually, but somehow connected.'

She'd been intentionally late for breakfast, waiting until Dulcie and Sarah had finished and Gina had gone to collect the eggs. Alice and Mac looked up with interest, as she'd known they would. The two older women often discussed their dreams, but Ellen usually preferred to keep hers to herself. Not this time, though – talking about it might clear the confusion she had felt when she woke to find sunlight streaming through the curtains.

'In the first part of the dream, I was looking for someone – I don't know who. It was raining, and the track was slippery with mud.'

Alice glanced at Mac but said nothing.

'I came to the ridge above the first causeway and the creek was way up, higher even than last winter. A woman was standing on the bank. She was oddly dressed in tight fitting trousers and a red padded coat with a hood. I'm sure it was nobody I know, yet somehow, in the dream, I felt I knew her very well. She had a stout bough in her hand, testing the water for depth as she waded in. I shouted a warning, but the torrent grabbed her and I could do nothing but watch as she was swept downstream. I was certain she must have drowned, but then the scene changed, and I saw Mary pull her out. Don't ask me how I know it was Mary, I just *knew*.'

Mac nodded, her eyes bright with interest behind her thick spectacles. 'And then?'

'This is the strangest part. I woke up – or thought I did – and went to the bathroom to run a hot bath for her – the woman who fell into the creek, I mean. Mary carried her in and laid her on the floor and...' Ellen shrugged. 'I woke and it was morning.'

'That is a strange dream,' Alice said thoughtfully. 'I don't know what to make of it.'

Ellen frowned. 'I was hoping you would. I still feel quite odd, as if I'm out of place or something.'

'Nay, hinny, it's the other lass. And it's not out o' place she is, but out o' time.'

Alice and Ellen looked at Mac curiously. 'What do you mean?' Alice asked.

Mac didn't answer. Her eyes were unfocused, her expression vacant.

'Mac?'

'Barragunyah dreams are slippery. Where are they born? When will they end?' Mac's eyes refocused. She looked at them, startled, as if surprised to see them sitting there, then shook her head. 'I canna say for sure, but I think we'll hear more of yon lassie. She's travelling back, trying to find us…'

Alice glanced sharply at her old friend. Mac was eighty now and her mind sometimes wandered a little. Was she experiencing one of her odd premonitions, or succumbing to the eccentricities of aging? It was impossible to tell with Mac.

'Well, she found me, so perhaps she'll move on,' Ellen said lightly. She pushed her chair back from the table. 'I don't suppose it means anything really. Who can make sense of dreams? If you'll excuse me, I'll see if Gina's back with the eggs. Dulcie and I plan to do some baking this morning.'

Mac smiled secretively and sipped her tea as Ellen headed for the kitchen. Alice, frowning slightly, was watching Mac. Neither of them saw Ellen change direction.

Ellen pushed open the bathroom door. There was nobody in the room, but the bath was filled almost to the brim. Nobody at Barragunyah would waste so much precious water. She stared at it for a moment, then plunged her arm into the tepid water and pulled the plug.

# JULIA

When I emerge from the darkness, I'm lying naked on the bathroom floor with no memory of how I got here. My sodden clothes are in a pile beside me. The tap is running and clouds of steam rise from the old claw-footed bath. I am freezing and nothing has ever looked so inviting. Grabbing the edge of the bath, I haul myself upright and lower myself gingerly into the water. The heat is like needles piercing my icy flesh, but as my body warms, I relax and lie back, my hair floating like seaweed around my face.

I don't know how long I lie there. My has brain switched off, my world is reduced to sensations – warmth, comfort, silence, peace. When the water cools, I stagger naked along the veranda to my bedroom and slide into my sleeping bag where I sleep dreamlessly until I wake to the all too familiar sound of rain on the roof.

I've lost my watch in the creek and have no idea what time it is, or even what day it is, but two things suggest I've slept for a long time. The bucket I placed under the leak in the ceiling is overflowing, and all that's left of the fire in the stove is cold ashes. The floor can't get much worse, so I dress and deal with the fire first, then I fill the kettle and set it on the hotplate. By the time I've emptied the bucket and mopped the floor, the water has boiled. I make a pot of tea and sit down to gather my thoughts.

It takes only a mental nudge – a single word – to open the floodgate of memory.

Peter.

I see him again through the deep pools of Mary's eyes and remember everything. Grief overwhelms me. Despite his bullying and arrogance, he was my brother, the only family I have left. *Had left* – for I am in no doubt that Mary showed me the truth. I think of all those lost years, the distance between us, the lack of understanding. I cry for a long time.

Eventually, my tears dwindle to snotty sniffles. I blow my nose and admit I was weeping for myself as well as Peter. It doesn't take a genius to see that I'm up the proverbial shit creek without a paddle. The instant I acknowledge this, an awful dread grips me and I can hardly breathe. Shadows crowd in on me, and all I can see is the blood on Peter's face.

Will I be next?

I am still sitting at the kitchen table, but I think I must have blacked out or something because when I sip my tea, it is cold. I have never fainted in my life, but then I've never been pregnant either. Or seen my brother die. Or been holed up alone in the middle of nowhere, faced with running out of food. Or… What? Behind all those undeniably frightening facts lies something darker and older. Something I would rather not think about. I reach for my phone and press buttons mindlessly, hoping for a spark of life. Nothing.

Nothing I can do but sit here staring into space, listening to the rain on the roof, thinking about Peter, feeling sorry for myself.

After a while I get up, go to the sink, and splash my face with cold water. Then I toast the last two slices of stale bread on the hotplate, make more tea, and assess my situation as calmly as I can. First the facts: Peter is dead. I am flooded in. Nobody knows I'm here. I cannot contact anyone. My pretence at calmness falters, and again I struggle for breath. My skin feels clammy. My hands are shaking. Falling to pieces is not an option, but it takes an act of will to ignore my fear.

I force down the last piece of toast. I must eat. I am pregnant and should be eating for two, but that's not going to happen. Even if I ration my remaining supplies stringently, I will run out of food in – what? Three weeks? Four? I refuse to think about what such a restricted diet will do to my baby.

Giving in is also not an option, nor is escape. I cannot risk my life, and the life of my unborn child, on another excursion like yesterday's fiasco. My only choice is to sit it out and hope the rain stops soon. By anyone's reckoning, one choice is no choice.

With rain still thundering down in biblical proportions, it's easy to believe it will last forty days and forty nights. By then, I'll be ravenous enough to eat one of Noah's elephants. I attempt a half-hearted chuckle at my little joke, but it sounds so fake it fails to convince me there is anything remotely funny about my situation.

If there's a bright side to this mess, it's in knowing that the creeks of Barragunyah subside even faster than they rise. Experience tells me that if the rain stops for a couple of days, I'll be able to cross the causeways. Then all I have to do is trek twenty kilometres to the main road and hail a passing car to take me to Darrobine. It's been a while since I've done any serious hiking, but I used to do that distance in under four hours.

Not on a slippery track thick with mud, whispers logic, and not if you are weak from lack of food. But what use is logic in this situation?

I pass the days immersed in journals, letters, photographs. These things are food for thought when I'm hungry for bread, meat for the mind, sustenance for the soul. I unpack Gran's clothes from the black bags into which I had stuffed them, and play dress-ups like a child. It is not all play though – my own clothes are smelly and mouldy. I wash my undies and dry them over the towel rail on the

Aga, but it's easier to wear Gran's things than attempt to dry jeans and jumpers.

Her divided skirt looks good on me with a cream silk shirt and a long cardigan knitted from soft green wool. The cardigan smells of the cedar chest it was stored in to keep away moths. I try to imagine Gran wearing it when she was Gina, the *lively bundle of energy* Alice describes in her journal, and questions besiege me. Why did Gran never mention she was born in London, or that her mother risked a deadly pandemic to bring her to Australia? But when I think back, I realise that Gran seldom spoke of herself – all her stories were about Barragunyah.

So, I'm surprised when I find her book of dreams at the bottom of the tin trunk. It's just an old, lined notebook covered with brown paper, not an elegant cloth-bound book like Alice's journal, or Ellen's with its hand-painted covers. A card decorated with butterflies is pasted in the centre of the brown paper with *Gina's Dream Book* scrawled carelessly across the top. The pen has left two ink blots. I fan through the pages and see that some entries are dated, others are not. The first one is, so I begin with that.

# GINA

*August 22, 1933. Another dream about the lost girl. They always start with her calling my name, then the part where she's following me. I'm on a horse and she's not, but in the way of dreams, she keeps pace. This time, as I try to outrun her, I find myself surrounded by water. Floods are on my mind because it's been raining like the devil these past few days. If it doesn't let up soon, we'll have to move the cattle into the hill paddock and hope we've enough feed to see them through. So, I suppose the water part of the dream is the weather playing on my mind, but it doesn't explain why the girl is crying. And as for what happened today, in broad daylight, when Molly and I came home after checking the fences – well, nothing can explain that!*

'Who's that?' Gina asked, as she and Molly trudged through the mud towards the veranda.

Molly, who'd been living at Barragunyah and working with Gina for six months, narrowed her eyes against the driving rain. 'Who? Where? I don't see anyone.'

'There, on the veranda. Hey, isn't that my new cardigan she's wearing?'

'What?' Molly glanced at Gina, her expression puzzled. Then she giggled. 'Oh, stop teasing. If I really wanted a long cardigan like yours, I'd knit one!'

Gina looked again. The visitor had gone, but suddenly, as if she'd been slapped in the face, she knew who she was. It was the girl from her dreams.

And that was impossible.

She laughed to cover her confusion. 'As long as you know you're not borrowing mine. Off you go, now. You can have first shower.'

'You sure, Boss?'

'Yes, I want to talk to Mac. But leave me some hot water or I'll feed you to the wombats.'

Molly grinned and bounded up the veranda steps, heading for her room. Gina followed more slowly, deep in thought. She had seen the visitor for only an instant but her pale, worried face had been as clear as Molly's, and the cardigan she wore, the one Gina's mother had knitted for her birthday, looked so real she could almost feel the soft texture of the wool. She hoped Mac could make sense of it because she sure as heck couldn't.

Gina balanced the tray carefully and pushed open the door to Mac's room. Her breath caught when she saw the filmy eyes wide open, staring blankly. 'Mac? Are you all right? Did I wake you?' She winced, aware that the tremor in her voice let her down. Mac didn't need to see her to know what she was thinking.

'Nay, Ginny, I wasna sleeping, but dreaming.' She chuckled. 'It seems the two don't necessarily fit together as I move nearer the other side.'

'Don't say that,' Gina snapped, more sharply than she intended.

As Mac aged, she had struggled with the cold and damp and this winter, the wettest anyone could remember, had left her with a nasty cough she couldn't shake. She made light of it, but they all knew it had to be pretty bad to keep her in bed. If the causeways hadn't flooded, Mother would have had the doctor to her by now.

'Dulcie's made you some mutton broth. Will you try it?'

'In a wee while. Help me sit up.'

Gina placed the tray on the bedside table and stared at the beloved old face. Mac's wild wiry hair was now completely white, her freckled skin pale and creased by the years. As Gina plumped the pillows and straightened the quilt, she knew she was stalling, but seeing Mac so fragile made her hesitate. Was it fair to burden her with odd dreams and the like when she was so ill? She helped her put on her spectacles and was slightly shocked, as always, at how huge her eyes appeared behind the thick lenses.

'I'm glad you're here, Ginny. We need to talk about the lost lassie.'

Gina's eyes widened. 'How did you know?'

'She's in my dreams too, sweeting. Your mother's and Alice's too, I suspect, though they keep silent to spare me.'

'Then I'm not saying anything either,' Gina said. 'We'll speak of dreams when you're better.'

'There'll be no getting better, lovey. My time here is almost over.' Mac patted the bed. 'Sit. Nay, don't look at me like that, Ginny. I've had a grand life, but this old body can't do my bidding anymore and I'll be glad to shed it. Dyin' is naught to be feared – a leap across the creek and a whole new adventure begins. Who could complain about that?'

'Does Grandmother know?' Gina's voice shook.

Mac sighed. 'Aye, though she won't admit it. But she's strong, is Alice. She'll be all right.' She coughed and grasped Gina's hand, holding tightly until the spasm passed, then lay back on the pillows, exhausted. 'Enough of me. Let's talk of this lost lass. You do know it's you she's searching for?'

'Yes, but why? She calls my name and follows me in my dreams, only...' Gina hesitated, her face puzzled. 'The thing is, I don't think we're meant to meet yet.'

'Yet?'

Gina blinked. 'I don't know why I said that. It's just…' She shot Mac a bemused glance. 'There's something else.'

'Go on,'

'I saw her today. It was only for a few seconds, but it wasn't a dream. She was real. She was on the veranda, wearing my clothes.'

'Well now, that's a new one to ponder.' Mac frowned. 'I don't know what she wants, Ginny, but she doesn't belong in this time.'

'You think she's a ghost from the past?'

'Not necessarily. Time's a slippery thing, sweeting. We like to think it moves ahead orderly-like, the present following the past and leading to the future, but sometimes things come undone, and you catch glimpses of what was, or what might be. My granny – her with the *sight* – reckoned that time can occasionally loop back, slip sideways, even jump ahead.'

Gina looked at her doubtfully. 'Even if that were true, it doesn't explain why *I* saw her. You have the *sight,* but I don't.'

'Don't be too sure of that, Ginny. Write down your dreams, try to work out what she wants of you.'

'I do that. It hasn't helped. Besides, I don't think it's just me she's looking for. One night I dreamt of her rummaging through Grandmother's things.'

'What things?'

'Those journals she writes in. Her private letters too.'

'Mayhap she's searching for somethin' in particular…' Mac sighed. 'I canna fathom what it is, but we mustn't forget Mary's part in this. Your mother dreamt Mary saved the lassie's life, so we know she's important to Barragunyah.'

'Maybe she just felt sorry for her.'

Mac shook her head. 'Mary's nae one for pity. She does nothin' that's not in Barragunyah's interest.'

Gina shrugged. 'I think you and Grandmother make too much

of Mary. Why would the ghost of an old servant care what happens here now?'

'Ginny, Ginny... Don't you know? Mary's no servant. Mary *is* Barragunyah.'

# JULIA

The days slip by, one blurring into the next with such a numbing sameness that I no longer know how long I've been here. Two weeks? Three? A month? Maybe I should have drawn lines on the wall like prisoners do in movies. I could start now, but what's the point?

It's funny how changed circumstances can change one's personality. For example, where I once enjoyed solitude, I'm now desperate for company. I used to love rainy days too. Ha! Right now, I'd kill for a glimpse of blue sky. Is too much of something you love a kind of torture? I should write that on the wall – a philosophical question on which to ponder when I don't want to think about my current reality.

A lot of things have changed since Peter… No, not going there. Since I've been trapped here. For a start, my dreams have become more vivid, more disturbing. Even my waking thoughts lead me astray, unravelling memories I'd rather forget, raising questions I cannot answer.

Gina's dream book offers no comfort. Quite the opposite. Each time she refers to her so-called lost girl, I feel a tightness in my chest that makes it hard to breathe. I've taken to skipping those parts. I think I was hoping her words would remind me of Gran and reveal some of the metaphorical roads young Gina travelled to become the grandmother I loved. But the Gina who writes seems so unlike Gran they might as well be two different people. I'm not even sure I like Gina, but then I didn't like myself at that age either.

I try to imagine what it's like to be a grandmother. Not a mother – if I think about that, all the fears I keep pushing to the back of my mind surge up and I have a panic attack. Being a grandmother, on the other hand, is set so far into the misty future it feels safe. I picture myself years from now, dispensing wise advice and nourishing food to my grandchildren, resolving their arguments, telling them stories. That's as far as I get. It's impossible to concoct a future when I can't see past today.

Anyway, it's probably better if I don't think beyond today. Better if I don't think about what I'll eat when I've devoured the last stale biscuit, the last can of baked beans, the last carton of long-life milk. Better if I don't think about how starvation rations might affect my baby. Better if I don't think about giving birth here, alone. Better to reach for another journal and return to the congenial, sunlit world of Barragunyah's early days.

Only it wasn't always like that.

This time, when I open Alice's journal and read what she wrote, I cry for the rest of the afternoon. I am falling apart…

*October 15, 1933. I have put off writing this. For a long time, I could not find the words to express my loss, yet this great hole in my life – in all our lives – cannot go unrecorded. We buried Mac in the graveyard of Darrobine church a month ago. I wish I could believe, as she did, that life goes on, that death is not an ending but a beginning. But sorrow clouds my vision and all I can see are the empty spaces she once occupied with her indomitable presence. All I can hear is the silence she once filled with her gentle wisdom. I try to remind myself that she was eighty-two and did not regret a single day of her long life. I try to remember*

*the smile on her face as she took her last breath – such a joyous smile, it surprised us all. In time I will accept her passing, as I must, but now, if not for Gina and Ellen, I would not know how to go on.*

I'm falling apart over the death of someone I never met. A woman who, from Alice's account, lived a long and mostly happy life. A woman who died years before I was born.

I can't continue like this, so I've decided to become a Stoic. If I remember my philosophy correctly (I probably don't), Stoics were unmoved by joy or grief, surrendering without complaint to all situations. I begin by gazing through the window and accepting the unrelenting rain without resentment. It works. I become calm. What shall I practise on next?

Soft laughter disturbs my thoughts. She thinks I'm deceiving myself. Doubt creeps in. What if I've overestimated the usefulness of stoicism? What if fear finds me again? What if I get sick or depressed? What if my eyes leak despite my ban on weeping?

But she doesn't know the value of Gran's handkerchief drawer. I smile. Stoically.

Those fine lawn handkerchiefs will be soft on my nose, the large cotton ones good for mopping up tears. The delicate lace hankies are of no practical use, but when nameless fears clutch me, I like to hold the initialled ones; *A.M.L* for Alice Meadows Larson, *E.M.L* for Ellen Moran Larson, *G.L.P* for Georgina Larson Parker. I run my thumb over the silken embroidered letters, and it is as if my foremothers are with me, holding my hand.

The handkerchief I like best offers a little mystery to keep me entertained. It is pale pink cotton, roughly hemmed, with *Mother* clumsily stitched in crimson thread. Which of the women who lived at Barragunyah was the recipient of this childish love-gift? Not

Alice, for she had only a son, and this is a daughter's handiwork. Did Gina give it to Ellen? Did my mother give it to Gina? Time stretches as I muse on the small pink square.

And the dark creeps closer. As I knew it would.

I realise I am shivering, so I rouse myself and stoke the stove. I must eat something soon, but the longer I delay, the longer my rations will last.

Meanwhile, the handkerchiefs are restless with stories. I smooth out the crepe georgette one printed with the British coat of arms for the coronation in 1937. The name Edward VIII has been blacked out and George VI printed beneath. That's a story in itself.

My thoughts drift... What were the women of Barragunyah doing in 1937 when the prince who never expected to be king was crowned?

# GINA

Gina skipped to one side of the narrow lane separating rows of horse stalls as four young riders headed their ponies towards the show-ring. She smiled, admiring the ponies' gleaming coats and neatly plaited manes and tails, remembering herself at that age, her determination to win the blue ribbon and make her mother and grandmother proud. Closing her eyes, she soaked up the atmosphere; the aroma of horse droppings and fresh hay, the sounds of pigs and poultry and cattle reminding her how she'd missed the hustle and bustle of show-time.

Wending her way down dusty walkways busy with people, Gina found the cattle section and ran an expert eye over a small herd of Herefords milling about in their enclosure. There were some fine-looking beasts among them, but none that could hold a candle to Barragunyah's Black Angus. She wasn't sure she believed in prayer, but said one anyway. If Barragunyah took out the prize for best in show, it would lift everyone's spirits – and such a lift was badly needed.

Grandmother had been down in the dumps since she fell from her horse not long after her seventy-fifth birthday. She claimed it was only her pride that was damaged, but her limp had worsened until she'd been forced to agree with the doctor that her riding days were over. The trouble, Gina mused, was that Grandmother's interest in Barragunyah seemed to have been shelved along with her saddle. Between her lack of enthusiasm, Mother worrying that another war was on the way, Dulcie and Sarah about to retire and live in town, and Molly planning to get married, Gina felt as if the world she knew was shifting beneath her feet.

Of course, things were topsy-turvy everywhere; infantile paralysis crippling kids all over the country, some fancy German airship crashing in America, and in England there was King Edward giving up his throne for that woman.

Gina frowned, realising that her thoughts echoed conversations between her mother and grandmother. Much as she loved them, she ought to have her own opinions now she was nearly nineteen. Anyway, that was enough gloomy thoughts for the day – she was at the show to enjoy herself.

Leaving the cattle enclosures, she sauntered towards the tea-rooms where she'd left her mother and grandmother inspecting the baking displays with Dulcie. Getting them to the show this year had taken all her powers of persuasion – Mac would turn in her grave if she saw what hermits they'd become. They really needed that *Best in Show* to snap them out of it. Head down, deep in thought, she pulled up short as she ran into someone.

'Sorry! My fault,' Gina smiled apologetically. 'Wasn't looking where I was going.'

The man grinned, tipping his Akubra. 'You can run into me any time you like.'

Gina blushed. She wasn't used to men, particularly young good-looking ones. 'Oh. Well, sorry anyway. I'd best be off then.'

Unaccountably, her feet refused to move. It was his eyes, she thought. No eyes should be that green. She shifted her gaze, took in the brown boots, the smart moleskins, the navy jacket over the white shirt, the blue tie, the curly chestnut hair peeking from under his hat. She wished suddenly that she'd worn the pretty dress her mother had made for her instead of a divided skirt and comfortable old boots. Thank goodness her cream silk blouse was new.

'You look like you're heading for the tea-room,' he said. 'Can I buy you a cuppa?'

She shrugged awkwardly. 'Um, I'm meeting my mother and grandmother there.'

'Fair enough. I'll buy them a cuppa too. They won't eat me, will they?'

Gina laughed. 'My grandmother might.'

She resumed her walk and he stepped into place beside her. 'Tom Parker's the name. What's yours?'

'Gina Larson.'

'Larson?' He raised one eyebrow. 'Not one of the Larsons who own those Black Angus breeders back there, are you?'

Gina bristled. She knew people gossiped about the women who ran Barragunyah. 'I am indeed,' she said coldly. 'What of it?'

'You're just not what...'

'Not what they told you? Not as old and witchy as you expected?'

He chuckled. 'Witches or not, you breed bloody good cattle – excuse the language. I have a buyer for that lot, if you're interested.'

'We sell our breeders through Lockhart and Willcox.' Gina lifted her chin, stared him down. 'I doubt your buyer could afford them, anyway. We always get top price.'

He grinned disarmingly and held out his hand. 'Let me introduce myself properly. Tom Parker, new stock and station agent for Lockhart and Willcox. Haven't been in the district more than five minutes but I do have a buyer lined up.'

Alice, Ellen, and Dulcie were debating the merits of the coronation cakes in the baking competition. 'I wouldn't have picked that one as a winner,' Dulcie said. 'All those silver cashews sprinkled among the red, white, and blue make it look common. It might have suited that Wallis woman, but Lady Bowes Lyon has class.'

Ellen hid a smile. 'You should have entered a cake, Dulcie. I'm sure everyone's missed your famous duck-egg sponges these past few years.'

'Can't trust my hands to mix a light batter these days,' Dulcie sighed. 'And there's no way I'd let Barragunyah settle for second place.'

'You never know, Dulcie,' Alice said. 'If you ask me, the competition is not what it was.' She pointed to the seating area in the cavernous shed. 'There's a vacant table over there. Do you mind if we sit down? My hip is playing up again.'

Crossing the sawdust-covered floor, they claimed the table and sank gratefully onto the wooden chairs. Alice smoothed her new dark green skirt, tugging it down in an attempt to gain length. 'I'm not sure I like this new hemline, Ellen. I feel rather exposed.'

Dulcie pursed her lips. 'Won't catch me showing my ankles.' She eyed Ellen's calf-length floral dress. 'Not that you don't look a picture, love, but who'd want to see my old pins?'

'You both look very smart,' Ellen said, smiling. 'I'll fetch us a pot of tea and something to nibble.' She stood up and strolled over to the big makeshift bench where a bevy of country women chatted amiably as they dispensed tea from giant teapots. She ordered three cups of tea and a plate of scones and was about to pay for her order when Gina arrived.

'Hello, Mother. We'll have tea and scones as well if you're ordering,' she said.

'And I'm paying, remember?' Tom added. 'A bloke doesn't go back on his word.'

Ellen glanced at the young man beside Gina and felt a pang of anxiety. Who was this tall, handsome stranger with her daughter?

'Mother, this is Tom Parker, the new agent at Lockhart and Willcox. Tom, my mother, Ellen Larson.'

Ellen took a deep breath and smiled. She mustn't be overprotective. Gina worked her heart out for Barragunyah, she deserved to relax with someone her own age.

In fact, it seemed Gina was working still. 'Where's Grandmother? Tom has a buyer for our heifers. I can't wait to tell her!'

Later that night, as Gina snuggled under her eiderdown, she felt for the crepe georgette handkerchief under her pillow. It was a silly thing, a flawed coronation souvenir with King Edward's name blacked out and King George's printed beneath, but Tom had bought it for her and strangely, that made her happier than the *Best in Show* ribbon her favourite cow had won. She smiled as she drifted off to sleep.

# JULIA

Grey days fold into black nights and neither sun nor moon penetrates the thick blanket of cloud. I sleep a lot, whiling away the time between what passes for meals in dreams that leave me exhausted. All my dreams are of the old Barragunyah, the one in the journals. Sometimes they're so vivid that when I wake I'm no longer sure what is real. Maybe that's a good thing – the stories of my ancestors hold more colour and substance than this damp, gloomy present.

When I can't sleep, I prowl, wandering from room to room, opening cupboards and drawers, climbing onto chairs and disturbing dust in high places, poking and prying like some old Shylock looking for a pound of flesh. Sometimes a place I know I've already searched will yield a surprise. Like this morning, when I discovered a large, flat box on top of a wardrobe in one of the bedrooms.

I open the box and find a wedding dress carefully packed in tissue paper. I remove the tissue and shake the dress to release the creases. The cream silk and antique lace have yellowed in places, but it is still beautiful.

I have never desired to be a bride in a glamorous gown. For a brief period, when I thought Stuart and I might marry, I imagined a celebrant, a summer garden party, cool, casual clothes. But as I stroke the smooth folds of this dress, I know it was destined for me.

I strip to my undies, shivering in the cold, and slip the gown over my head. The sleek fabric clings to my hips and forms a pool like sunlit water at my feet. I fasten the jewelled clasp at the waist, then gaze into the oval mirror in the middle door of the wardrobe.

Someone else peers out at me.

Someone with my colouring but younger, and with a vibrant beauty that I have never possessed. She is slim and elegant yet somehow looks uncomfortable, as if the floor-length silk and long sleeves are foreign to her.

As I watch, she frowns impatiently.

# GINA

Gina tugged at the fitted lace sleeves and frowned at her reflection. 'Honestly, Mother, I wish you hadn't talked me into this dress. It seems overdone for such a small wedding.'

'I know it's not what you had in mind, darling, but you do look beautiful. Think of it as your gift to me and your grandmother.'

'But you didn't bother with a wedding dress when you married. I'll bet Grandmother didn't either.'

'Exactly. You're making up for us.' Ellen turned to the older woman sitting on the bed. 'Isn't that right, Alice?'

Alice smiled. 'Yes, indulge us, Gina. I wasn't there to see George marry your mother, so to see his daughter looking so lovely on her wedding day will be a consolation.'

Turning her back on the mirror, Gina gazed at them fondly. Her mother's hair was steel grey now, her grandmother's white. Both strong, indomitable women, they had risen above their shared grief over the death of her father to make a good life for themselves and for her. Now, all the talk of another war had reawakened their sadness, so if a silk frock and a veil would make them happy for a day, why make a fuss?

'Fine. You know me, more at home in boots and dungarees, but of course I'll wear it.' She grinned. 'Just promise me you won't organise a big wedding like Molly's parents did last year. Everyone in Darrobine must have been there, to say nothing of all their rellies from out of town!'

'Relatives will hardly be a problem since Tom has no kin and you have only us,' Alice said. 'Have you settled on who you want to invite?'

'We haven't changed our minds about keeping it small, if that's what you mean.' Gina counted the names off on her fingers. 'Tom's mates from Lockhart and Willcox will come with their families; eight altogether, I think. Molly's my maid of honour, so John's coming too, plus Lizzy and her Dave. Then there's Dulcie and Sarah, Vera, and Maud. Have I forgotten anyone?'

'Your mother and grandmother, it seems,' Ellen said dryly. She stood up. 'Let's get you out of that dress. Then you can go to the kitchen and explain to Vera that her cooking won't be needed because you're having the reception in Darrobine.'

Gina laughed. Vera and her daughter Maud had been employed when Dulcie and Sarah retired to live in the cottage Alice bought for them in Darrobine. Maud was a mouse of a girl, but Vera was the most bossy, opinionated person Gina had ever met. She cooked like an angel and cleaned like a demon, but if it hadn't been for Ellen's firm supervision, Vera would have tyrannised them all.

But even Vera was quiet that evening when the Prime Minister spoke on the wireless. *Fellow Australians*, he said. *It is my melancholy duty to inform you officially that, in consequence of the persistence of Germany in her invasion of Poland, Great Britain has declared war upon her, and that, as a result, Australia is also at war.*

As Mr Menzies' mellow voice continued, Gina glanced at her mother's white face, her grandmother's tight mouth. Speculations about the likelihood of war had been rife for months, but now, hearing it confirmed, Gina finally understood how they felt. The wedding was barely a month away, but she knew Tom would enlist.

Ellen leaned forward and turned the knob on the large mahogany wireless cabinet, cutting off the Prime Minister mid-sentence. 'That's that, then.' She looked at Gina. 'Has Tom said what he'll do?'

Gina shrugged. 'He'll volunteer, of course. He reckons every young bloke in the district will sign up. God knows who'll run the farms.'

'Women and old men, the same as last time,' Alice said, her lips pursed. 'Some properties will go under. We'll manage, but it'll be hard to get help when we need it.'

'Maybe you should consider moving your wedding forward,' Ellen said.

Gina frowned at her mother. 'Nothing will happen in a month, surely!'

'Who knows? Talk to Tom, find out when he intends to enlist.'

Gina felt her eyes prick with unshed tears at the sight of Tom's huge grin as she walked down the aisle towards him. Silly to cry when she felt nothing but gladness – glad he wasn't in uniform, glad they'd have two precious weeks alone before he began training, especially glad that their wedding photograph would be different from her parents'. She was even glad of the wedding gown now. Superstitious it might be, but Gina had convinced herself that anything that distinguished her own marriage from her mother's would lead to a different outcome; unlike her father, Tom would return when this war was over. She kept these thoughts to herself.

Some of Tom's mates had signed up immediately and were already training at Ingleburn. When Gina had tentatively suggested he could go with them if they moved their wedding forward, Tom had laughed and kissed her. 'It took me two years to get you to the altar, love,' he said. 'If I can wait, so can the war.'

Yes, Gina thought, the war could wait. There was only this moment; Tom smiling, Mother wiping away a tear, Grandmother's faded blue eyes filled with love. And a long silk gown that whispered, as she walked, of a bright and sunlit future.

# JULIA

When the candles burn low and shadows are deepest, Mary comes like a shiver in the dark, loosening the ties that divide then and now, distorting truth with trickery. I never know what to expect. Will she uncover another of Barragunyah's secrets? Will she provide a gift to divert me, a puzzle to intrigue me? I like to think that in her own mysterious way she is trying to make amends for keeping me here.

On the other hand, perhaps she wants me alive for reasons of her own. That's what I thought this evening when I found two skinned and gutted rabbits on the veranda. But Mary is not Hades and I'm not Persephone on a hunger strike, so I roast the rabbits and enjoy every mouthful.

Afterwards, I wander into the living room and find my grandfather's service papers in the bottom drawer of a sideboard that was empty last time I looked. A drawer I had no reason to open again and yet… There's my hand, reaching for the knob all by itself, the drawer sliding open with barely a catch, where before I'd had to tug it. And there are the papers, discoloured and mottled with brown spots, lying there, waiting.

A cursory glance at the documents tells me they're another gift from Mary. But why? What on earth could be in Tom's service record that she wants me to know? Whatever her reasons, delving into the past is preferable to imagining my uncertain future, better than frightening myself about limited rations and poor nutrition affecting my baby.

So I spend the rest of the night deciphering the hand-written entries. Reading the faded ink by candlelight is hard on my eyes, but this is what I learn: My grandfather fought in North Africa, Greece, Crete, and Syria. After Japan bombed Pearl Harbour in December 1941, most of his division were brought home to defend Australia while Tom's brigade was sent to Ceylon. He was finally granted leave in July 1942.

I think about all those battles. All those theatres of war staged by men who run the world and claim the glory. Men who seldom look behind the scenes to where the real players are prepared for slaughter.

When Tom took leave, he'd been in combat for over two years. Given all he'd seen and done, it was unlikely the man who came home was the same man Gina kissed goodbye two weeks after they married. And what of Gina herself? Had she spent those years longing for his return? Or was she too busy running Barragunyah to miss him?

A memory slips unbidden into my thoughts; my mother telling me she'd had a sibling who died before she was born. Which means Gina must have been pregnant when Tom left.

# GINA

Gina prowled the length of the front veranda, her eyes scanning the road. It was still muddy, but not so much that the post couldn't get through. It had been weeks since her last letter from Tom, long miserable weeks in which she'd been unable to ride or do the work that needed her attention. She felt well enough now, but could scarcely believe how ill she'd been in the first months of her pregnancy. Naturally, now she had all the energy in the world, she was the size of an elephant and riding was out of the question.

She always seemed to be waiting these days – for a letter from Tom, for a response to her advertisement for farm hands, for the baby to be born so she could get on with things. She frowned irritably. Would the post never come?

Pain lanced her belly, a cramp so intense she had to grab the veranda railing for support. She straightened as it passed, feeling suddenly anxious. It was too soon; the baby wasn't due for three weeks. Pushing her fear aside, she gingerly resumed her pacing. The pain struck again. She felt a wet trickle down her leg, then a gush of fluid pooled at her feet. She staggered towards the door, calling for her mother.

Ellen smiled tiredly. 'A perfect, beautiful boy,' she said as she cut the cord. 'He's small, but you can tell he's a fighter.'

Gina held out her arms. Her eyes, shadowed by exhaustion, were focused on her son and she did not see her grandmother's uneasy glance.

Leaving Gina to nurse her baby, Ellen headed for the laundry with the soiled towels, surprised to find Alice following on her heels. 'I can do this. You stay and admire your great-grandson.'

Alice shook her head. 'There's no time, Ellen. They must leave Barragunyah. We'll rent Gina a house in Darrobine.'

'What are you talking about?'

'Mary won't want a boy here. I told you about George.'

Ellen dumped the towels in the tub and sighed. At seventy-six, Alice was usually unruffled and logical, the tower of strength she had always been, but it had been a long night for all of them. 'That was a long time ago, Alice dear. I'm sure the baby will be fine.'

'He will if we get him away. It's not too late.'

'You know Gina won't leave. She's been chafing at the bit for months about her plans for Barragunyah.'

'She must go!' Alice was trembling. She peered anxiously into a shadowy corner of the room where the light didn't quite reach. 'Mary will take him otherwise.'

Alarmed by the older woman's intensity, Ellen tried to calm her. 'Alice, if Mary didn't want the child, wouldn't she have told Gina? Like she told you all those years ago?'

Alice stared at Ellen, confused. 'I don't know… That makes sense, I suppose.' She hesitated. 'You don't think I should say anything?'

'I think it would be kinder if you didn't. We can talk about it again tomorrow if you like, but for tonight, let her enjoy her son.'

Gina sat in a well-cushioned chaise on the veranda, admiring her baby as he suckled contentedly. 'Just wait till your father sees you,

James Thomas Parker,' she whispered. 'He'll be so proud.' Her eyes lifted momentarily to the paddocks beyond the house fence, taking in the soft golden-brown tints in the pale winter sunlight. She laughed softly. All those jobs that had seemed so urgent before were suddenly unimportant. Nothing mattered but her son. Barragunyah could wait.

She looked up as Ellen placed a cup of tea on the table beside her. 'What tales are you telling my grandson?' she asked, smiling.

Gina shifted the baby to her other breast. 'I was thinking about how I always used to put Barragunyah first. Even Tom had to wait in line.' She grinned. 'Now I don't care. I'm totally besotted with my son and everyone, Tom, you, Grandmother – even Mary – will have to get used to it.'

Ellen froze. 'Mary? Why mention her?'

'Oh, some silly dream – I think it was a dream – it was early in my pregnancy, when I was sick. She was insisting I had to leave because I was carrying a boy. Some rigmarole about Barragunyah not wanting him.' Gina shrugged. 'I've forgotten the rest.'

'And did you agree?'

'Of course not. I told her I'd never leave. That she had no right to ask.'

'And then?' Ellen looked at her daughter breathlessly.

'Then nothing. She went away. Why?'

But her mother had fled inside, calling for Alice.

# ELLEN

Ellen stopped knitting and frowned as she heard Gina yelling at the Land Army girls again. If she didn't rein in her temper, they wouldn't stay a week, let alone the month they'd been assigned to Barragunyah. They were lucky to have them at all, as farms like theirs were not usually allocated AWLA workers, and with calving season upon them and Alice unwell, the help was welcome. Gina needed to give those poor girls a break.

But Gina hadn't wanted the girls at all, and wishing she'd go easy on them was like wishing for a miracle. Gina didn't go easy on anyone these days, herself least of all. It was as if her cheerful, light-hearted daughter had vanished that ghastly morning she'd found little James dead in his bassinet. She'd lost weight and her face had grown hard and gaunt, an unsmiling mask with little resemblance to the daughter she loved. If only she could cry, Ellen thought, it might release some of her anguish.

Gina hadn't even cried at the funeral service when they'd watched the baby's tiny coffin placed in the earth not far from where Mac was buried. It was as if she'd built a wall around her deepest feelings, and none of Ellen's explanations about the randomness of infant deaths had made the slightest impression.

It was Alice who'd shed the most tears. Who was still crying three months later, although she wept in private and thought nobody knew. Ellen sighed. She also mourned her lost grandson, but for Gina and Alice, their grief was weighted with guilt and anger at

Mary. Ellen felt a measure of guilt herself, wondering if things might have been different if she'd listened to Alice the night James was born. In her clearer moments, she doubted it. Barragunyah's heart held ancient secrets and a purpose no one could fathom, but it was unlikely a baby's life would be sacrificed to serve that purpose.

Not for the first time, Ellen wished Tom would come home. She'd failed miserably to comfort her daughter, but perhaps – if the army ever gave him leave – she might be healed in her husband's arms.

# JULIA

Sometimes, as if to tease me, the rain pauses long enough to give me hope. I know it's a trick, but I make the most of the reprieve, replenishing the baskets with wood and foraging for food. Some trees in the old orchard behind the woodshed still bear fruit, so lemon in hot water provides a substitute for the tea bags that ran out days ago, and for breakfast I eat oranges and sour apples. In what was once Gran's prolific vegetable garden, cherry tomatoes, cucumbers, lettuce, parsley, and coriander have self-seeded and grow wild among the weeds. I toss them together to make a salad, or poach them in lemon juice to add to my strictly rationed pasta or tinned tuna. I crave bread.

Yesterday I invented a fortune-telling game to play with the weather. If the rain has stopped when I wake up, my baby will be a boy and I'll have to leave. If it's raining when night sets in, I'll have a girl and Barragunyah will keep us. Only now, when I think these two scenarios through, it's clear that either way I cannot win.

But there are other games.

There is the one where I slide into dreams, or slip between thoughts, poking around until I discover something I didn't know. Dreams and thoughts and feelings are ingrained in the woodwork here. Barragunyah hoards everything.

When I creep into Alice's dreams, I can hear her soul wailing, though not a sound escapes her tightly sealed lips. She thinks her descendants are being punished for the massacre committed by her husband. Maybe we are.

Gina is a problem. Once we were close, but now, she won't play my games; won't even acknowledge my existence. I can no longer tell what she's thinking or where she goes when she stops. The letters I found are of little help. I imagine her excitement when she opens this message from Tom, but somehow I don't think I've got it right.

# GINA



*May 25, 1942.*

*My Darling Gina,*

*Sorry for the brief note. We're about to go on patrol, but I wanted to let you know I've got leave in July. I won't be home long though, so I'm hoping you can meet me in Sydney. We could stay in a hotel, make it a second honeymoon. After all this time apart, I think we deserve it. I miss you, sweetheart. Can't wait to see you again.*

*All my love, Tom.*

Gina sat on her bed, staring at the clumsily scribbled note. If she stared at it long enough, she thought, it would all come back to her – what he looked like, the way he laughed, why she loved him. And she did love him. Of course she did. She'd married him, hadn't she?

But that was a lifetime ago. What made him think she could rush off to Sydney just because he asked? Had he forgotten how much work she had to do here? Probably. He'd apparently forgotten other, more important things.

By the time she showed the letter to her mother, Gina was fired up with righteous anger. 'He's got a hide expecting me to stop everything and go to Sydney, don't you think?'

'Gina, you've been apart for over two years. He misses you,' Ellen said. 'It's not so busy this time of year, we'll manage. We might even be allowed some Land Army girls while you're away.'

'Pfft, those city girls are useless without me to keep an eye on them.' Gina snatched the letter from Ellen's hand. 'I'm not going. I don't know why he thinks I would. Why can't he come here?'

'I expect he's hoping to spend time alone with his wife. It won't be much of a leave for him here if you're dashing off every five minutes to tend to things.'

Gina shrugged and looked away. 'You'd think he'd want to come. He hasn't seen James's grave yet. When I told him… Well, he wrote back as if he cared, but now I wonder if he does.' She shook the letter angrily. 'There's not one word about his son in this. What does that tell you?'

'Gina, Tom explains why the letter is brief.' Ellen sighed. 'Look, I understand how you feel but …'

'No, you don't. How could you?'

Ellen felt like shaking her. 'It's true I don't know what it's like to lose an infant,' she said. 'But I do know how easily war robs women of the men they love. If you don't go to meet him, Gina, you may regret it for the rest of your life.'

Perversely, by the time she convinced Gina she should go, Ellen herself was having second thoughts. Japanese midget submarines had entered Sydney Harbour and torpedoed a ship, killing over twenty sailors. Barely a week later, two large subs had bombarded both Sydney and Newcastle. The enemy was on Australia's shores, and that changed everything.

'It's getting too close for comfort,' Ellen said to Alice as they listened to the news on the wireless. 'Tom will have to come here.'

Alice agreed. 'We'll book them into Darrobine hotel where they'll have some privacy. At least they'll be safe there.'

'Who'll be safe where?' Gina asked. She'd been out mending fences all afternoon and looked bushed.

'You will, darling. And Tom,' Ellen said. 'Sydney's been attacked again. It's best if Tom comes here after all. He'll understand.'

Gina frowned. 'No, he won't. He's been fighting this war for years. He'll think I'm a coward if I refuse to go. You're not changing my mind again.'

He looked different. He was thinner, his face leaner, harder, and his eyes… Surely his eyes had been a brighter green, less shadowed? Gina looked at the man who sat across from her in the hotel dining room and wondered who he was.

He reached over and ran his thumb lightly down her cheek. 'It was imagining your face that kept me going,' he said. 'I lost your photograph when my tent got shelled, but it was already imprinted on my mind. The thought of you…' He took one of her hands between both of his, turning it over and staring at it as if he were a palm reader.

Gina pulled away and gazed around the slightly shabby room. 'Grandmother recommended this hotel. She stayed here with my father during the Federation celebrations.' She smiled uncertainly at Tom. 'That was years ago, of course. He was only a boy and I suppose the hotel was new then. It looks rather worn now. Do you think we should go somewhere else?'

'I don't give a damn where we stay as long as I'm with you.' Tom clasped her hand again. 'Gina, love, what's wrong? You haven't given me more than a peck on the cheek since I arrived. In fact, you haven't even looked at me, not really.' He put his finger under her chin, tilted her head. 'If there's someone else, you'd better tell me now.'

'Someone else?' Gina stared at him, startled. 'What do you mean?'

'I've been away a long time, love. I've seen enough mates get bad news from home to know how it goes. If you don't love me anymore, just tell me. I won't like it, but I won't blame you either.'

Gina shook her head. 'It's not that, it's…'

'What?'

'Well, James, of course! You don't write about him. You haven't asked. It's as if you don't care!'

Tom's jaw tightened. He let go of her hand and looked away. 'Oh, sweetheart, he was my son. Of course I care. I felt terrible that I wasn't there when he was born, then when he… I haven't said much in my letters because I was scared I'd say the wrong thing. I didn't want to upset you more…'

Gina watched his eyes fill with tears and felt something hard and cold dissolving inside her. 'I'm sorry. I should have known you… It's just that I miss him so much, Tom. I wish you'd seen him. He was so beautiful…' She smiled and ran one finger across Tom's eyebrows. 'Everyone said he had your eyes.'

Tom leaned forward, resting his arms on the table. 'Tell me more,' he said. 'I want to know everything about him.'

*Barragunyah,*
*October 30, 1942,*
*Dearest Tom,*

*I'm in Darrobine Post Office scrawling this on a new aerogram I just bought so I can post it today. Mr Gibbons (remember the old postmaster?) says it will get to you quicker than an ordinary letter.*

*I've been to the doctor, and it's good news. Wonderful news! Remember what I said while you were on leave? I was right! Our baby is due in March next year. Surely the war will be over by then – I want you with me when this child is born. I am well, no morning sickness at all so far – touch wood.*

*I have a lot to do while I'm in town, but couldn't wait to share this with you. I'll write at length tonight. I miss you. Take care and come home to us soon.*

*All my love, always, Gina*

# JULIA

What is it like to birth a child, then lose it to something as random as cot death? What is it like to love a man and lose him to something as indiscriminate as war? Tom's service record shows he was killed in New Guinea on October 28, 1942 – two days before Gina wrote to tell him she was pregnant again. It would be a girl this time, but Tom would never know her.

That baby was my mother, Annie. Did her birth help heal Gina's grief for James and Tom? I know she gave Gran plenty to grieve over as she grew up, but perhaps, while she was still small and biddable, she brought joy rather than heartache. I like to think so.

I like to think a lot of things.

It's all I have at the moment, my thoughts. I feed them on journals and letters, dress them in old-fashioned clothes, wipe their tears with embroidered handkerchiefs. I rein them in when they stray too far, refuse, as befits a Stoic, to give in to hope or despair. But the rain keeps falling and the sky remains grey, and I cannot help thinking that Barragunyah has seen more deaths than births, more sorrow than happiness. And I can't help wondering if I'm next on her list – me and my baby.

To be honest, I try *not* to think about that.

Annie was born in March 1943. Australia had been at war for four years by then, and would fight on for two more, but it was all over for Tom. And Gina? I think women die in pieces during war. A little bit at a time. I think that's what's happening to me now, even though the only thing I'm at war with is the rain. And Barragunyah.

I think too much.

Alice died in the winter of 1943. Her death jolted me. I opened Ellen's journal and there it was in just two entries. Alice is ill. Alice is dead. Well, Ellen was more forthcoming than that, but that's how it hit me. And I'm furious with her. With Ellen. If she hadn't written those words, Alice would still be alive for me.

It is hard not to think about death in this place.

Is sudden death easier to accept than watching someone you love die slowly? Gran died slowly. My mother died in an instant. And Peter… How did he slip into my thoughts? I don't want to think about him lying out there in the rain all this time. How long has it been now? I don't know. I don't know much, actually. I don't know how long a body takes to decay, for instance. Isn't that something everyone should know?

Time means nothing here and ghosts are everywhere.

I wish I could talk to Gina. Not to Gran, to Gina. I know it's the same person – I haven't lost all my wits – and yet, in a way, they're not the same at all. I want to talk to the woman who hasn't yet come to terms with the death of her baby and her husband. The woman who was around my age when her own grandmother died.

When I think about it, Gran lost a lot of people she loved during her long life. I've lost a few myself in a life that's short compared to hers. Maybe Barragunyah is running a competition, a test to see who cracks first. That's the crazy way I think when my brain goes into overdrive and it all becomes too much. I think, why is she showing me all this? What am I meant to do with it?

All this thinking is doing me no good.

What I need is someone to give me a hug and tell me I'll be okay, and that my baby will be okay. What I need is for Peter to drive up the track in our hired Jeep and start hectoring me when he sees I haven't finished what we came here to do.

If only…

My thoughts are uncontrollable. Rebellious. What I'm thinking now is that my future is uncertain and that the past holds more interest for me than the present. So I'm going back to see what Gina is up to. She's hard to read, but not hard to find. There she is, standing on the edge of an abyss, watching the next sorrow rise out of the pit.

Gina was my grandmother. Alice was hers. I want to know how she felt, what she thought, when Alice died.

# ELLEN

*July 19, 1943. A cloud of gloom hangs over the household since Alice became ill. Everyone is low, even the indomitable Vera. But though it is Alice's heart that falters, it is Gina who worries me most. I hoped the baby would lift her spirits after Tom's death, but she seems indifferent to the poor little mite, feeding and caring for her as if it were a chore – so unlike the joy she found with James. For herself, she cares nothing at all. She sometimes goes days without bathing, and I don't know when she last washed her hair. The only time she seems at peace are the afternoons she spends with her grandmother. I don't know how she will cope when Alice goes. I am not sure how I will cope either. Dear God, I will miss her.*

Ellen reached for the crying baby. 'Let me take her for a while, darling. You rest.'

'She's all right. I'll put her down for a nap.' Gina headed down the hall to the nursery. Through the open door, Ellen saw her plonk the infant in the cot as if she were a parcel. The screams grew louder.

'Does she need changing?' Ellen called.

Gina ignored her. She slammed the door, not quite shutting out the baby's cries, then went to her own room, slamming that door behind her as well.

Ellen sighed. Opening the door to the nursery, she lifted the child from the cot and held her close. 'Mummy doesn't mean it,' she whispered. 'She's just unhappy. She misses your daddy, and she's worried about your great-grandmother.' She placed the screaming baby gently on the change table, unpinned her nappy, and cleaned her soiled bottom.

Ellen, of all people, knew what Gina was going through. Hadn't she been through the same herself when she lost George in the Great War? But her daughter's reactions were so different from her own she did not know how to help her. That madness after Gina got the letter from the war office, trying to drown her sorrow in work, running herself ragged right up until the baby was born. And since then, this awful lethargy, the personal negligence, the lack of interest in anything, including her own child. The only thing she seemed to care about was Alice. Ellen had tried to connect with her through that, through their shared concern for the woman who had shaped Barragunyah and had such a huge influence on her and Gina. But getting through to Gina was like talking to a machine.

'Give her time,' Alice had said. 'She's still grieving for Tom and I know she worries about me. The baby's presence hasn't really sunk in yet.'

But it was more than that and Ellen was beginning to worry about her daughter's sanity. The way she was always looking over her shoulder, the incoherent mumbling, the wild looks. Last night, as Ellen was getting ready for bed, she thought she heard voices coming from Gina's room. Who on earth was she talking to? She knocked on Gina's door and pushed it open without waiting for a response. Gina was lying on the bed, staring at the ceiling. There was nobody else in the room.

'Are you all right? I thought I heard you talking to someone.'

Gina stared coldly at her. 'I'm trying to read.'

Ellen refrained from pointing out there was no book in sight. 'That's odd, I was certain I heard…'

'Please, Mother. Just leave me alone. I need to think.'

And Ellen had left, chastened. Now, as she folded a fresh nappy beneath her squirming granddaughter and reached for the safety pins, she wondered if it were she who was going mad. She'd been sure there were two distinct voices, yet she had seen for herself there was no one else there. Perhaps it was this relentless rain playing tricks on her mind. Except for essential chores like milking, collecting eggs and bringing in firewood, the weather had confined them to the house for days, a sharp reminder of the winter Mac had died. Ellen picked up the baby, rocking her gently. 'Sleep, little one,' she whispered. But a troubling thread was unravelling in her thoughts.

The winter Mac died was the year the lost girl invaded their dreams. Had she returned? Was that who Gina had been talking to? She frowned. What had Mac said about her? Something about being from another time. A visit from some time-travelling ghost was the last thing Gina needed in her present state of mind.

She was startled out of these disturbing thoughts by a sharp cry from Alice's room. Not waiting to put the child down, she hurried down the hallway, sharing a worried glance with Gina who appeared beside her.

Alice was pale and sweating, her hand on her chest, eyes squeezed shut against the pain. Gina reached for the tablets on the bedside table. 'Pop this under your tongue. I'll call the doctor.'

'No doctor. The pill will help.' Alice opened her eyes. 'Just sit with me, both of you. Mary will be here soon. I feel better when she's around.'

Ellen hesitated. 'Shall I give you some morphine?'

'No. It will pass. I must be clear.'

Gina pulled up a chair, sat down, and reached for her grandmother's hand. Ellen stood helplessly on the other side of the bed, holding the baby. What use were her nursing skills now?

Alice's face relaxed as the tablet did its work, and the pain diminished. She smiled at Ellen and patted the quilt. 'Here, put Annie beside me. Gina, help me sit up a bit.'

Gina lifted her tenderly and plumped the pillows, glaring at the baby as Ellen placed her on the bed. 'She'll only start screaming again. Put her back in the cot, Mother.'

Alice put out a veined hand and touched the baby tenderly. 'No, leave her. Allow me to spend a little time with my great-granddaughter.'

The baby gurgled and grabbed Alice's finger. Alice stared fondly at the infant for a while, then turned her gaze to Gina. 'She has Tom's green eyes and his copper hair; you must love her for that alone. And she's strong, Gina, like you. See how she kicks her legs and grips my finger? It makes me happy that another spirited girl will care for Barragunyah one day.'

Gina looked at her grandmother, stricken. 'But I don't…'

Alice raised her hand. 'Shhh… or my voice will give out before I say what I need to.' She looked at Ellen. 'Gina and I have talked a lot these past few weeks, mostly about Barragunyah, which she'll inherit along with what is left of my fortune after death duties.'

Ellen nodded. 'Gina will manage the property well.' She paused, tears filling her eyes. 'But how we will manage without you, my dear, I can't begin to imagine.'

'You'll do what you need to do, just as we did when Mac left us. I haven't forgotten how hard that was, but I know you won't wish me to linger on in this miserable state.' Alice smiled. 'You've been more than a daughter to me, Ellen. You and Gina have made my life richer than I dreamed possible all those years ago in England.'

'Stop it!' Gina snapped. 'Stop talking like that, as if…' She stifled a sob.

'As if I won't be here tomorrow? But that's my dearest wish, Gina love.' Alice sighed. 'Perhaps I'm weak, but I'd rather not face another day of pain and uselessness. Wish me well and let me go, sweeting.'

Gina shook her head, and Alice reached for her hand. 'You must learn to accept what you cannot change, Gina. These past years have been hard on you, but you're stronger than you realise.'

'Next you'll be telling me time heals all wounds.' Gina's lip curled derisively.

'No, sweeting, I won't tell you that – after all these years I still ache for my son – but I know from experience, Gina, that our wounds are the source of our strength.' Alice's grip loosened, but her eyes held some of their old fire as she stared at her granddaughter. 'It's the hard times that force us to rethink our lives, force us to change even if we're not ready. But never forget it's our choices that determine whether we change for good or ill.' Her hand fell to the bed beside the baby, who gurgled happily. 'Choose wisely, Gina.' She groaned softly and glanced at Ellen. 'I think I might have that morphine after all.'

'I'll get it now.' Leaving the baby on the bed, Ellen hurried from the room.

'Grandmother…' Gina's voice cracked. 'I've made an awful mess of everything, and I don't know how to fix it. How do I stop being angry? How do I put things right with Mum? With Annie?'

'Just love them, sweeting. And let them know you do. In the end, that's all that matters.'

When Ellen returned with the morphine, Gina was curled beside Alice, crying softly.

*July 30, 1943. The rain eased long enough for us to lay Alice to rest beside Mac and little James, but it has come back in force, as if the sky itself is weeping. Everything is damp and sorrow spreads like mould throughout the household, etched on our faces, spilling through our daily tasks, seeping into our conversations. I should be glad that Alice is out of*

*pain, but instead I long for her to be back, even as she was in those last weeks, just so I can talk to her. As I write this, I realise that for the first time in my life, I am truly lonely. There is a hole inside me that even Gina and baby Annie cannot fill. I feel disconnected from everything and the drumming of rain on the roof is driving me mad. Will it never stop?*

# JULIA

I wake in the middle of the night aware that something is out of kilter. A light shines through the window and in the eerie silence, my heartbeat steps up a notch. Shivering in the chill, I slip out of bed, creep along the wall, and peer obliquely through the glass. A full moon sails serenely in a starry sky. I catch my breath, scarcely daring to hope. The unfamiliar silence, I realise, is the absence of rain, the moonlight a sign that the thick cloud cover has moved on. Excitement stirs in my belly and I long for morning so I can determine how fast the sodden earth is draining. How many hours till dawn?

Time has always moved differently at Barragunyah, but now, with my watch lost in the creek and my phone dead, there is only day and night, only my body clock ticking off cycles of hunger and sleep, interest and apathy. It's all relative. When I'm engaged in something that interests me, time moves quickly. When I can't be bothered doing anything, the days drag. Now, anticipating a day in which hope overcomes despair, I've stepped into a dimension where impatience makes time stand still.

Knowing I won't sleep, I get dressed, stoke the fire in the Aga, and fill the kettle. As I wait for the water to boil, my excitement at the change in the weather gradually gives way to melancholy, as if the sadness trapped between these walls refuses to acknowledge the promise of a brighter dawn.

I think of Alice grieving for Mac, Ellen mourning Alice, Gina struggling to come to terms with Tom's death so soon after the death of their son. Ellen's journal suggests the birth of a daughter did nothing to assuage Gina's grief and may even have made it worse; I suspect these days she'd be diagnosed with postnatal depression. Which comes first? Does the depressed mother create a fractious baby? Or does a difficult baby make the mother depressed?

I try to keep these thoughts separate from my own situation, but questions bubble up through the mud of my fear. Is there such a thing as pre-natal depression? Will the dread that simmers beneath all my thoughts filter through to my child?

The face I see in the mirror is gaunt, and my limbs seem thinner, although my belly has rounded slightly. I know this should tell me something, but given my confusion about the passing of time, I have no idea when my baby is due. Twice now, I have woken in terror from dreams of giving birth alone while Mary watches from the shadows.

But now the moon has appeared, shining a glimmer of hope through the windows of my mind, making those questions redundant. That's what I tell myself, anyway.

To pass the time until daylight, I put my fragile anticipation aside and slip into the past like the shadow-walker I've become. There, I watch Gina find a way through the maze of her grief and begin to understand where she garnered some of the wisdom that would later guide me through my own upheavals. And I watch that fractious baby grow into a difficult toddler, an unruly child, a rebellious teenager. My mother, Annie.

It is Ellen's journals, rather than Gina's, that reveal my mother as a child. Reflecting on the tragedy that war had wrought on the region, Ellen's stories of Annie are set amid tales of battles. For years I believed I was the cause of my mother's bellicose nature, but Ellen shows me it was part of her personality from the beginning.

# ELLEN

*May 9, 1945. Germany has surrendered and the war in Europe is over. If Japan would only do the same, I might feel like celebrating. Yet when I think of all those lost lives, what is there to celebrate? Around here, women and old men struggle to manage properties they expected to pass on to their sons. Darrobine, small though it is, has borne a heavy burden, Tom being one of many young men who won't return. It's the same all over the country.*

*Despite everything, Barragunyah prospers under Gina's management. Thankfully, she has stopped trying to do it all herself and hired two of the young women who worked here with the Land Army early in the war. Ruby and Gillian came looking for work after being sacked from their factory jobs when the men returned. Gina was reluctant to hire them until they told her they'd loved working here despite the grumpy boss. That made her laugh, and she agreed to give them a try. So far it has worked out well and Gina seems happier for their company.*

*I wish I could say the same about my granddaughter. At two years old, she is a difficult child. With Gina so busy on the property, Annie is in my care for most of the day and I find I am constantly questioning myself, wondering what I am doing wrong. My approach is no different to the way I raised Gina, but perhaps it should be, as she is nothing like her mother at that age.*

Ellen shook her head in exasperation as her granddaughter threw herself on the floor, kicking and howling. 'Annie, darling, you can scream till the cows come home, but you're still not having cake before dinner.'

The yelling stopped. Annie sat up and looked at Ellen curiously. 'Cow come home?'

'Of course. Daisy and Moo always come home.'

Annie's tiny eyebrows knitted together over her green eyes. 'Moo eat cake?'

A clatter of boots on the veranda saved Ellen from answering. Annie scrambled to her feet. 'Mumma! Wooby!' She scampered down the hall to the mudroom.

A few minutes later she returned, her little arms wrapped around Gina's neck, her legs around her chest. She grinned at Ellen. 'Mumma piggyback!'

'I can see that.' Ellen smiled at her daughter. 'You look tired, darling. Did you finish the drenching?'

'Yes, all done, thank God.' Gina reached up and swung Annie to the floor.

'More piggyback, more!' Annie stamped her feet.

'Later, Annie. Mummy needs a shower.'

Annie's feet stepped up a pace. 'Now! Piggyback now,' she yelled.

Gina looked at Ellen helplessly. 'Who'd have thought there'd be anything harder than drenching?'

Ellen laughed and scooped up the screaming child. 'Mummy needs a shower, Annie, she doesn't smell nice.'

The yells subsided. Annie sniffed noisily, squirming in Ellen's arms to lean towards Gina. Her snub nose wrinkled. 'Mumma smell bad!'

'I do? Then I'd better have a shower right away.' Gina planted a kiss on Annie's forehead, shot a grateful look at Ellen, and headed for the bathroom.

Next morning, after surviving yet another tantrum over breakfast, Ellen headed for the veranda to enjoy a welcome cup of tea while Annie rode her dinky. Annie made a couple of noisy runs along the timber decking, then hopped off and began teasing the dog.

'Leave Jip alone, Annie. He's too old and tired to play with you.'

Annie ignored her, pulling the dog's ears and laughing when he shook his head. As she looked for something to distract her, Ellen heard Vera call from the kitchen.

'The Prime Minister's on the air. You'll want to hear this!'

Ellen hurried inside. Would it be the news everyone was waiting for? Vera and Maude were at the sink, staring at the small Bakelite wireless on the shelf near the window as if it were about to perform a magic trick. When Mister Chifley began speaking, Vera turned up the volume.

*Fellow citizens,* he said, *the war is over. The Japanese Government has accepted the terms of surrender imposed by the Allied Nations and hostilities will now cease...*

He continued speaking, but the three women were too busy hugging each other to hear what he said. Vera was the first to pull away. 'Hang on,' she said. 'He's not finished.'

*Let us remember those whose lives were given that we may enjoy this glorious moment and may look forward to a peace which they have won for us.*

'About time!' Vera dabbed at her eyes with a corner of her apron.

Maude looked at her. 'Don't cry, Mum. We should be celebrating.'

'Indeed, we should,' Ellen agreed. She took one of Annie's crayons from her apron pocket and circled the date on the calendar tacked to the wall. 'Fifteenth of August. A day to remember for all the right reasons.' She smiled at Maude. 'Will you watch Annie for me? I'm off to the yards to tell the others.'

*August 25, 1945.* It's been ten days since the war ended and we all look forward to life returning to normal. Yet there was nothing normal about the new bombs the Americans dropped on Japan to end the war. Reports say they "seared every living thing to death". How is this possible? I know something drastic needed to be done, but I cannot help wondering what kind of future is waiting for Annie in a world where such weapons exist.

# JULIA

The rain holds off, so I decide to go for a walk to see if the creek's gone down. Grabbing my parka from the hook by the door, I put it on, then pull Gran's gumboots over my socks – and instantly feel something is wrong. I stare out across the wet paddocks, and everything looks normal – soggy plains, dripping trees, mud – it's just my overactive imagination at work again. But as I give Gran's boots a final tug, something clicks in a corner of my mind. Didn't I lose these boots when I fell in the creek? I pick at the memory, but it's like attempting to recall a dream – the harder you try, the faster it vanishes. A thread of doubt makes me pause. What if I didn't fall into the creek? What if I dreamt it? What if… I make myself stop. I'm going stir-crazy. I need this walk.

I can feel my nose and cheeks reddening in the cold as I splash through sheets of groundwater, trudge through mud. An icy wind makes my eyes water, but the exercise lifts my spirits and the sense of unease evaporates. Here and there, tiny blades of grass peep through shallow puddles, giving me hope the land is beginning to drain.

Those hopes are dashed when I reach the creek. It's still a roaring torrent, reaching high up the banks on either side. And I know immediately that my memory of falling in was no dream. I did lose Gran's boots. Mary saved me. Through her eyes, I saw Peter die. Ellen ran me a hot bath; fragments of memory that I cannot properly fit together.

I linger aimlessly beside the turbulent water until it begins to rain again. I look up at the leaden clouds and my mother's face peers at me through the gloom. But which Annie is it? Is it the mother whose temperament was so unlike mine that we brought out the worst in each other, or the mother I was beginning to know and love? It hardly matters I suppose. Hating me or loving me, she never stayed around long enough to form a real relationship.

Back at the house, I rummage through diaries and photo albums, letters and newspaper articles, watching the years slip by as I search for my mother. A page torn from the *Darrobine Weekly* heralds the introduction of television in 1956. Some tattered newspaper cuttings of the Melbourne Olympic Games are dated the same year. Annie would have been thirteen by then. Was she excited about Australia's first Olympics? Did she pester her mother to take her to Melbourne, or demand a television so she could watch? What was she like, that young girl trembling on the brink of womanhood? What were her hopes and ambitions? One of Gina's journals offers a clue…

# GINA

*August 15, 1958. Annie has been expelled from yet another boarding school, the third in as many years. The official letter from the school cites the usual – failure to follow rules, disturbing influence on other girls, skipping classes. More worrying is an "incident" in which Annie is said to have attacked another student. Details are vague as the girl's parents are apparently considering legal action, although I'm not sure whether it's against the school or me. When I picked up Annie from the railway station this afternoon, I asked for her version of the event, but she was her usual uncommunicative self. I'm at a loss to know what to do with her. She's always been a difficult child but if she would only talk to me, I'm sure we could find common ground. Part of the trouble, I think, is that Annie herself does not know why she behaves as she does.*

# ANNIE

Annie lay on her bed, staring at the ceiling. She hated Barragunyah, yet here she was, back again, with nobody to blame but herself. Two years ago, she'd been excited about going to boarding school – anything had to be better than being tutored at home – but she hadn't known then that she'd be expected to share a dorm with girls who hadn't a brain between them. Girls whose conversation revolved around fashion, film stars, and who they'd marry. She certainly hadn't known there'd be so many stupid rules – food rules, uniform rules, study rules, even bed-making rules.

She'd lasted six months at that first school, then spent the rest of the year being miserable at Barragunyah until another school agreed to accept her. She'd blown that too. How her mother found a third place willing to enrol her was a discussion she'd chosen to avoid.

Annie frowned, wishing she hadn't thought about her mother. All those questions coming home in the car! She knew Mum was only trying to help, to understand her side of the story, but how did you explain what was going on in your head when you weren't even sure yourself?

She'd had the best of intentions this time, was determined to follow the stupid rules as if they mattered. But for a school that offered scholarships to disadvantaged girls, nobody seemed to care the place was rife with privilege and bullying that made the lives of those girls miserable. Annie hated unfairness with a passion that sometimes got out of control. She hadn't meant to punch anyone, but she wasn't about to let them get away with ganging up on that poor kid.

'No school will accept you after this.' the snooty principal had told her. 'You're a bright girl, but university is out of the question now. You will need to reconsider your future.'

She had said a lot more than that, but Annie hadn't heard a word after the bit about university – her one chance of escaping Barragunyah. She didn't care what she studied, but she *had* to go to university!

From the time she was old enough to think about the kind of life she wanted, Annie had imagined herself at eighteen, living in Sydney in her own flat like her grandfather had when he was at university. She'd pictured herself exploring the city, having coffee in little cafes, walking along the foreshores of the harbour, catching a train to the suburbs, going to the beach, listening to jazz in smoky dives. She could see now these musings were the daydreams of a child, drifting aimlessly from one scene to another without achieving anything. She had no real plans, no idea what she wanted to do with her life. The only thing she was sure of was that she had to get away from Barragunyah.

And how was she to do that now? Her mother would never provide money for her to live in Sydney without a valid reason like uni. Annie sat up and reached for her journal. Giving up was not an option; there had to be a way out. She began to jot down a list of possibilities.

# GINA

*April 1959. Annie has been impossible since she left school last year. She does her chores under protest, is usually missing when an extra pair of hands is needed, and is often deliberately obstructive. I could put up with all that if she spent her time studying, but she won't even look at the brochures I had sent from the correspondence schools. Her sulking and outbursts of anger make life miserable for all of us. I know Mother wonders why I let her get away with it, but how can I explain that it's because I blame myself?*

*Annie would sneer if I said I know how she feels, but her behaviour is so much like mine was after she was born it's as if I infected her. Lost in my grief for James and Tom, I failed to love her as she deserved, and I suspect her difficult personality is the result. It's hard to criticise her for something I almost certainly caused.*

*Unfortunately, while this insight helps me to understand my daughter, it's of little use to her. She's so confused it breaks my heart. She has no plans for her future yet harps on about leaving Barragunyah to live in the city, as if that will solve everything. Surely, like me all those years ago, she'll eventually let go of her anger and find something she enjoys? Today I found reason to hope.*

*I was doing the books, a task I've always hated, and Annie was doing her best to annoy me, leaning over my shoulder, pointing out errors, criticising my handwriting. I was ready to scream when Ruby came in to tell me that one of the heifers was calving. I left at once, glad to escape both the books and my daughter. Two hours later, with the heifer and a healthy bull calf both on their feet, I reluctantly headed back inside to finish the dreaded bookwork the accountant requires. When I opened the door to the study and saw Annie sitting at my desk scribbling in the ledger, my heart sank…*

Annie looked up as her mother opened the door. Closing the large red ledger, she leaned back in the swivel chair and stretched her arms above her head.

'What have you done?' Gina asked sharply.

Her daughter rolled her eyes. 'Corrected your mistakes, finished what you started, made sure the bloody accounts balanced. Which they didn't before.'

'Don't swear, Annie,' Gina said automatically. Fighting to contain her temper, she went to the desk and opened the ledger. 'This isn't a game, Annie. You know I have a meeting with the accountant on Monday.'

'Maybe he'll be glad to see you for once,' Annie scoffed.

Gina's anger faded as ran her eyes over the neat columns of figures. 'These look…'

'Balanced? You really don't trust me to do anything right, do you, Mum?'

'It's not that I don't trust you, but bookkeeping isn't easy, it's…'

Annie smirked. 'Not for you, obviously.'

Gina flipped through the pages, noting how neat Annie's handwriting was compared to hers. She shook her head in bewilderment. 'You've actually finished? How did you know to do a summary?'

'Easy, I just copied what your accountant did last year. It was interesting. Better than most of the stuff you make me do.'

Gina pulled up a chair and sat facing her daughter. 'I don't know what to say, Annie. When I was your age, being asked to stay inside and write in a ledger would have been a form of torture.' She shrugged. 'To tell the truth, it still is.'

'Yeah, well, I'm not you.' Annie frowned. 'Haven't you worked that out yet, Mum? You expect me to drench cattle, fix fences, drive a tractor, ride the boundaries. You might like that sort of stuff, but I hate it!'

Gina sighed. 'Annie, I know that, but you can't sit around all day doing nothing. I suppose I keep hoping you'll eventually get a feel for the place and begin to love it like I do.'

'Fat chance!'

'Yet you actually enjoyed putting all those tedious entries in the ledger?'

'Sort of. It was the challenge I suppose.' Annie grinned, a rare sight that warmed Gina's heart. 'I wanted to prove I could do it better than you.'

'Well, it looks you've succeeded. I'll get the accountant to check it.'

'Ha! I knew you wouldn't trust me!' Glowering, Annie flung herself from the chair.

Gina reached out and grabbed her hand. 'For goodness' sake, don't go off in a huff! It's the accountant's job to check it! Look, why don't you come to town with me on Monday? We'll show him what you've done.'

Frank Cooper closed the ledger and looked at Gina over his glasses. 'I'm pleased you took my advice and got some help. Makes my job easier, and it'll save you money in the long run.'

Gina beamed at Annie. 'We can thank my daughter for that.'

Cooper raised his eyebrows. 'I didn't know you were studying bookkeeping, young lady. When did you start your training?'

Annie shrugged. 'Who needs training? It's only numbers.'

'Indeed, but a lot of people make hard work of numbers, including your esteemed mother.' He winked at Gina and returned his gaze to Annie. 'How old are you, lass?'

'Sixteen.'

'Well, you come and see me when you've finished school. I might have a job for a girl who knows her way around numbers.'

'I'm finished school already,' Annie looked at him defiantly. 'Any chance of a job right now?'

The accountant's eyes narrowed. 'Possibly. But you'd need to lose that attitude.'

Annie sat up straight, her eyes wide. 'Really? A paid job?'

'That would depend on how you shaped up on a written test and in a formal interview.' Cooper glanced at Gina, who was leaning forward, her expression filled with doubt. 'And whether or not your mother is agreeable.'

'You wouldn't stop me, would you, Mum?' Annie's eyes shone. 'I mean think of it, a real job!'

'I don't see how it's possible, Annie. How are you going to get here? Even when the road's freshly graded, it takes hours to get to town.'

'That's so typical of you!' Annie sprang to her feet. 'You complain about me not working, then when I get a chance to do something I actually like you try to stop me!' She glared at her mother, then turned to the accountant. 'Please excuse my bad manners, Mr Cooper. I really want that job and I'll do the test and interview any time you say. And don't worry about me getting to work on time – I'll live in Darrobine.'

Gina gaped as her daughter strode from the office, her head held high.

Cooper tried unsuccessfully to hide a grin. 'A spirited lass, you've got there.'

'That's one way to describe her.' Gina shook her head. 'She's sixteen, Frank. I'm not letting her live alone in town.'

'Of course not.' He steepled his fingers under his chin, frowning thoughtfully. 'What if someone respectable was to take her in as a boarder? My sister might be willing. Wouldn't be the first time. Josephine says being around young people keeps the cobwebs away.'

Gina sighed. 'If you're going to offer her a job, I suppose I'll have to think about it.' She tilted her head. 'Are you sure though? You've seen what she's like.'

'Hmm. The smart ones can be tricky, but I've been around long enough to know that having a job can settle 'em down. Give her some responsibility, Gina. She'll rise to it.'

# JULIA

I found another skinned rabbit on the veranda this morning. I was hungry enough to eat it raw, but I haven't quite come to that yet. I stewed it with scavenged vegetables and sucked every scrap of meat from the bones. Afterwards, I felt more substantial and could think clearly for the first time in days.

My thoughts are not encouraging.

I think I'd expected the history of this place would seep into my brain cells as I explored my foremothers' stories, but in fact the opposite is happening and Barragunyah is absorbing me. I feel as if I'm dissolving into the walls of the house, the mud of the land, the wetness of the sky. I'm like a ghost, drifting aimlessly through certain spaces in uncertain times.

I'm not alone. Many ghosts inhabit this land, unsettled still about the way my great-great-grandfather imposed his will through this house, these fences, those boundaries. That massacre? Perhaps. Mostly, I'm content to observe them and acknowledge their presence. At other times, something that is still me emerges to ask if there's any purpose to their existence. Or mine.

These dark questions often overwhelm my frazzled imagination.

In my clearer moments, when I'm aware my sanity trembles on the edge of an abyss, I sift through the lives of the women who've gone before, hoping for a lifeline, a thread to lead me through the labyrinth in which Barragunyah has imprisoned me.

My mother used to tell me how trapped she felt growing up at

Barragunyah. I didn't understand then. I do now. And while I dance around the fact my imprisonment is totally different to hers, knowing she escaped gives me hope.

Annie's letters are bundled together and tied with string so dry it's impossible to undo the knot. I cut it with a knife and open the envelope on the bottom of the pile. The address at the top of the single sheet of paper says Newtown – a Sydney suburb I know well, although the street name is unfamiliar.

I'd known since I was a kid how she got there, how she roared into a new and exciting life riding pillion on the motorbike of a man she barely knew. It was one of many stories in which my mother was the central character and as a child it seemed to me like a fairy-tale, the young man a knight in shining armour, my mother an imprisoned princess. Now, as my eyes strain in the flickering candlelight to read her small, neat handwriting, I see a young woman, just nineteen, bravely steering her life into uncharted waters.

# ANNIE

*May 11, 1962*

*8 Holt Street, Newtown*

*Dear Mum,*

*I know you'll never understand why I left, so let's just say that the thought of living around Darrobine for the rest of my life gave me the heebie-jeebies. Working for Mr Cooper was all right, but that job was only ever meant to be a stepping-stone to what you know I've always wanted – a city life. I've written to Mr Cooper (belatedly, I admit) to tender my resignation and apologise for not giving notice. I hope my sudden departure didn't cause too much of a ruckus (especially as I've asked him for a reference). I hope you and Nan will forgive me (eventually), but if I'd failed to grab the opportunity to head for the bright lights when it presented itself, I'd never forgive myself.*

*And Mum, now you have my address, please, please do not arrive on my doorstep thinking I need rescuing. I'm nineteen, old enough to manage my own life and make my own mistakes. If I need you, I'll let you know. Give me a chance to do this on my own.*

*I love Sydney! Love it! Andy and I have found a little flat in Newtown, a shabby old suburb which doesn't suit its name (although I suppose it was new once). We're renting the second storey of a terrace house only ten minutes' walk from the railway station, and fifteen minutes by train to work.*

*Yes, we've both found jobs! Andy works as a mechanic at a motorbike shop near Central Station, and I got a job in a*

*delicatessen at Wynyard, right in the heart of the city. We're both
keeping our eyes peeled for something better, but for now at least
we can pay the rent.*

*I'll write again soon. Love to you and Nan and everyone.*

*Annie xxx*

Annie shifted from one foot to the other, trying to ease the ache
in her legs as she scrubbed salty slime from the preparation bench
at the back of the shop. It was a disgusting job, leaving her hands
as pale and wrinkled as the pickled pork soaking in the brine tub.
There had to be something better than this, despite what Andy said.
She hated everything about it, the work, the stench, her lecherous
boss with his sleazy suggestions.

At least Andy was doing something he'd been trained for and
enjoyed. She rinsed the dishcloth, wincing as the hot water stung
her hands. Her problem, the reason she was stuck in this filthy job,
was that unless Mr Cooper forgave her abrupt departure and sent her
a reference, she had no evidence that she was trained for anything.

Of course, even a reference might not be enough in a big city like
Sydney; all the bookkeeping jobs she'd seen listed in the newspapers
demanded a certificate. Annie knew she was smart and a fast learner,
but proving it was something else. Not that she particularly wanted
to be slaving over musty old ledgers, but all the other jobs advertised
for girls were even less appealing. She didn't want to work in a shop
or a factory. She didn't want to be a typist, a nurse, a teacher or a
hairdresser, yet work for girls didn't offer much else.

She heaved a bucket into the sink and turned on the tap. All
the stuff she'd done growing up on Barragunyah – horse-riding,
milking, fencing, branding cattle, driving a tractor – would look
good on a resumé if she was a boy, but… Annie paused, oblivious to
the water splashing over the rim of the bucket. Who said a resumé
had to be true? A slow smile dawned on her face.

She was startled out of her reverie by a sharp pinch on her bottom and spun round to see her boss grinning at her. 'Piss off,' Annie said, giving him a shove.

His grin vanished. 'Watch your mouth,' he growled. 'Don't forget who's paying your wages. And turn that bloody tap off!'

'Turn it off yourself,' Annie snapped, tossing the dishcloth at him. 'I quit.' She couldn't wait to tell Andy.

Annie still got shivers when she remembered how everything changed the instant she met Andy. There she was in boring old Darrobine, doing her job, rushing to get to the bank before it closed, and bam – she'd pushed open the door and slammed into a black leather jacket.

The wearer of the jacket stared at her boldly, his eyes as dark as his slicked-back hair. 'Well, look at you,' he said, his mouth curved into a lazy half smile. 'Just when I was beginning to think there were no hot chicks in the outback.'

After that, things happened so fast Annie barely had time to think. One minute she was standing on the step gawking at him, the next she was on the back of his motorbike, her arms wrapped around his chest as they powered out of town, the wind in her hair and her heart beating like a drum.

They were well out of town when he skidded to a stop on a rise near the creek. She slid off the pillion, her legs shaking. He stood the bike on its stand. 'Whatta ya reckon? Only way to travel, eh?'

Annie shrugged. 'Wouldn't want to be on it in winter.' She stared at him. 'Did you really come all the way from Brisbane on that thing?'

'Hey, don't insult the old girl!' He patted the bike seat. 'She got me here, no trouble, and she'll get me to Sydney, too.'

'You're going to Sydney? When?'

'Tomorrow.' He tilted his head, his eyes full of questions she wasn't sure she wanted to hear. 'Unless some pretty sheila wants me to hang around for a bit?' He ran a finger down her arm.

His touch was like fire and ice. She shivered and looked away, unwilling to meet his eyes. 'What are you going to do in Sydney?'

'Hey, you're cold! Can't have that.' He pulled her close, wrapping his arms around her, resting his chin on top of her head. 'Sydney? Meet up with a coupla mates. Get a job. Hang around and see what turns up.'

Annie could barely breathe. Her heart was pounding so hard she was sure he'd feel it right through his leather jacket. She tilted her head to look up at him. He smiled that slow, lazy grin again, then bent his head and kissed her.

Her stomach did a strange little lurch. Then, amazingly, she was kissing him back as if she actually knew what she was doing, her mouth opening, her tongue curling round his with a fierce hunger, her body responding feverishly to the touch of his hands. She became aware of him undoing her bra, his mouth on her breast, her skirt being pushed up to her thighs.

'Andy, stop!' She pushed him away.

He moved back, staring at her with an unreadable expression. 'The way you were kissing me… I thought you wanted it.'

'I don't know what I want,' she said shakily. 'It's just… I mean, we only just met. I thought…'

He took a deep breath and shrugged. 'Yeah, fair enough. C'mon, I'll take you back to town.'

Annie shook her head. 'I don't want to go back. Not yet. Can't we just talk? Get to know each other?'

That grin again. The way her stomach flipped. The way her hands wanted to touch his hair, stroke his bare skin.

'Sure. What do you want to talk about?' He sat on the grass, his back against a tree, looking up at her expectantly.

Annie sat down beside him. 'You,' she said. 'Tell me everything.'

Sitting at the kitchen table in their shabby little flat, Annie made a list of anything she could think of that would look impressive on a resumé. She was chewing on the end of her pencil, trying to work out which lies she could get away with, when she heard Andy clumping up the stairs. She jumped up, hurried to the tiny bathroom, ran a brush through her long copper hair, and strolled out casually as Andy opened the door.

His eyes lit up when he saw her. 'Hey, you beat me home for once. Get an early mark for being a good girl?'

She laughed. 'Actually, I was a bad girl. I quit.'

Andy's grin faded. 'So, where's the rent money gonna come from?'

'We can manage on your wage until I get a better job. Look, I've made this list...'

'To hell with that!' He snatched the paper from her hand and threw it to the floor. 'You shouldda asked me. I traded my bike today. Had to take out a loan. We need your money to get by.'

'What? How much did you borrow? Why do you need a new bike anyway? You'll have to take it back!'

His eyes narrowed. 'You're not my bloody wife, Annie, just some sheila I picked up along the way. Don't tell me what to do.' He turned and headed back out.

Annie winced as the door slammed behind him. His boots on the stairs sounded louder than they had on the way up. She fought back tears. *Just some sheila he picked up along the way.* He was always saying stuff like that. Later, when they made up, he'd say he didn't mean it, but she was beginning to think he did.

When they'd first arrived in Sydney and had to sleep on the floor of his mate's flat, he'd gone to the pub every night without giving a thought to how she felt left alone in some stranger's room in a city she didn't know. She'd said nothing, swallowing her anger, hiding her humiliation, convincing herself things would get better when they found work and got their own place. And it had been better for a while; coming home to him at night, cooking his meals, sharing a beer while they laughed about nothing and whinged about their jobs. And later, in bed, exploring each other's bodies, for her a discovery of sensations so unexpected she sometimes didn't know whether to laugh or cry.

Even that became an issue when Andy decided contraception wasn't his responsibility. 'I'm sick of bloody condoms,' he said. 'You need to get that new pill everyone's talking about. Blokes at work reckon it's the best thing since sliced bread.'

Annie giggled. 'Yeah? How does sliced bread stop me getting pregnant?'

'Very funny. Anyway, I'm done with the old rubber. It's up to you. Get it sorted.'

Flicking through the telephone book, Annie had found a local doctor, made an appointment, asked for a prescription. The doctor refused. 'The contraceptive pill is for *married* women, Miss Parker, not girls like you.'

'Girls like me?' Annie looked at her in shock. She'd chosen a woman doctor, thinking she would understand. 'I'm just not ready to have kids yet,' she gulped.

'Then abstain from sexual relations until you are. Is there anything else?'

Bestowing her iciest glare on the woman, Annie left with her head held high, but outside she leant against the wall shaking, trying hard not to cry. How dare that old biddy judge her? To hell with doctors! Andy would just have to put up with condoms.

But Andy wouldn't. 'Joe's girl found a doc in Kings Cross. I'll get the number.'

Screwing up her courage, Annie made the appointment as Mrs Wilson, slipping a cheap fake-gold band on her finger as proof.

Leaving with the precious script in her hand, she hoped she wouldn't have to prove her identity to the pharmacist. She tested the new name to see if it fit. Mrs Andrew Wilson. It sounded all right, but did she really want to marry Andy?

She hadn't thought that far ahead when she'd left Darrobine with him. Caught up in the excitement of the moment, the thrill of breaking rules and escaping the stifling conventions of a small town, she hadn't thought about anything much. Now, she knew when it came to marriage, city slickers were as narrow-minded as country folk. It still grated on Annie that they'd had to say they were married before they could rent the flat, but Andy reckoned they wouldn't let them have it otherwise.

Andy would say anything to get what he wanted. It was all a game to him, but if she played by the same rules, he'd twist things around and use them against her. *Just some sheila he picked up along the way.* That hurt. Yet it wasn't as if she loved him. At least she didn't think she did. How could anyone be sure of something like that? Her mother reckoned she'd loved Annie's father the minute she set eyes on him. Annie frowned, remembering all the wild feelings she had when Andy first kissed her. She still felt like that sometimes, but if she was honest, it was more to do with lust than love. Or was that all love was? She wished she could ask her mother. Not just about that. About lots of things.

Annie took a deep breath. She was an independent woman living a life she'd chosen for herself. It wasn't up to her mother to land her a decent job, pay the rent, or work out how to deal with Andy. She'd got herself into this, it was up to her to sort things out.

She picked up her list of bogus skills from the floor and stared at it for a long time.

# JULIA

I was not expecting these revelations. My mother was an expert at shooting down my fantasies, but she'd given no hint that the knight in shining armour I'd pictured as her rescuer would turn out to be a jerk. As a child, I used to tell myself she would have loved me more if Sir Andy and Princess Annie had done the happily ever after thing. Clearly, I was wrong.

It was years before my mother and I worked out how to get along despite our differences and, eventually, we came to love each other. But I never understood her. I can see now this is because there are huge gaps in my knowledge of Annie's life, of what she achieved, her motivations and ambitions, her beliefs. And I want those gaps filled. I want to know what she was like before I was born, and what she did during the years we lived apart, those silent years when I pretended not to care.

I reach for another of her letters…

*28 St John's Road,*
*Glebe,*
*November 29, 1962,*
*Dear Mum,*

*Please note the change of address. Andy and I have split up and I've moved into a flat with Erica, a girl from work. My new work, that is. I've scored a job as a copywriter in a small advertising agency. Mr Cooper came through and sent me a reference, but it turned out I didn't need it. All the grammar and creative writing*

*Miss Phelps drummed into me when I was a kid has paid off and I'm actually pretty good at coming up with jingles, snappy advertisements and slogans. The people in the agency are mostly around my age, or not much older, so it's a great place to work.*

*Tonight, a group of us are off to Chequers to see Shirley Bassey. Have you heard her on the radio? I think you'd like her.*

*Sorry I didn't get home last year as promised. Life was a bit messy at the time. All okay now. Please give my love to Nan. Tell her I'll write soon.*

*Love to you, too – and stop worrying, I'm perfectly fine. Life is good.*

*Annie. xxx*

# GINA

Gina paced the floor while Ellen read Annie's letter. 'What do you think?' she asked as her mother handed it back. 'Should I be worried?'

'I think she sounds happy,' Ellen said. 'She has a job she enjoys, workmates she likes, and she's rid of that young man who was making her miserable.'

Gina snatched up the letter and read it again. 'But what does she mean by *life was a bit messy at the time*? And Chequers – isn't that a nightclub? I don't think she should be going to that sort of place at her age.'

'She's almost twenty, Gina,' Ellen said gently.

Gina's face crumpled. 'She doesn't want anything to do with me, does she?'

'She just needs to find her own way, darling. You have to accept that.'

'I know.' Gina sat down and ran her fingers through her hair. 'I've been kidding myself that she'd get the city out of her system and come home, but she's happy there like she never was here. If I'd been a better mother, maybe…'

Ellen reached out and took Gina's hand. 'Don't go down that path, Gina. As parents, we do the best we can, but we're all imperfect. Annie's a strong young woman with a mind of her own. That's not a bad outcome.'

Gina raised her head and stared at her mother. 'You're right. I have to let her go her own way. I'm just sorry...'

'About what, darling?'

Gina shrugged. 'That there'll be nobody to care for Barragunyah when I'm gone.'

'Do you know what Alice would say to that?'

'What?'

'That Barragunyah was around long before we came along, and will be here long after we've gone. I don't think we ever really own anything, Gina. We're just caretakers. All we can do is make the most of what we've been given while we're here.'

# ANNIE

Erica sat on the edge of Annie's bed, watching her throw clothes haphazardly into her new suitcase. 'You can still change your mind, you know. We can spend our holidays here. We'll go shopping for the tiniest bikinis we can find, then bake ourselves brown on the beach.'

Annie tossed out a pair of red Capri pants and added a thick jumper. 'I wish I could, but Mum keeps on about me turning twenty-one. She'll never forgive me if I alter my plans at the last minute like I did last year.'

'Your choice.' Erica shrugged. 'Actually, I'm looking forward to meeting your mum. A woman who runs a cattle station practically single-handed has a lot going for her, in my opinion.'

Annie looked up from her packing. 'Yeah, she is pretty amazing. It's just that we have different ideas about what makes life worth living.' She paused. 'The thing is, I haven't been back since I left in a hurry with whatsisname.'

'That creep! I never understood what you saw in him.'

'Me neither, but he got me out of Darrobine and away from Mum.'

Erica raised her eyebrows. 'Is that what this is about? The prodigal daughter's afraid to face the music?'

'Maybe.' Annie emptied the contents of her suitcase onto the bed, then sat cross-legged on the floor looking up at her friend. 'I mean, what I did was kinda wild. It would have kept the gossips talking for a year. Mum never mentioned it, but it must have hurt. And my grandmother hasn't been well since I left – I can't help thinking my running off might have had something to do with that.'

'Oh, come on, all will be forgiven when you turn up.' Erica glanced at the mess of clothes on the bed and sighed. 'Which will clearly never happen unless I do your packing.' She stood up and began sorting through the jumble. 'Now watch how an expert does it.'

# GINA

Gina glanced at Ellen as the train whistle cut through the still morning. 'Do you want to wait in the car, Mother?'

'What, and have my granddaughter think I'm decrepit?' Ellen smiled wryly. 'You may have to help me out, though. I am feeling rather stiff this morning.'

'My fault for making you sit so long. If I'd remembered they'd sealed the Lurradallan road, we could have left an hour later.'

Gina got out of the car and went around to help her mother. At seventy, Ellen was still a beautiful woman. Her hair, pulled into the same loose bun she'd always worn, was now silver, but her creamy English complexion was barely lined. Only a slight limp betrayed her age, making her glad of her daughter's arm as they walked towards the station.

Ellen looked around curiously. 'You know, this place hasn't changed since I first saw it. You were just a baby and Alice met me in Sydney so we wouldn't have to make the train journey alone.' A shadow crossed her face. 'Dear Alice, she must have wondered what to make of me. I was so prickly. It was an awkward meeting as I recall, and of course, the masks didn't help.'

'Masks? I think you might have dreamt that one.' Gina glanced at her mother uneasily. She said some odd things at times.

Ellen frowned. 'Age has not warped my memory, Gina.' Spanish Influenza was rampant. Everyone had to wear masks.'

'Really? I didn't know that.'

'It's rarely mentioned, yet that flu killed more people in twelve months than the Great War did in six years. Too much of our history is conveniently forgotten, if you ask me.'

Gina nodded, but said nothing. In her opinion, the stories that made the history books were mostly tales written by men in love with blood and glory, whereas ordinary people connected to the past through what touched them personally. She often lay awake at night wondering what her life might have been if the war hadn't taken Tom. If rewriting history could bring him back, she'd do it in a heartbeat.

The whistle sounded again, and the chugging of the steam engine grew louder as it rounded the bend. Those old coal-driven locomotives would be history soon too, Gina thought; even here, in this backwater, change was inevitable. She clutched Ellen's arm nervously; the only question that mattered now was how many changes had two years in the city wrought on her daughter?

# ANNIE

'And here we are at the gates of hell,' Annie said as the train pulled into Lurradallan station with a hiss of steam and a grinding of metal. 'Don't say I didn't warn you.'

Erica grinned. 'Change the record, will you? For someone who's trying to be cool, you're doing a good imitation of nervous Nellie.' She stood up and heaved her suitcase down from the luggage rack. 'Come on, they're not going to crucify you.'

'All right for you to say. You don't know my mother.' Annie peered through the window at the two women standing on the otherwise deserted platform. She waved vaguely, not sure if they'd seen her, and was surprised to find her eyes pricking with tears as she rose from the cracked leather seat to retrieve her luggage.

A half-forgotten sinking feeling gripped Annie as her mother turned the car off the main road onto Barragunyah's gravelled track. She turned to Erica sitting in the back beside Ellen. 'Prepare for a bumpy ride,' she said. 'It's like this all the way to the house.'

'I don't mind, although my bladder's complaining,' Erica said. 'If I'd known it was so far, I'd have gone to the loo at the station.'

'Would you like me to stop?' Gina asked. 'You can go by the roadside.'

'Um, no thanks. Don't fancy meeting a snake with my pants

down. I'll be right.'

Ellen patted her hand. 'The house is almost an hour away, dear. And snakes are more afraid of you than you are of them.'

Annie laughed, her mood lightening. 'Yeah, pull over, Mum. I'll go with her.'

Gina stopped the car beside a large eucalypt and turned to smile at Erica. 'There, you've even got some privacy. Take your time.'

Erica climbed stiffly out of the car and followed Gina behind the tree. 'Are you sure there's no snakes?'

'It's not something you can actually be sure *about*,' Annie said seriously. 'You never know until you feel their fangs.'

'What!' About to squat, Erica pulled up her knickers and looked around wildly. 'You bloody bitch,' she said as Annie laughed.

'Welcome to the bush,' Annie chuckled. 'Go on, you'll be right. I'll keep a lookout for slithery things while you pee.'

Back in the car, Erica gazed through the window. 'The country here is really beautiful,' she said. 'I didn't expect it to be so green.'

Gina nodded. 'Yes, it's the best season we've had for ages. Perhaps it put on a show for Annie's return.'

'I haven't returned, Mum. I'm just visiting.'

There was an awkward silence, then Ellen said, 'Of course, and we want to make it a special visit. We thought you might like a party to celebrate your twenty-first.'

'God, no! Who on earth would you invite?'

'We thought we'd leave that up to you,' Gina said tersely. 'Ask anyone you like. We can have it at Barragunyah or hire Darrobine Hall if you prefer.'

'Mum, there's no one around here I'd want to ask.' Annie sighed. 'Look, if we must celebrate, get Vera to cook up a roast and buy a bottle of bubbly. That'll do.'

'Bubbly?' Ellen looked at Erica and raised her eyebrows.

'Champagne,' said Erica, smiling. She leaned over and tapped Annie on the shoulder. 'Be glad you're being given a choice, kiddo.

Remember the massive bash my parents threw for my twenty-first?'

Annie laughed. 'Yeah, total disaster – although you've got to admit it improved after the great escape.'

'Why, what happened?' Gina asked quietly.

'Well, it was a really big deal for them,' Erica said. 'They invited their friends, all the rellies, the neighbours,' she shrugged. 'Unfortunately, they didn't bother asking my friends.'

Ellen looked at her sympathetically. 'That must have hurt. How did you handle it?'

'Drank bubbly, smiled until my face ached, then snuck out to a nightclub with the people who mattered to me.' Erica paused. 'Actually, it *was* an unforgettable birthday, but not for a good reason. That was the day JFK was shot.'

'My goodness!' Gina exclaimed. 'What a horrible way to mark your birthday.'

'Yeah, it was weird,' Erica said. 'We were wandering around Kings Cross blearily looking for somewhere to have breakfast when we saw the headlines. Remember, Annie?'

'Yep. Hard to forget. As I recall, it sobered us up quick smart.'

Erica pulled a face. 'And that night, on the TV... the footage of him being shot and Jackie scrambling out on the back of the limo. It was awful.'

'I think it upset everyone,' Gina said. 'It seemed so... so barbaric.'

They were quiet for a moment, then Annie laughed. 'Enough gloom. Hey Erica, let's go to a nightclub for my birthday when we get back.'

'Okay. But I think your mum still wants to know how to celebrate while you're here.'

'I've already said.' Annie glanced at her mother, whose eyes were fixed on the road, her mouth a thin line of disapproval. Or was it disappointment? Annie reached over and lightly touched her arm.

'It's not that I'm not grateful, Mum. I just don't want a fuss. I'll bet you and Nan never had big celebrations.'

'I certainly didn't,' Ellen said. 'Nobody made much of birthdays back then. And of course the Great War had just started…'

Gina raised her eyebrows. 'How odd, Mother. I've never made that connection.'

'Why is it odd?' Annie asked.

'Because the Second World War began around the time I turned twenty-one.'

'That's creepy,' Erica said. 'I hope Annie's doesn't signal World War Three. Vietnam's looking grim right now.'

'Yes, it is,' Gina said, frowning. 'I don't understand what that benighted country has to do with us.'

'And I can't agree with Mr Menzies on conscription,' Ellen added. 'A huge mistake, if you ask me.'

As the Holden ate up the miles and the conversation flowed, Annie relaxed. She was glad Erica had come – she could talk to anyone. Maybe the next two weeks wouldn't be as bad as she'd expected.

Sprawled on a chaise piled with cushions, Annie watched Erica in a long floaty kaftan leaning on the veranda railing as she stared into the distance. Ellen sat at the head of a large table with mismatched chairs, pouring from a china teapot decorated with roses. Erica turned as Gina came through the French doors carrying a tray laden with scones, a dish of jam, and a bowl of thick clotted cream.

'How do you stand all this… this vastness?' Erica gestured vaguely. 'All that sky, all that bush, no evidence of humans at all. Doesn't it make you feel a bit… um, insignificant?'

Gina smiled and placed the tray on the table. 'Every day. But then, I think we *are* insignificant in the larger scheme of things. Barragunyah was here long before a human foot trod this land and will be here long after the last human is dust. We scarcely matter.'

Annie frowned. 'That's stretching it a bit, Mum. Aboriginal people were here thousands of years before our ancestors stole this place from them.'

'Indeed, but that doesn't alter the truth of what I said.' Gina set a stack of plates on the table. Ignoring Annie's belligerent expression, she smiled at Erica. 'You're in for a treat. Vera's scones are unrivalled.'

'They sure look delicious.' Erica pulled out a chair. 'You on a diet, Annie?'

Annie joined her friend. 'Don't joke. We'll be like porkers when we go back.'

Ellen handed them fine bone china cups and saucers with the same rose pattern as the teapot. 'It looks a lot, but Ruby and Gillian will be in soon, and they're always hungry.'

Erica helped herself to a scone. 'Who? I thought this was the whole family.'

'Ruby and Gill work for us,' Gina explained. 'But we think of them as family.'

'Ruby practically brought me up,' Annie said. 'She's a darling.'

Gina winced. Why did her daughter always make her feel so guilty? She heard footsteps on the back veranda. 'Here they are now,' she said brightly.

Erica looked up as a wiry woman in jeans, checked shirt, and riding boots strode along the veranda. Her hair was dyed a vivid red. She grinned at Annie. 'Hey, look at you all grown up.'

'Ruby, it's so good to see you!' Annie stood up and hugged her. 'Where's Gill?'

'On her way. Just checking on a poddy.'

Annie introduced her to Erica, then settled back on the chaise as Ruby helped herself to a scone. 'So, what's new with you?'

'Nothing. And that's how I like it.' Ruby piled jam and cream on the scone and devoured it in two bites while she studied Annie. 'Can't say the same about you, missy. A real city girl now, eh? Not planning to ride in those fancy pants, are you?'

Annie smoothed her white capri pants and laughed. 'Not planning to ride at all.'

'That's a pity,' Ruby grinned. 'Gill's gonna be disappointed on two counts.' She turned as another woman clattered up the veranda steps. Apart from her greying hair, she looked enough like Ruby to be her twin. 'You owe me a fiver,' Ruby said to her.

Annie hugged Gillian, then tilted her head to one side. 'Did you two have some sort of bet on me?'

Gillian pulled a face at Ruby. 'You told her?'

'Nup. But she reckons she's not riding. Gone all citified, she has.'

Trying not to laugh, Annie glared at them. 'So, what was the bet?'

'Not telling,' Gillian grinned. 'But listen, come to the stables tomorrow morning. I've got the cutest little filly to show you.'

Gina frowned. 'Gill, don't you dare! Annie hasn't been on a horse for years.' She shook her head as Annie's expression turned defiant. 'Believe me, darling, you do not want to go near Gill's filly. Now, can we please decide what we're doing for your birthday?'

# JULIA

The rain stopped three days ago, and the sky remains clear and blindingly blue. It's hard now to believe how excited I was to see the sun, how my spirits soared as I made my way to the creek and saw the water level had dropped enough for me to try crossing. Yet for some reason I hesitated. I told myself it was a long walk to the road, that I should go back, get a bottle of water and the remaining biscuits to keep up my strength. It was good advice, but I was deceiving myself. I know now something else was holding me back, some primitive *knowing* buried in my psyche.

I ignored it and crossed anyway.

And found myself back inside the house observing a rite of passage – the twenty-first birthday of my mother Annie, celebrated among a coven of ghosts.

The birthday girl sat at the head of the table looking awkward, gifts piled in front of her like offerings to a goddess. Gina was setting out glasses while Ellen arranged place settings. Ruby and Gillian were helping Vera and Maude set out a feast that made my mouth water. Erica was opening a bottle of champagne, something I recalled her doing quite often when I was a child.

As for me, I was the watcher in the shadows, a wallflower, a knot in the wood that, in a certain light, had anyone looked, may have seemed like a face.

But no one looked.

I've crossed the creek twice since then. I get halfway before I'm swirled into another time and my own life becomes tangled with all the other lives Barragunyah holds captive. I don't know who – or what – is doing this. It's beyond my understanding, beyond my control. Only one thing is sure: That creek has become both a boundary and a portal.

# ANNIE

*28 St John's Road,*

*Glebe,*

*November 30, 1965,*

*Dear Mum,*

*I'm sorry to hear that Nan hasn't been well. I hope she's feeling better now. Please give her my love and tell her I'm sending hugs and kisses.*

*Here, all we talk about is the war in Vietnam. We're furious that Menzies has turned conscription into a bloody birthday lottery. A friend at work had his number come up and now he's being trained to fight in a war he's totally against. Erica's boyfriend joined an anti-war group and we're all going to the next meeting.*

*I hope to make it to Barragunyah for Christmas, but I'll let you know later. As you can imagine, things are crazy here.*

*Take care of Nan and yourself and give my best to Ruby and Gill.*

*Lots of love,*

*Annie xxx*

# JULIA

Stuck between then and now, I read my mother's letters and watch the years turn. I witness Gina's bewilderment when Annie writes of politics and protests but shares nothing of her personal life. I watch Ellen grow old and frail, and Gina morph into the Gran I loved. I count Annie's promises to visit and pair them with her excuses. She writes passionately about the virtues of love over war, but doesn't spare a thought for the love she denies her mother. A long-held anger at my mother's selfishness returns to plague me, and once again I'm powerless to express it.

After all, I'm not even born yet.

I am there, nonetheless.

I am there as the once-indomitable, bossy Vera becomes increasingly confused and forgetful. I am there to see Maude, her silent, obedient daughter, make the first solo decision of her life and insist they retire. Following Alice's tradition, Gina sets them up in a cottage in Lurradallan, where Maude can get help for Vera if needed. They are sorely missed. I miss them myself – those delicious scones with clotted cream and home-made jam were a feast for my soul, even though my body could not partake.

Of course, Vera and Maude are not entirely absent. Like everyone who serves Barragunyah, they leave part of themselves behind.

But they are not around in the spring of 1966 when I watch Ellen die.

Gina is out riding with Ruby, checking the calves. Agnes, the new housekeeper, a bustling little stick of a woman, is in the garden picking beans for dinner. Gillian is fetching wood from the shed. So I am the only one who sees Ellen gasp and clutch her chest. She grabs the back of a chair to steady herself, takes a deep breath. Her face grows ashen, her forehead is beaded with perspiration. She rubs her arm, her hand moving to her throat as she struggles for breath. She needs help, but what can I do? I am a phantom drifting in the loops of time.

But Ellen's eyes widen, and I realise she's seen me. More surprisingly, she remembers me. Together, we relive the night Mary rescued me from the flooded creek, the night Ellen ran me a bath and wondered next morning if she'd dreamt it. Then deeper memories flicker in her eyes, love and loss and grief and healing, the richness of companionship, the comfort of solitude. I wait with her until the last fleeting moments of her life unfold like wings and soar into the ether.

Annie will have to come home now.

# ANNIE

Erica shot Annie a grin as the motorcade approached Hyde Park. 'Ready to show LBJ what we think of his dirty war?'

Annie laughed. She could barely hear her friend above the uproar, but she was ready for anything - the brownnosers waving their yank flags were in for a shock. 'At least the bloody singers have shut up,' she yelled to Erica. 'If I hear the *Yellow Rose of Texas* once more, I'll spew!'

'Hey, there's Rob and Tim!' Erica pointed across the road to where a group of angry university students pushed against the police cordon, their chanting growing louder by the minute… *One, two, three, four, we don't want your fucking war…*

'We need to get over there,' Annie shouted.

Erica nodded. But as they shoved through the crowd, several protestors broke through the police barricade and flung themselves onto the road in front of the President's car. Police horses reared up in alarm, the car stopped, and security men rushed to surround it. The students were dragged from the road, but others flung themselves down to take their places and a new chant rose above the chaos: *Hey, hey, LBJ. How many kids have you killed today?*

The noise was deafening, the response everything the campaigners had hoped for. As the car inched forward, they could see the President talking into his intercom, Ladybird beside him looking anxious. Premier Askin, his doughy face red with anger, leaned from the window and bellowed to his driver, his words just audible over the din.

Annie's eyes narrowed, and she turned to Erica, shouting into her ear. 'Bloody Askin just told his driver to run over those guys!'

'Yeah? Let's hope *that* gets reported,' Erica yelled back gleefully.

As the crowd exploded into pandemonium, she grabbed Annie's hand and they sprinted across the park towards the Art Gallery with the other demonstrators, all determined to get there before Johnson began his speech.

# GINA

'I phoned again and again, but nobody answered,' Gina said. 'I didn't know where you were. Your workplace didn't know where you were. I was worried sick, but I couldn't keep postponing Mother's funeral.'

Annie grimaced. 'Sorry. There was this massive protest, and I got arrested so…'

'You were in jail when I called?'

'Only for a few hours – Erica posted bail. But I'd sprained my ankle, so I spent the next couple of days at Rob's place.'

Gina glared at her. 'You should have let me know.' Her voice trembled with the effort to keep her anger checked. 'Why didn't you phone me?'

'I did! I got your message when I went back to work, and I called straight away. Nobody answered. I tried again the next day and Ruby told me you'd all been at Nan's funeral.' Annie's face coloured. She looked away. 'I feel terrible that I missed it.'

'You knew your grandmother wasn't well. You should have stayed in touch.'

'Look, I've said I'm sorry, all right? I feel guilty enough without you rubbing my nose in it.' Annie folded her arms across her chest. 'Anyway, I don't see what you hoped to achieve by charging down here.'

Gina sighed. 'I was worried about you, Annie.'

She barely recognised her daughter. Her copper hair hung halfway down her back, her eyes were heavily outlined in black, her lips painted pale pink, and the dress she wore with long white boots barely covered her bottom. Gina took a deep breath, trying hard not to say something she'd regret. She nodded towards the living room where a long-haired, bearded young man sat on the floor strumming a guitar. 'Since I *am* here, are you going to introduce me to your friend?'

'Sure, that's the guy I was staying with. Come and meet Rob.' Annie fled into the room as if she'd been given a reprieve.

Gina followed, her eyes narrowing when she saw the boy push her daughter away as she tried to kiss him.

'Geddoff,' he growled. 'Can't you see I'm playing?'

'Yeah, well, stop for a minute and meet my mum.'

Rob put the guitar down but made no effort to stand. 'Hi, welcome to the big smoke.' He nodded to Gina. 'Annie tells me you don't get down here too often.'

'That's true.' Gina felt Annie watching her closely, waiting to pounce on any perceived misstep. 'Nothing but concern for my daughter could drag me away from Barragunyah.' She laughed to make light of her words, but the effort was wasted.

'I didn't ask you to come.'

'I know that. But Annie…'

'Yeah, Annie's told me a bit about your place,' Rob interjected. 'Sounds like it'll make a good bolthole if I need one.'

'Bolthole?'

'If my number comes up.'

Gina stared at him blankly.

'The Birthday Ballot? The Lottery of Death?' Rob shook his head. 'Geez, is that place of yours on another planet?'

'Mum, I've told you how conscription works,' Annie snapped.

'I know what he means, Annie. I just don't see how Barragunyah comes into it.'

Rob rolled his eyes. 'It's an escape. A bolthole, right? Living in the sticks has gotta be better than dying in Vietnam.'

'I see. But isn't National Service compulsory if you're called up?'

'If they can find ya. That's my point.' Rob frowned. 'The irony is, I could've got a student deferment if I hadn't dropped out to protest the bloody war. But hey, that's how it rolls, right?'

'So you're a conscientious objector? Doesn't that give you the right to appeal?'

'Yeah, only it's a bit hard to prove.'

'The point is, he shouldn't have to prove anything, Mum,' said Annie, jumping in before Gina could respond. 'What the government's doing is immoral. We're planning another demo soon – they're in for a big shock!'

Gina pursed her lips. 'I can see you feel strongly about it, and I'm not saying you're wrong, Annie, but if you've already been arrested once...'

'That's a price I'm willing to pay!' Annie scowled. 'You taught me to stand up for what I believe in so don't go judging me for doing it.'

Rob laughed. He stood up and pulled Annie into his arms. 'That's my girl!'

'I'm not judging you, Annie. I just don't think having a criminal record is...'

'You really don't get it, do you?' Annie untangled herself from Rob's embrace and glared at her mother. 'You never will. The world needs fixing, but all you care about is Barragunyah. When are you going to wake up and realise that there's more to life than cattle and barbed wire fences?'

Gina clenched her teeth. 'That's not fair, Annie. We're aware that...'

'Aware? You have no idea! Christ, Mum! People are dying. Not just soldiers. Women and kids! And you're worried about me being arrested? Why? Are you scared the red necks in Darrobine might look down their noses at you?'

'Stop it, Annie!' Gina wanted to slap her. 'That's enough!'

'No, it's not. It's never enough. I've barely started…'

Annie paused and Gina thought she was calming down until Rob slipped his arm around her shoulders and said, 'You tell her, babe.'

'Why bother?' Annie snarled. 'This whole conversation's a waste of time. You know what, Mum – just go back to Barragunyah and leave me to get on with my life.'

Gina was shaking with anger. 'If that's what you want.' Turning her back on them, she picked up her overnight bag, opened the front door and walked out.

# JULIA

Gina returns to Barragunyah shadowed by anger and grief. 'I was worried about nothing,' she tells the others, giving them a sketchy account of Annie's anti-war protests that make her seem almost heroic.

Agnes, who has been living at Barragunyah for two years without ever setting eyes on Annie, nods absently and returns to her work. Ruby and Gillian know something isn't right, can see Gina's unhappy, but assume she's missing Ellen. 'She'll come good,' they tell each other. 'She just needs time to grieve.'

They don't know that Gina is mourning the loss of her daughter as well as her mother.

Only I see the hopelessness that permeates her thoughts during those sleepless nights when she prowls the house, searching for answers to shape despair into meaning. Only I see how the weight of each loss has built on the next, how one grief magnifies another until it feels as if her world has been emptied of all she once loved. She grieves for Mac, and Alice, and Ellen. For Tom and their baby son. Most of all, she grieves for her lost daughter.

Gina is forty-eight and still a good-looking woman, but within weeks of her return to Barragunyah her supple slenderness becomes gaunt, her face is lined with sorrow, her dark curly hair threaded with grey. She's working harder than ever, but finds no joy or satisfaction in any of the tasks she once loved. For beneath the questions that ebb and flow endlessly through her thoughts is a chilling undercurrent linking Barragunyah to each loss.

There's a full moon the night Gina leaves the house. I follow her to the stables where she saddles her mare and gallops across the moon-silvered paddocks. For the first time in months she is acting with purpose, yet something about her demeanour makes me anxious and I follow uneasily, watching and wondering what has initiated this midnight excursion. When I see who is waiting for her, I understand my disquiet.

Mary.

She's lurking in the clearing by the creek where the dark people lived before John murdered them. Her eyes are the colour of the moon, shadowed and distant.

Gina is unaware I've followed her, but Mary knows. Mary, who could return me to the house in an instant if she chose, who could tumble me forward into my own time, or back into Alice's with one blink of her silver eyes. I can do nothing but wait to see what she decides. She likes tossing me around, playing games with then and now, asserting her power. This time, for no reason that I can fathom, she allows me to stay.

I watch Gina dismount and join Mary at the edge of the creek. It has been raining for days and the water is deep and turbulent. Gina's gait is strange, stiff and jerky, like a marionette, as she follows Mary into the water. She stumbles on the stony creek bed and Mary catches her as she falls, pulling her out into the centre until they are both immersed and all I can see are two dark heads silhouetted against the moonlit water.

Then, as I watch from my nowhere space, I see Mary rise naked and dripping from the water until she is hovering upright several metres above the clearing. In her arms, Gina lies like a broken doll, limp and still as death.

Darkness takes me.

When I wake, I'm in bed cocooned in my sleeping bag, and it's raining again.

The rain gives me an excuse to avoid the creek. The creek where the causeway is, I mean, not the one where Gina died and was reborn.

I wish I knew what happened that night after I was banished. The Gina I knew was strong and compassionate, a grandmother who cherished me when my mother could not, whose wisdom guided me through a rocky childhood. But from what I saw that night, I think that if it wasn't for Mary, Gran wouldn't have been around to help me at all. Maybe I'm being fanciful, but there's nobody here to say I'm wrong.

While I wait for the kettle to boil, I rummage through my depleted stores and open the last can of baked beans. I spoon it straight from the can into my mouth. I don't bother with plates these days, as I have nothing to put on them that looks remotely like a proper meal.

I crave bread and milk, cereal, and pasta. Eggs. Real tea. Coffee. Cravings that have nothing to do with pregnancy but quite a lot to do with hunger. I keep hoping Mary will leave me another rabbit, but she probably won't. I try not to feed my expectations.

When I've scraped every morsel of sauce out of the baked beans can, I squeeze a lemon into a mug of boiling water, take it to the window seat and gaze out at the tearful sky.

My thoughts turn again to Gina and how she was broken and remade.

It was Annie who broke her. My mother, with her noble battles for justice, her deeply passionate caring for everyone and everything but those who really needed her.

# ANNIE

The wipers on the little VW beetle were working overtime in the torrential rain, but Annie could barely see the road. It didn't help that she was crying.

It was two years since she'd last seen her mother. Two years since that terrible row after Nan died. And now, despite everything, here she was, running back to Barragunyah like a whipped hound.

That she was dreading their meeting was nobody's fault but her own. If only she'd kept in touch, written thank-you notes for the gifts her mother sent for Christmas and birthdays, maybe even sent gifts herself, though she seldom bothered with that stuff. She could have phoned, of course, but what would they talk about? Her mother had called once or twice, but it was always awkward – like the time she'd phoned after the Prime Minister disappeared from some godforsaken beach in Victoria. Had she honestly thought that talking about a politician's mishap would somehow reconnect them?

Then again, Annie herself had nearly called Barragunyah this year wondering what her mother thought of the moon walk. *One small step for man, one giant leap for mankind,* Armstrong had said. And maybe, if she'd made that one small step of her own, the breach between her and her mother might have healed. In the end, she hadn't bothered. The truth was, they had so little in common that Annie hadn't even told her when she and Rob got married.

Tears ran down her face and she dashed them away angrily with the back of her hand. What a joke that turned out to be! Marriage was just a game to Rob, like everything else he did. Their romantic wedding on the beach at Byron Bay meant as little to him as the anti-war protests he took part in – just another way to make himself the centre of attention.

He was almost disappointed when his number didn't come up in the conscription lottery. He'd been planning to go to Byron and join some mates who'd dodged the draft, and suddenly he was sidelined. At a loose end, he'd decided they'd both go and turn the trip into a wedding. Annie had gone along with the idea. Why not? She loved him – at least, she thought she did. Getting married was a tad traditional, but the setting, and their hippy friends, made it seem wild and impetuous. She sniffed and wiped her eyes again, remembering how beautiful it had been, both of them in long white kaftans, her hair woven with flowers, their bare feet on the golden sand, a weekend of bliss before they went back to work.

It was all downhill after that, hitting rock bottom a few months later when Annie discovered she was pregnant.

'You're joking,' Rob said when she told him. 'You told me you were on the Pill.'

'I am. I was.' Annie shrugged. 'I must have forgotten to take it or something.'

'Christ, Annie! Can't you do anything right?' Rob took another drag on his joint. 'Anyway, not my problem, babe. Get rid of it.'

'What if I don't want to? I mean, we're married, so why not…'

Rob's eyes narrowed. 'No bloody way. You want to keep it? Go right ahead, but don't expect me to hang around.'

Annie pulled over to the side of the road and rested her head on the steering wheel. She'd been a fool to think he might have second thoughts once she started to show, but she never dreamed he'd go against everything they believed and enlist. Still, when had Rob ever believed in anything? He used causes to get himself noticed. Used people for the same reason, without a thought for the consequences. The war was being scaled down, so he probably reckoned he'd finish up in some cushy admin position in Sydney. Instead, he'd been shunted off to Kapooka for training, then straight to Vietnam. Annie smiled bitterly. It was a dirty war, but it would be just his luck to come back unscathed.

Meanwhile, she was heading to another war zone called Barragunyah, and she had no idea how that would end.

# GINA

The sound of the telephone ringing woke Gina from a deep sleep. She swore as she glanced at the clock on her bedside table – nobody would ring at this time of night unless it was serious. Grabbing her dressing gown from the chair near her bed, she ran barefoot down the hallway and picked up the receiver.

'Hello? Mum? It's me.'

'Annie? What on earth? Are you all right?'

'Not really. I've run out of petrol and nothing's open in this pisspot town.'

'Where are you?'

'Lurradallan. Public phone box.'

Gina gasped. 'You're on your way here?'

'Yeah. I've been driving all night. I'm stuffed.'

'All right. So first you need to get some sleep. Go to Johnson's pub on Angus Street. Knock on the door, tell them who you are. They'll put you up. Charge it to me. You can fill your tank in the morning.'

There was silence at the end of the line.

'Annie?'

'I thought you'd come and get me.'

'That's not exactly practical, Annie. It would take me over three hours to get there, then we'd have to drive back in separate cars anyway. You won't want to leave yours there.'

'Oh.' Silence again. 'I guess not.'

'Have a shower. Get some sleep – you must be exhausted – and order a hot meal when you wake up. Then phone me when you're leaving. I'll ask Agnes to cook something special for dinner.'

'Kill the fatted calf for the prodigal daughter, eh?' Annie's laugh sounded hollow.

Gina hesitated. 'Are you really all right, Annie? I mean...'

'I'm fine. See you later.'

Gina winced as the line went dead. Why did conversations with her daughter always end so abruptly? Had she said something wrong? Not done enough? She sighed. Whatever she did, it would never be enough. Only one thing was certain – Annie wouldn't come home unless she needed something. It remained to be seen what it was.

It was just on dusk when the little VW pulled into the driveway. Gina hurried out, reaching the car as Annie emerged stretching her arms and rolling her shoulders to relieve the kinks.

'Annie! It's so good to...' Gina blinked and looked again. 'You're pregnant?'

'Good guess, Mum.' Annie's eyes were bloodshot and swollen, but she lifted her chin defiantly. 'You're going to be a granny. How do you feel about that?'

Gina smiled. 'It's a wonderful surprise.' She hugged her, ignoring her daughter's stiffness, her inability or unwillingness to hug back, then held her at arms' length. 'I have lots of questions, but I can see you're exhausted. Come inside and put your feet up. Ruby will bring in your luggage.'

'Do I get a last meal before the inquisition?' Annie laughed bleakly. 'I'm married, if that's what you want to know.'

'I want to know everything, darling.' Gina slipped her arm around Annie's waist as they walked towards the house. 'But there's no hurry. You're h…' About to say home, she corrected herself, '…here, and that's all that matters.'

Annie glanced at her with raised eyebrows, then shrugged. 'I can't promise to tell you everything, but I'll give you the general rundown on your wayward daughter's crazy life.'

The following afternoon, Gina was pleased to see Annie looking a lot better. They'd all gathered on the veranda for afternoon tea, Annie settled on the cane chaise with cushions plumped behind her back as she added to the bare facts she'd told Gina the previous night.

'So, he ran away to join the army as if it was a bloody circus?' Gillian shook her head. 'Deserting you is bad enough, but enlisting to cop-out on his responsibilities is pretty insulting to all the young blokes who died over there.'

Ruby frowned. 'I thought he was one of those anti-war protestors like…' She hesitated, glancing at Annie.

'Like me?' Annie shot her a weak grin. 'He was. Or so I thought. But Rob's a chameleon. He changes when it suits him.' She sighed. 'Not this time, though. He told me he didn't want kids, but I had no idea how far he'd go – literally – to escape.'

'You don't need him, anyway,' Ruby said. 'You've got us.'

Gillian gave her friend a cautionary look. 'Annie hasn't said she's staying.'

'That depends on Mum.' Annie looked at her mother. 'I'm pretty annoying to have around. She might not want me.'

Gina, who had said little while Annie's tale unfolded, leaned over and touched her daughter's hand. 'You're my daughter, Annie, of course I want you to stay, but…'

Annie frowned. 'There's always a *but*.'

'If your child's a boy he'll be unwelcome at Barragunyah. We can't run the risk.'

'You're going to turf me out because of that old story?' Annie glared at her mother. 'I don't even believe that rubbish!'

'Neither did I,' said Gina quietly. 'Your brother paid for my disbelief with his life.'

Ruby and Gillian exchanged glances, then Gillian said, 'To tell the truth, we didn't believe the stories, either. We thought Mary was one of those old bushman's tales – until we saw her.' Gillian shrugged awkwardly. 'At least, we assumed it was her.'

'When? Where?' Gina looked at them sharply.

'Yesterday. On the veranda. It was late afternoon, and hard to see against the glare, but she was tall and dark like the stories say. When she turned and looked at us with those creepy eyes, I thought I'd wet myself.'

'The weirdest thing,' Ruby added, 'was what happened next. She dropped a couple of skinned rabbits on the veranda and a woman came out of the house and took them inside. While we were looking at her – the woman, I mean – Mary vanished.'

Annie laughed. 'What were you guys smoking?'

'I know how it sounds,' said Ruby, 'but I swear…'

'What did she look like?' Gina asked. 'That woman.'

'Hard to say.' Ruby looked away. 'Anyway, we went inside but couldn't see anyone.'

'She looked like you, Gina,' Gillian said firmly. 'A younger version of you.'

'The lost girl,' Gina whispered. 'I haven't seen her since my grandmother died.'

'Oh, for Chrissake!' Annie looked at them all impatiently. 'Another ghost? As if mad Mary isn't enough!'

Ruby ignored her. 'Who is she, Gina? One of your ancestors?'

'I don't know.' Gina stared into space, frowning as she tried to cast her thoughts back over the years. 'I remember Mac saying she could as easily be from the future as the past. I used to dream about her a lot back then, and once I saw her in broad daylight, too.' She glanced at Ruby and Gillian. 'Right here, on the veranda.'

'Come off it, Mum,' Annie scoffed. 'You're kidding, right?'

Gina shook her head. 'I wish I was. The question is, why is she back now, after all this time? Is it a warning?'

'Warning of what?'

'I'm not sure, Annie, but I'm guessing it's to do with your baby.'

# JULIA

They're asking the wrong questions. They think I've come back when I've actually been here since the beginning. Okay, maybe not the beginning, but since Alice. What they should ask is why they can see me again now. That's something I'd like to know too. Is Gina right? Is it a warning to Annie about the Peter foetus growing in her belly?

My belly, carrying its own little enigma, is tight as a drum. I could easily devour those scones that sit untouched on the cane table beside Annie's chaise. I drool over the clotted cream, ache for the sweetness of strawberry jam, but they offer me nothing. Why would they? To them I'm just a puzzle to be solved. So they talk around me, over me, through me, linking me to past events as if I signify something, as if I hold answers to Barragunyah's mysteries.

As if I am more than merely a silent witness.

As they talk, I watch my mother and my grandmother, observing the dissonance between them, their tangled emotions, their chaotic, frustrated love. All those times when Gina wanted Annie to stay and Annie wanted only to escape are now reversed. Gina insists her daughter must leave Barragunyah; Annie, feeling rejected, perversely wants to stay.

I am able to leap ahead of them because I know how this part of the story ends. Peter will be born at Lurradallan Hospital and Gina, besotted with her grandson, will offer to buy Annie a house in Darrobine so she can be close to family. Annie, wilful as ever, without money, home, or a job to pay the bills, will insist on returning to Sydney, creating an impasse that could easily carry their fractious relationship beyond repair.

In a flash of insight that has eluded me until now, I realise that the way Gina deals with this ongoing mother-daughter conflict is part of what made her the Gran I knew and loved. Gina simply surrenders. Just as she surrendered to Mary that night in the creek, Gina gives up her long-held dreams for Barragunyah. When Annie returns to Sydney with her baby son, she has enough money to buy a house and investments to provide her with an income.

And Barragunyah is considerably smaller.

That's the part of the story I know.

What I didn't know was that my father was such a loser. And what I don't understand is why my feisty mother allowed that loser back into her life so they could make me.

# ANNIE

*2 Don Street, Newtown,*
*November 13, 1972.*
*Dear Mum,*

*I heard Whitlam give the most inspiring election speech today and I just know the coming election will be life changing. Labor's got this brilliant campaign song, "It's Time" (so true!) sung by all these famous people hoping for a new government (look for it on the tele). Erica and I are involved in the grassroots of the campaign (did I tell you she broke up with her boyfriend and moved in with me?). We're using the front room downstairs for meetings, printing flyers and stuff, so my dear old terrace is always buzzing with people coming and going. It's great fun!*

*Pete is going to Australia Street Infants School, a ten-minute walk from here. He seems to like it and it keeps him out of my hair during the day so I can get on with things. The photo I've enclosed was taken on a swing at the school.*

*The other news is that Rob's back from Vietnam. I haven't seen him yet, but we have mutual friends, so I'm bound to run into him sooner or later (unfortunately).*

*Anyway, must rush to pick up Pete from school.*
*I hope you're keeping well. Love to you and the girls.*
*Annie xxx*

The post-election party had spilled out into the street, Annie's neighbours in the working-class suburb as keen as the campaigners to celebrate Whitlam's win. There were kids everywhere, the older ones playing cricket on the road, the littlies running riot through the house as they made the most of being allowed to stay up late. Erica, a bottle of sparkling burgundy in one hand and glasses in the other, stepped aside as Pete, followed by two little girls and a boy, charged up the hallway towards the kitchen where Annie was throwing together some sandwiches.

Food had been an afterthought – a few bowls of chips and nuts – but people arrived with cheese and crackers, sausage rolls, pickled onions and cocktail frankfurts. Old Mrs Roberts from the adjoining terrace supplied a fruit cake, Val from across the street nipped home to get an egg and bacon pie she had in the oven, Maria from down the lane wandered in with a huge dish of lasagne. All the men had brought beer in Eskys filled with ice.

Annie raised one eyebrow at Pete and his mates. 'You lot again! I've only got fish paste or vegemite left. What'll it be?'

'Vegemite,' the girls yelled, holding out grubby hands. The older boy hesitated, but Pete wrinkled his nose. 'We want cheese.'

'Too bad.' Annie shrugged. 'Go see if there's any left on the plates with the crackers.'

The boys raced off, followed more sedately by the girls, munching happily. Annie cut the remaining sandwiches into triangles and arranged them haphazardly on a plate. That was her done. What she needed now was another glass of champagne.

'Which one's mine?'

Annie looked up to see a man slouching in the doorway. It took her an instant to realise it was Rob. With his hair cropped short and his beard shaved off, he looked quite ordinary. 'What the hell are you doing here?'

He smiled mockingly. 'Not much of a welcome, Annie. I expected a kiss at least.'

'Fat chance! What do you want, Rob?'

'Like I said, just wondering which kid's mine. I'm guessing that little boy who just ran past. The one in the blue shirt.'

'So, what if he is? You made it clear you wanted nothing to do with us.'

'Hey, give a guy a break. Things change. The kid needs a dad and here I am.'

Annie stared at him coldly. What had she ever seen in him? 'You gave up that right when you left. Do us a favour and leave again. Now.'

He folded his arms across his chest and grinned. 'Nice place you've got here, Annie. I hear these old terraces are worth a bit now. Had a look around upstairs. Hope you don't mind.'

'I do mind. I don't want you in my house or my life, Rob, so piss off.'

'A little bird told me your mum bought the place for you. Living the good life, eh, Annie? No rent, no mortgage. I hear you don't even have to work now, so I'm guessing Mum slipped you some money too, eh?'

'I work from home,' Annie snapped. 'I freelance.' She took a deep breath, forcing herself to remain calm. 'Anyway, it's none of your business, so piss off or I'll have you thrown out.'

He laughed. 'Nobody's gonna throw out a wounded veteran, Annie.'

'Wounded? Pfft! I know you, Rob. You'd make damned sure you stayed clear of the action.'

'Yeah? What's this then?' He pushed himself away from the doorjamb, grabbing the crutch he'd concealed behind him. 'Leg's full of shrapnel. Pain like you wouldn't believe.'

Annie tilted her head. 'Yet you climbed all those stairs to count my bedrooms? Why put yourself through such agony?'

His face twisted into a snarl. 'Because, little wifey…'

Erica pushed past him without a glance. 'Annie, enough with the sandwiches! Jim and Ali just arrived with real champagne and... What's wrong?'

'Him.' Annie jerked her chin and Erica spun around. It took her a few seconds to recognise him.

'Rob? Where'd you spring from? Didn't see you arrive.'

'Came through the backyard and up the back stairs. Man, that's a massive basement. Enough room in this place to house an army, let alone one wounded soldier.'

Erica glanced at Annie with raised eyebrows. 'You're letting him move in?'

'Not in a million years.'

'We'll see about that,' Rob smirked. 'I'm a returned soldier; that gives me kudos. Plus, we're still married, and the kid needs a dad. Law's on my side, babe.'

# JULIA

I'm rifling through the trunk looking for evidence as if I'm demented. My mother believed in social reform, women's rights, Indigenous land rights, freedom. She was selfish, stubborn, argumentative, challenging, aggravating – not the sort of woman anyone pushed around. Why on earth would she let that creep back into her life? I empty a shoebox stuffed with letters onto the floor, then pause.

That creep was my father, and there are always two sides to a story. But when I look at the yellowing papers scattered around me, I know I won't find Rob's version among them.

Gran would know. She didn't like Rob and there's a good chance she vented her anger in one of her journals. I push the letters aside and begin a new frenzy of searching.

By the time I give up, the floor is strewn with journals, newspaper cuttings, scrapbooks, photos, letters, albums, old recipes that make my mouth water – but I cannot find my father.

I know he came here once with Mum and Peter before I was born, so he's been in this house. He's passed through these rooms where nothing goes unnoticed and nothing is forgotten, where memories weep from the walls and ghosts watch and wait. Barragunyah hoards everything, collecting moments and squirreling them away until she finds a use for them. She knows every secret and story connected with this place, including Rob's.

And I'm hungry for secrets. How can I persuade her to tell me what I want to know? Is there something she wants? Should I promise her my baby?

In the dream, my father is holding me and I'm hitting him, my small hands clenched into fists, beating against his chest. He is laughing, but I'm angry, frustrated because I am too little to have any impact, because I'm powerless to stop him from going away again. Suddenly I know what I must do. I cease hitting and put my chubby starfish hands on either side of his face and stare at him. I can't make him stay, but I can make myself remember how he looks and feels and sounds. But as I stare, the dream shifts and I'm no longer a child, I'm me, grown-up Julia, and I know with the certainty of dreams that this is a true memory of my father.

And he is not Robert Brennan.

# GINA

The train was late, allowing Gina an extra hour to fret about what she'd say and remind herself of all the things she couldn't say. She was always on the defensive with Annie, and had hoped this time, they could forget their differences and enjoy each other's company, but there was little chance of that, now she'd decided to bring Peter. Gina had been on edge for days, worrying that something awful might happen to him while he was here. But when she'd mentioned her concerns to Annie on the phone, her daughter had brushed it off as if it were nothing. Still, when had Annie ever listened to her?

Peter was five now and Gina hadn't seen him since she went to Sydney for his second birthday. He won't remember me, she thought guiltily. Phone calls, birthday cards and Christmas gifts were all very well, but she should not have left it so long between visits. Now she'd reduced the herd and sold the northern paddocks to the new owners of the Enright property, she'd make an effort to visit more often. But that was in the future – it was now that worried her.

The sound of the approaching train put an end to her speculations. She stiffened her back and tried on a smile. One week, Annie had said. They'd just have to make the most of it and hope nothing went wrong.

A man followed Annie and Peter off the train, but it was only when Annie turned to speak to him that Gina realised it was Rob. She felt as if a lump of lead had dropped into her stomach. Annie hadn't said a word about him coming, but of course she knew he'd be unwelcome. Gina's jaw tightened, the one and only meeting with her son-in-law still as fresh in her mind as if it were yesterday – the offhand way he'd proposed hiding out at Barragunyah to evade conscription, his smug grin as he goaded Annie into a confrontation with her. He looked different without the beard, and with that awful long hair cropped military-style, but his irritating smirk as their eyes met was exactly the same. Annie had said she was going to divorce him. Why hadn't she?

A quick glance at her daughter's stony face and Gina swallowed her questions. Whatever had prompted this visit would unfold in due course. Smiling, she moved forward to embrace Annie, dodged a half-hearted kiss from Rob, and crouched down to hug Peter. The boy pulled back, glaring at her.

Gina laughed awkwardly and stood up. 'No hug, Peter? I don't suppose you remember me. We'll have to get to know each other all over again.'

'Say hello to your grandmother, Peter,' Annie snapped.

He shook his head, his eyes angry, his mouth forming a tight, stubborn line.

Rob grabbed him by the shoulder and gave him a shake. 'Do as you're told, kid, or your granny'll feed you to the dingoes.'

The boy looked up at her, his eyes wide.

'I'll do no such thing,' Gina said, concealing her anger. 'Do you like cake, Peter?' He nodded. 'Excellent! Because you know what? My friend Agnes is in the kitchen right now, making the world's best chocolate cake to welcome you to Barragunyah.'

Gina introduced Peter to her old mare. 'Give her the carrot,' she said. 'Hold your hand flat, like this. She won't hurt you. Her lips are like velvet.'

Peter threw the carrot at the mare's feet and turned away. 'Can we go now?'

'I thought you might like to ride her.'

'No.' He looked at his grandmother as if she'd suggested eating worms.

Gina sighed. 'Well, what would you like to do?'

'I wanna go home. I don't like it here.'

I could have predicted that, Gina thought, gazing at her grandson. He was a quiet child, too serious for his age, and with a disconcerting habit of looking at adults as if he didn't trust them. Just as he was looking at her right now.

'You only arrived yesterday. What don't you like?'

He spread his arms. 'It's too big, and… and…' His arms fell and he gave her an odd sideways glance.

'What?'

'There's ghosts,' he whispered.

Gina's heart skipped a beat. She forced her voice to remain light. 'Really? Where are these ghosts?'

'In my bedroom.' His little jaw jutted out pugnaciously, daring her to disbelieve him. 'I saw them last night.'

'Did you? Were you afraid?'

He shook his head vigorously, although his eyes suggested otherwise. 'The old one doesn't like me. She's…'

'She's what, Peter?'

He looked down, scuffing his shoes in the dust. 'I dunno. Wild. Like a wolf.'

Gina knelt and took his hand. 'Think carefully, Peter. Did she say she would hurt you?'

He shook his head again. 'She said she'd wait for me.' His lip trembled. 'What does she mean, Gran?'

'I'm not sure, darling…' Gina thought for a minute. 'I've got an idea. Why don't you sleep in my room tonight? We could put up a camp bed. Would you like that?'

His eyes lit up for a second, then he looked away. 'Mum won't let me. She says I've got to sleep by myself now I'm big.'

'Well, I'm Mum's mum,' Gina said, standing up. 'And this is my place, so I say you can.'

'Can what?' Annie said, coming up behind them.

Gina turned, smiling, as she felt Peter's hand slipping into hers. 'I said he can set up a camp bed in my room tonight. I thought we might look at the stars.'

Annie shrugged. 'Fine.' She glanced at Peter. 'Go find Dad. I want to talk grown-up stuff with Gran.'

'But I wanna ride the horse.'

'Later, Peter. Go. Now.'

Oblivious to her son's furious glare and dragging feet as he headed towards the house, Annie turned to Gina. 'We didn't get a chance to talk alone last night… I know you're wondering why Rob tagged along.'

'Well, I'm wondering why you didn't tell me he was coming. It's been awkward. The sleeping arrangements…'

'Sorry about that, but there's no way I'm sharing a room with him.' Annie scowled. 'I hope you don't think I invited him. I don't know how he got wind of it – maybe he heard me booking our seats, maybe he looked through my diary – he's always sneaking around. We were halfway here when he suddenly lurches down the aisle grinning that stupid grin and plonks himself in the seat next to us. I told him to get lost, but he threatened to make a scene.'

'So, you're not back together?'

'God, no! I should've divorced him when he left. It didn't seem to matter one way or another then, but now…'

Gina shot a sharp look at her daughter. 'Now what?'

'He wants to play happy families, goes on about Pete needing a dad. I know damn well what he really wants is my house. He thinks the world owes him, thinks I owe him! He turns up at all hours, usually drunk or stoned, then sits in the gutter sobbing about me chucking him out. I've called the police a few times, but they're on his side. You know, "give him a fair go, missus, poor bugger's a returned soldier." I need to get rid of him, Mum.'

Gina frowned, aware that Annie was staring at her as if she expected her to do something. 'I don't know what to say, darling. I've had no experience… Surely there are laws?'

'Laws!' Annie laughed scornfully. 'Laws are for men! We're working to change that, but it won't happen overnight. I need Rob gone now. I don't plan on being one of those battered wives.'

Gina looked at her in horror. 'You think he'd hit you?'

'He's come close a few times. And he's rough on Pete.' She looked away, staring across the horse yard to the distant paddocks. 'I came here to get away from him, but when he turned up on the train, I knew I'd have to do something more drastic. That's when I had this idea…'

'You'll divorce him?'

'That won't stop him unless I give him my house. There's no way I'm doing that.'

'Then what? You said you'd thought of something?'

Annie was silent for a moment, then shrugged uncomfortably. 'I was hoping you might offer him a job. He's got a big ego so he'll think you're on his side, that you're welcoming him into the family.' She glanced sideways at Gina. 'But Barragunyah won't want him, will she?'

'Well, no. And I…'

'So, he might have an accident. Like great-grandma's husband. The one who murdered those Aborigines.'

Gina blanched. 'Where did you hear that?'

'I read it in one of those old journals.'

'You read Alice's journals? You had no right!'

'Why not? She's my ancestor too. Anyway, who cares? The point is, Barragunyah got rid of him and…'

'Annie, stop! Please!' Gina grasped her daughter's hands. 'There's so much we don't understand about this place, this land. But whatever Barragunyah is, however she may appear to us, this is not a force we can use to serve our own ends.'

'You're scared!' Annie's eyes narrowed. 'What if I told you I was scared too? Scared Rob might hurt Pete, hurt me, hurt the baby?'

'Baby?'

'I wasn't going to tell you yet, but yes, I'm pregnant. And before you ask, no, it's not Rob's.' Annie's eyes filled with tears, which she brushed away angrily. 'I don't know what he'll do when he finds out.'

'I see.' Gina remained outwardly calm, but her thoughts were spinning. A new grandchild, perhaps a granddaughter who would love Barragunyah as she did. Rob must not be allowed to hurt her. She squeezed Annie's hands, forced herself to smile. 'Does the father of my future grandchild have a name?'

'His name's Jack. I can't tell you his last name – he's married.'

Gina frowned. 'So, you'll both have to divorce?'

'Jack won't. He made that clear from the beginning. He's well known, says he has a reputation to consider. It's rubbish really – it's 1975, for God's sake – not that I care.' Tears trickled down her face, making a mockery of her words.

'Does he know? About his child, I mean,' Gina asked quietly.

Annie nodded. 'He's fine with it. Pleased actually – his wife can't have kids. He'll support us, visit when he can. It's not ideal, but it's more than I had from Rob after Pete was born.' She sniffed and looked at Gina through reddened eyes. 'It's not Jack I'm worried about. If I can't do something about Rob, there may not be a baby.'

# JULIA

The rain has held off all day, and I can hear magpies warbling hopefully from a nearby tree. For myself, I have little hope, despite stray beams of sunlight conspiring to persuade me otherwise. For now, it is enough to be free of the thundering torrent on the roof, enough to feel a measure of stillness washing through me like a balm. In the midst of all this benevolence, I sit on the floor surrounded by the scattered debris of my search, sipping hot lemon juice and thinking about my father.

I was born on the same day as the infamous *Dismissal* – the day the Whitlam Government was sacked – and my mother never quite forgave me. My arrival not only prevented her from attending a rally to support her political hero, but also kept Jack from being with her for the birth, as he'd promised. The way Annie told it, if I'd waited another week to be born everything would have been different – Kerr would have supported the elected government, Fraser would not have become Prime Minister, and Jack would have been at her bedside when she needed him.

It was my fault justice failed that day.

Her twisted little story suggests Jack was connected to the government in some way, but tells me nothing about who he was, or how they met. My dream of him has lost its edge now, but the feeling remains, and I know I loved him for the short time he was part of my life.

I also know that Rob drowned a few months before I was born.

What *I don't* know is why my mother let me think he was my father. A sudden thought hits me – what if she didn't? What if, as a kid, I simply overheard her telling Peter about his dad and assumed he was mine too?

Once, when Mum was out, Pete showed me Rob's funeral notice and after that, whenever I was angry with her, I'd dig it out of the drawer and imagine how much better my life would have been if he had lived. I memorised the details: *Robert Gary Brennan, 28-8-1940 to 20-7-1975, in a tragic accident. Beloved husband of Annie, loving father of Peter, dearly loved son of Jane and Albert (dec), son-in-law of Georgina Parker.* Now I know the truth, I sidestep all those conventional lies about being loved and loving and wonder what has been left out of the story. There is no gravestone; Rob was cremated and his ashes scattered. It's all suspiciously convenient…

But suddenly I couldn't care less. I'm no longer even curious. Did my mother and grandmother collude to get rid of him? Did Barragunyah play a part in his fatal accident? Those are questions about Rob – let somebody else ask them if there is anyone left who cares. My father's name was Jack.

Something – some barely formed memory – tells me that's what I called him; Jack. Were 'daddy' and 'father' forbidden words? Questions bubble to the surface of my thoughts like a spring that has been unblocked. Is he still alive? How can I find out when I don't know his surname? Why did he leave us if he loved my mother and wanted me?

A few tantalising memories rise through the murk of forgetfulness. They have no beginning or end, they simply are…

A day at the beach shimmers in a corner of my mind as if it were rare and special – riding on his shoulders as we trek through bushland, the shrill of cicadas, the lemon scent of the scrubby trees, my surprise as he steps from the track onto a long strip of deserted sand. Cliffs pitted with rock pools guard either end of the beach. A wide sky is alive with seagulls, their strident cries competing with the growl of the ocean. Then Jack is holding me in his arms as the waves crash and swirl around us and, although it's scary, I feel safe because he is with me.

And there I am in bed on a cold winter's morning, snuggled between him and Annie, sniffing the aroma of fresh coffee and buttery croissants, watching Jack's mouth curve into a smile as he leans across me to kiss my mother. Another flash of memory has me on his lap in the living room of Annie's terrace house, watching our new colour television. A lady with an umbrella is singing and dancing with penguins. I'm in my pyjamas eating popcorn, and my mother is laughing as she hands Jack a glass tinkling with chunks of ice.

Then the feeling changes. I am outside a closed door and Peter is holding my arm, so I can't go in. My mother is crying and shouting. Jack's voice is deep and calm. I shake free from Peter's grasp and open the door just a tiny bit. 'Three years,' I hear him say. 'Then London for two more. It's too good an opportunity to pass up.'

'What about me?' My mother shouts. 'What about your daughter?' When he answers, his voice is so cold it frightens me. 'I never made you any promises, Annie.'

I'm about five years old. Old enough to understand that Jack is going away again. Old enough to wish my mother would stop yelling at him. Old enough to think that if she doesn't shut up, he won't come back.

Most of Annie's relationships ended in tears and shouting. Her passion and enthusiasm for causes drew people to her, and men were captivated by her beauty, intrigued by her intelligence. But she was not an easy person to love long-term. She demanded a lot of herself and expected everyone around her to step up, too. Sooner or later, the lover of the moment would feel the brunt of her anger, and that was it. Nobody was going to hang around waiting to be scorched by Annie a second time.

As I think about small Julia listening at the door to that last argument, another memory surfaces and I realise the last time I saw Jack is connected in some way to my first visit to Barragunyah.

# ANNIE

'For God's sake, Julia, stop whining! I told you we won't get to Gran's until tomorrow!'

'But I'm hungry. You said we'd have dinner when it got dark and it's dark now. You said I could have anything I want.'

Annie sighed. 'I didn't think it'd be so far to the next town. Just be patient. You don't hear Peter whining.'

'That's coz he's sulking. He hates Gran.'

Peter looked over his shoulder from where he sat beside Annie and shot his sister a murderous look. 'I do not. It's that place I hate. I've been there, you haven't, so shut up.'

Annie felt a rush of guilt. Maybe she should have left Pete with Erica. He hadn't had a great time on their last visit. She peered through the windscreen. 'Look, kids, see those lights in the distance? That's the town; we're nearly there. Let's hope the pub's still serving meals.'

Peter closed the farm gate behind the car and climbed into the front seat. 'This place gives me the creeps,' he said. 'I'm not staying.'

'Oh, don't you start,' Annie snapped. 'Isn't it enough I've got to deal with miss whiney in the back?'

'I'm not whining,' Julia protested. 'I love it here. Can I ride a pony?'

Peter twisted around in his seat. 'You have to ask the ghost first. She'll say yes, but then she'll tell the horse to buck, and you'll break your stupid neck.'

'Pete!' Annie glanced at him in dismay.

'There's a ghost?'

Peter ignored his sister, scowled at his mother. 'Well? I know she killed Dad.'

Annie gripped the steering wheel as the car shuddered over a pothole. The road never used to be this rough – her mother was letting the place run down. 'That's not what... Look, can we talk about this later?'

'A ghost killed Dad?' Julia leaned forward resting her arms on the back of Peter's seat. 'How? What happened?'

'Later, Julia!' Annie's voice shook. 'Not another word from either of you! Look, the last gate. We're nearly there.'

Annie glanced through the open kitchen door as she sat down to breakfast. Julia was nowhere to be seen, having gulped her cereal and gone off to find the dogs. Peter, on the other hand, squatted on the veranda steps looking miserable, elbows on knees, chin on hands, eyebrows knitted into a frown.

'I guess I didn't think it through,' Annie said, adding cream to her porridge. She looked at her mother. 'I know I should have planned things better, but I was in a hurry to get away. Too many memories of Jack.'

'Are you quite sure he won't be back?' Gina asked carefully.

'Not a hope in hell. Not after what I said to him.' Annie swiped angrily at the tears that filled her eyes. 'I don't want to talk about that. The thing is, I intended to leave the kids with you and go off by myself for a while – only I don't think Pete will stay.'

Gina nodded. 'Last night, he told me he was going to run away.'

'Bloody hell!' Annie sighed. 'Look I hate to ask, but if I take Pete with me can you put up with Julia for a couple of weeks?'

'Of course. I'd love to have her.'

'Really? Well, you only see her when you come to visit. She's a miserable little bugger. Always whining about something.' Annie shrugged. 'I'm not trying to talk you out of it – just warning you. She's not an easy kid.'

'We'll rub along nicely,' Gina said. 'What about you? You won't have much time to yourself if Peter's with you.'

'Oh, Pete's okay. We understand each other.' Annie gave a wry grin. 'It might actually be better with him tagging along. I won't have time to mope.'

# GINA

Gina watched her granddaughter urge the ageing pony into a slow canter around the yard, the little girl sitting easily in a saddle far too big for her. Both saddle and pony were borrowed, trucked in by a neighbour three days ago. If Annie had given her more notice, Gina could have picked up better tack at last week's farm fair. She was tempted to take Julia to the horse sale next week and buy her a pony of her own and some new gear, but there wasn't much point when Annie could turn up any day and whizz her back to Sydney. She sighed, wishing she could have more time with her granddaughter. God only knew when they'd be back.

Annie had been gone ten days and hadn't called once, not even to check if Julia was missing her. Thankfully, she didn't seem to be. Gina chuckled. After Annie's warning she'd been expecting tears and sulks, but Julia seemed perfectly happy, following her around like a puppy, asking questions, offering to help. At night, she begged for stories about the place, the people, the animals, pushing Gina to remember things she'd long forgotten and arousing in her a longing to share each day with this child who seemed to love Barragunyah.

Gina smiled as Julia brought the pony to a halt in front of her. 'That was perfect, darling. You're doing so well. I think you can ride out with me to check the herd tomorrow.'

Julia looked at her doubtfully. 'But that's a grown-up thing.'

'It certainly is. Don't you want to come?'

'Yes, only…'

'Only what, darling?'

Julia shrugged. 'Mummy says I get in the way when she's doing grown-up stuff.'

'Well, Mummy hasn't seen you ride. I think you'll do just fine. Now show me again how you dismount.'

The little girl slipped effortlessly from the saddle and lifted the reins over the pony's head. She dug a sugar lump from the pocket of her jeans and offered it to him, stroking his soft muzzle as he munched contentedly. 'You know what, Gran? I wish I could…' Her voice caught. She turned away, burying her face in the pony's mane.

'Could what?'

Julia turned, her eyes filled with unshed tears. 'Stay here with you. I don't want to go back with Mummy and Pete.'

This was so close to what Gina had been thinking all week, she felt as if a giant fist had clutched her heart. 'Mummy would be lonely if you did that,' she said gently.

'No, she wouldn't,' Julia scowled. 'She's got Pete.'

'She needs both of you,' Gina said, with more assurance than she felt. 'But I'll bet she'll let you come for holidays now she knows you like it here.'

'It's not the same.' Julia tilted her head to one side, her mouth set in a stubborn line. 'Mary wants me to stay. She likes me. She said I can stay forever if I want.'

Gina took a deep breath – in none of her stories had she mentioned Mary. 'When did she say that?'

'Last night.' Julia glanced at Gina uneasily. 'Mary's kinda scary, isn't she Gran?'

'Sometimes she is, yes. But you said she likes you?' Julia nodded. 'Then you can be sure she'll look after you. Come on, let's take Lucky back to the stable. You can rub him down and give him some hay.'

Gina woke around midnight to the sound of torrential rain thundering on the iron roof. Where the hell did that come from? she wondered, sitting up and switching on her bedside lamp. There hadn't been a cloud in the sky three hours ago. Now it was pouring hard enough to wake the dead. She got up, reached for her dressing gown at the foot of her bed, and padded down the hallway to check on her granddaughter.

Julia was standing at the window, peering out into the darkness. 'It's loud, isn't it?' Gina said, walking over to stand beside her. 'I expect it will stop before morning.'

'I'll run out of food before it stops,' Julia said, her voice flat.

Gina stared at her in alarm. 'We've plenty of food,' she said. 'You mustn't worry about things like that, darling.'

'The creek will flood. I'll be trapped.'

Gina shivered. She put her hand on Julia's shoulder. 'I think what we need is a cup of warm milk.'

Julia jumped at her touch. She turned abruptly and looked up. Her eyes were wide and blank, but as Gina watched, they gradually focused. 'Gran? Did the rain wake you too?'

'It sure did. I wasn't expecting it.' She hesitated. 'Are you afraid of rain, Julia?'

'No, I love it, but...' Her expression grew puzzled. 'I've been to Barragunyah before, haven't I?'

'Only in your Mummy's tummy, before you were born,' Gina said carefully.

'Was it raining then?'

'I don't think so. It was nearly six years ago. I can't remember.'

Julia frowned. 'I remember. The roof leaked... We had to use candles. Mary wouldn't let me leave.'

Gina looked at her granddaughter uneasily, questions chasing each other through the darker corners of her mind. Had she been dreaming, or... Something tugged at her memory, something Mac had said not long before she died, about the vagaries of time. But she'd been talking about the lost girl, so why was it pricking at her thoughts now?

'Did Mary say what...' Gina paused. Sometimes it was better not to know about things you couldn't change. 'Oh, never mind. Listen, I'm going to have some warm milk and cinnamon to help me sleep,' she said. 'Would you like some?'

Julia nodded.

'Get your dressing gown on then.'

They sat at the kitchen table in companionable silence, sipping the fragrant milk, then Julia said, 'I wish you were my mum. You never get cranky with me.'

'It's much harder being a mother than a grandmother, Julia. I used to get very cranky at your mum when she was your age.'

Julia giggled. 'Did you yell at her?'

'Quite often.' Gina frowned. 'To tell you the truth, Julia, I wasn't a very good mother when Annie was small.' Her thoughts drifted back to those difficult years and she sighed; this was not the sort of thing to share with a five-year-old.

But Julia was persistent. 'Tell me about when Mum was little.'

'Well, it was an awful time for everyone. Annie's father – your grandfather – died in the war, you see, and I missed him very much.'

'Were you sad?'

'Yes, I was. Angry too. For a long while, I couldn't look at my poor little baby without remembering that Tom was gone.' Gina sighed again. 'So I didn't look at her. I let my mother take care of her and do all the things I should have been doing. And by the time my sadness and anger faded, it was easier to let things continue as they were – me running Barragunyah and my mother looking after Annie. When she was your age, I never made time for her, not even to have a cup of warm milk on a rainy night.

And later, when I realised what I had done and tried to be a better mother, Annie didn't have time for me.' She smiled wryly at Julia. 'That's how it goes in life, darling. You get back what you give. Remember that.'

It was still raining the following afternoon when Annie phoned. 'Mum, can you hear me?'

'Barely. The rain's thundering down. You'll have to speak up.'

'It's the rain I'm calling about,' Annie yelled. 'The highway's cut. I can't get through.'

'Where are you?' Gina realised she was shouting too.

'Some tin-pot town south of you. Listen, I phoned Erica, and she said my best client has a big-paying job for me, but if I want it, I need to head back to Sydney now.'

Gina felt a butterfly of hope spreading its wings in her midriff. 'Do you mean to leave Julia here?'

'Yes, exactly. Can you put up with her until the rain stops, then pop her on a train?'

'I'm happy to have her here, Annie, but I'm not putting a five-year-old on a train by herself.' Gina hesitated, then forged ahead before Annie could respond – what did she have to lose? 'Annie, would you mind very much if Julia stayed here until the end of the year? I could bring her down on the train myself before Christmas.'

Annie was silent for a minute, her thoughts racing. It had been good to get away from Julia's whining and, if she was honest, those bloody eyes that reminded her of Jack. Pete was old enough to amuse himself, but Julia demanded constant attention.

'Annie? Are you still there?'

'What about school?' she shouted. 'She's supposed to start next term.'

'There's always School of the Air,' Gina said. 'But honestly, I don't think missing a year matters much at her age. She'd be learning lots of other things.'

'Yeah, okay. That'd solve a lot of problems.' Annie glanced around and nodded at the man waiting in the lobby of the pub to use the phone. 'Listen, Mum. I've got to go. I'll call you when I get home, okay? Give my love to Julia.'

# JULIA

The rain has eased to a drizzle yet still holds me prisoner. Back then, it poured for a week and set me free. I was only five, but I recognised a gift from the universe when it came my way; when my mother went home without me, I felt as if all my Christmases had come at once.

Yesterday, I stuffed things haphazardly back into the old tin trunk in an attempt to tidy the mess I'd made of the living room. Now, greedy for memories that are mine, I rummage through it again. This time I know what I'm looking for – the photo album with the pony picture on the front. The one Gran and I chose together on a trip to Lurradallan. I dig it out, open the cover and there, on the first page, is the reason we bought it.

It's a picture of Gran and me that Ruby took with her new colour camera and sent away to be enlarged. I remember the fuss she made trying to get us to be still, to get the light just right, to get us to smile at the same time, to get me to stop giggling. Despite my silliness, Ruby did a good job. In the photo, Gran and I are dressed up ready to go to the Darrobine show. We're sitting on the front steps of the veranda wearing matching Akubra hats, checked shirts, jodhpurs and brown boots. Gran is holding my hand, my head is tilted slightly, and we both have broad smiles, mine revealing a gap where my two front teeth had been. My hair is in two dark plaits, Gran's springy grey curls are partly hidden by her hat.

That's how it was that first year. I was Gran's shadow. Where she went, I went. I know she enjoyed my company because even when I messed up, which I often did, there was no, *get lost, Julia,* no, *Julia, you're giving me a headache,* no, *stop your whining, you little pest.* The truth is, I had nothing to whine about – every day was an adventure. Chores were challenges: Could I carry all the eggs home unbroken? Did I remember the difference between lettuce seedlings and weeds? Were my hands strong enough to milk Pet, the dairy cow, for two minutes more than I'd managed the day before?

A couple of pages into the album is a photo of me riding Pebbles. The day Gran took me to the horse sales and bought her for me I thought I was in heaven. I loved that little buckskin mare more than life and when she died of snake bite eight years later, I cried for a week.

I flip through the pages of the album, watching myself grow up, watching Gran grow old, but it is the photos from my first year at Barragunyah that I return to again and again. Because that year changed me. It changed who I was and the way I thought, it changed how I felt about my place in the world and where I belonged. And it changed my relationship with my mother and Peter. Mum never really understood that.

I know that in all those months I didn't miss her at all, and I'm pretty sure she didn't miss me. When Jack had been around, I was his darling and hers. Once he was gone, I was the whiney kid, the one who moped and complained, who picked at her food, who hid under the stairs when Mum's friends came over. To her, I probably seemed no different when I returned – I was still the difficult child, the kid with the sulky face.

I think I was always a mystery to Annie. Despite her quick temper, she was lively and outgoing, usually the centre of attention. She could talk to anyone about anything and make people laugh. I was her opposite, the silent observer hovering in the background, probably frowning or, as my mother would have it, sulking. It was years before I became aware of how we brought out the worst in each other, how my moodiness sparked her anger, how her anger caused me to withdraw even more. It was an ongoing battle, exhausting for both of us.

And in between was Peter. He'd always been smug about his big brother status, pushing me around, telling on me when I did anything wrong, siding with Mum when she got annoyed with me. He turned thirteen during those months I spent at Barragunyah, and by the time I returned to Sydney, he and Mum had established a comfortable relationship that left no space for me.

I felt like an intruder, an interloper in a family I couldn't understand and into which I never quite fit. I dealt with these feelings the only way I knew how; I withdrew, reinforcing their opinion of me as a sulky child that a year with Gran had not been able to cure. The battles resumed.

The following year, when school broke up for the long summer holidays, Mum took me to Barragunyah and left me there. It was a relief for both of us and became the pattern for the next five years. In between times, I escaped the conflicts of family life by imagining myself at Barragunyah, thinking about what I'd do, where I'd go, having conversations in my head with Gran, cooking with Agnes, joking with Ruby and Gill, riding Pebbles, playing with the dogs, swimming in the dam. It was a rich and wonderful world inside my head, and in my heart, I longed desperately for someone to wave a magic wand and make those daydreams real and lasting. It had happened once before – why couldn't it happen again?

# ANNIE

Erica tossed a pile of travel brochures on the kitchen table and grinned at Annie. 'Look through these, then tell me you don't want to go.'

'I didn't say I don't want to. I just don't see how I can.'

'Seriously, Annie, it's time we expanded our horizons. Most of our friends did Europe years ago.'

'Yes, when they were in their teens and early twenties. In case you haven't noticed, we no longer fit the backpacker demographic.'

'Pfft. Who said anything about backpacking? I'm talking about living and working in London, slipping over to the continent at weekends. God, it'll be divine!'

Annie pushed her coffee mug aside and flipped half-heartedly through the brochures. 'It's all right for you. You haven't got kids.'

'Are you looking for excuses?' Erica frowned. 'Look, you said you were going to let your hair down, make some changes once Pete was off to uni. If this doesn't fit the bill, I don't know what does.'

'What about Julia? She'll be home from Mum's in two weeks, ready to start high school.'

'So, tell your mother not to bring her home. The kid likes it better there anyway.'

Annie pulled a face. 'Too true. Only...'

'What now?'

'High school. There isn't one. She'd have to board, and she'll hate it. I certainly did.' Annie grinned wryly. 'I was expelled from three.'

Erica raised her eyebrows. 'You never told me that! Three boarding schools? You must have been a terror.'

'I was. I don't know how Mum put up with me.'

'Yeah, but Julia's nothing like you. She'll fit right in. Come on, Annie, stop looking for excuses. Let's do it!'

'Oh, God, I really want to, but… How long do you think we'd be away?'

'I don't know. A year or two? Why set limits? As you pointed out, we're not exactly spring chickens.' Erica paused, her expression suddenly serious. 'Look, I really want to do this together, Annie, but if you decide against it, I'm going anyway.'

Annie ran a hand through her long hair, flipping it away from her face as her thoughts raced. She couldn't bear it if Erica went to Europe without her. Besides, why sacrifice herself for a kid who didn't even like her? They'd both be miserable, and what would it prove?

'I guess Pete could house-sit,' she considered. 'It's an easy walk to Sydney Uni from here, so he'd have no trouble renting the spare bedrooms to other students. That'd cover his food and expenses.'

'Perfect. And Julia's already settled with your mother.' Erica rummaged through the brochures, found what she was looking for, and shoved it across the table. 'Look, these flights are really cheap if we book now. Say you'll do it, Annie. We'll have the time of our lives.'

Annie grinned. Her friend's enthusiasm was contagious. 'Okay, I will. Just give me a day to sort out the kids before we book.'

# GINA

'Mum, are you still there?'

Gina shook her head, frowning at the telephone receiver in disbelief. 'I'll get Julia,' she said at last. 'You'll want to tell her yourself.'

'No, she'll take it the wrong way coming from me,' Annie sighed. 'She'll say I'm abandoning her or some such rubbish. Get her to call me after you've told her. Oh, and could you find a boarding school that'll take her at short notice?'

'I don't know, Annie. Julia's looking forward to going to Fort Street High. She told me she was thrilled to be accepted.' Gina hesitated. 'Have you thought this through?'

'Oh, don't start lecturing me on the responsibilities of motherhood,' Annie snapped. 'You couldn't wait to send me off to boarding school. What's the difference?'

Gina sighed. It was pointless arguing. Annie knew quite well the situation was different. 'What if Julia insists on keeping her place at Fort Street?'

'She's twelve, Mum, she doesn't get to insist. Anyway, she won't. If she can spend every holiday at Barragunyah, she'll be happy as a pig in shit. Listen. I've got to go. Get her to call me when you've got things sorted.'

Gina broke the news gently, expecting tears, but it turned out Annie was right.

'Really? I can stay here? With you? All the time?' Julia's eyes lit up.

'Well, not all the time. You'll have to go to boarding school. But you'll spend every holiday here, not just the Christmas one.'

Julia's smile faltered. 'I don't want to go to boarding school. Why can't you teach me like you did when I lived here before?'

'You were six then, darling. I wouldn't know where to begin teaching high school subjects.' She put her arm around her granddaughter's shoulders. 'Are you very disappointed about Fort Street?'

'What? No! I don't care about that if I can stay here.' Julia pulled away, folded her arms across her chest. 'But I'm not going to boarding school, Gran.'

Gina looked at her uneasily. Annie had been too uncompromising and feisty to fit into boarding school life. Julia, although quiet and reserved, was equally strong-willed. 'I suppose we could get you a live-in tutor,' she said slowly. 'Like I had when I was a girl.'

'Yes!' Julia threw her arms around Gina's neck. 'Please, Gran, can we do that?'

'It might work.' Gina considered the possibilities. 'We'd have to find the right person of course. I was lucky to have Lizzie. Then there's all that junk in my old classroom, we'd have to...'

'I'll clean it up,' Julia said excitedly. 'I'll start now!' She gave her grandmother another hug and headed for the room Ellen had had built all those years ago.

Gina watched her go, unable to keep the smile from her face. Just when she thought Barragunyah's women had reached the end of the line, something happened to surprise her. Annie might not like the idea of Julia being tutored, but she doubted she would cancel her trip over it. And with Julia loving the place as much as she did, the future was looking brighter.

# JULIA

I want to remember those six years as a halcyon time, the golden age of Julia when I lived my dream. And at first it was. But Barragunyah, that old hoarder of gloom, will not let me forget the dark side, the horror of a drought so all-consuming it altered the lives of everyone I knew.

It began with an unusually dry summer a couple of years after Mum went to England. We scraped through that season relatively unscathed, thanks to our bores and creeks, but it was just a harbinger of the horrors ahead. Over the next three years, the lack of rain controlled our lives, tested our endurance, and ate up Gran's fortune. What we would have given then, to see a sky as sodden and grey as the one that currently rains on my parade. But the sky was relentlessly, cloudlessly blue, the sun merciless.

The lush green pastures I loved to explore on horseback turned crisp and brown, then disappeared entirely as hungry animals, both domestic and wild, ate the stubble down to bare earth. Gran ordered stock feed by the truckload which we dispensed from the back of the farm ute twice a day, but it was never enough and the sleek Black Angus cattle for which Barragunyah was renowned grew lean and bony.

As the drought tightened its grip, we were forced to reduce the herd, but with everyone in the same dire straits nobody was buying bloodstock so promising heifers and bull calves went to the abattoir, breaking Gran's heart. A prize bull, worth thousands, died bogged to his belly in the mud of a drying dam. Champion breeding cows struggling to give birth in their weakened state had to be shot, ending bloodlines that had taken generations to establish. Our fourth spring without rain saw the herd reduced to twenty cows and one young bull, Gran reduced to borrowing from the bank, and Barragunyah reduced to two hundred acres.

Over those years, I watched Gran's hair turn white and the worry lines on her face deepen. I watched her cry when she told Ruby, Gillian, and Agnes she could no longer afford to pay them. But now, remembering their responses, I smile.

'Of course, you can't pay us,' Ruby said, raking a hand through her impossibly red curls. 'We're lucky to have a roof over our heads. That's payment enough until it rains again.'

'Put the money towards stock feed,' Gillian added. 'Don't let that bloody bank manager get his hands on it.'

'How do you expect to feed everyone and keep the place clean without me?' Agnes asked stroppily. 'Unless you need my room, that is. Were you planning on letting it out?'

'What? Of course not,' Gran said. 'But I can't…'

'Well then, we'll get by. The vegetable garden's surviving on bathwater. Scraps and a bit of corn will keep the chooks laying. As for my poor house cows—well, nobody expects cream on their porridge these days.' And off she stomped, refusing to discuss the matter further.

I was seventeen then, and with everyone making sacrifices, it suddenly dawned on me I was Gran's biggest liability. Looking back, I'm appalled it took me so long to see it. I'd always helped around the farm, but there was little to do during the drought, so I spent most of my time studying for the HSC with Miss Adams, my tutor. And she was another financial burden Gran could do without.

Janet Adams was in her mid-sixties when she arrived at Barragunyah. Tall and bony, with sharp blue eyes behind half-moon spectacles, she had recently retired from teaching at a private girls' school and was a stickler for old-fashioned conventions (*you may call me Miss Adams*). Although she was inclined to correct my posture, my diction, and my manners as well as my essays, she was a brilliant teacher and we got along well despite her aversion to country living. Her idea of being outdoors was sitting on the veranda with a book and a cup of tea; she rarely ventured further. I never really understood why she'd applied for the position. Perhaps she'd hoped for a touch of rural hospitality, a few bush dances and country shows. If so, it was bad timing because, with the drought and everyone struggling to survive, all social events were suspended. I think it was only her commitment to seeing a job through to the end that kept her with us. And that was an issue I could resolve.

'I can get by without Miss Adams now,' I told Gran. 'I have my study materials and I can work perfectly well alone. To be honest,' I added, grinning, 'I think she'll be glad of an excuse to leave, and it'll save money.'

Gran shook her head. 'You need her more than ever in your final year. We'll manage.' Then she dropped the bombshell that changed everything. 'Julia, love, I think you should apply to go to university next year.'

'What? No way! I'm staying here to work Barragunyah with you. You said I could!'

'That was before the drought.' She took hold of my hands. 'The thing is, darling, I've had to borrow money from the bank. If it doesn't rain soon, I'll probably lose Barragunyah. Even if it doesn't come to that, I've had to sell off so much land it will never be the breeding stud it once was. You must think of doing something else with your life.'

I stared at her, speechless. I hadn't realised things were that bad.

'It's hard to let go of a dream, Julia. Believe me, I know. But sometimes we just have to deal with what we're given and make the best of it.' Gran smiled. 'Miss Adams tells me you're very bright.

She believes you could win a scholarship. I've asked her to send for the application forms.'

'I don't want to go to university,' I protested, fighting tears. 'I don't know anything about it. I'd be hopeless.'

'Miss Adams thinks otherwise. Talk to her, darling. Just think, you could be the first Barragunyah woman to get a degree. Wouldn't that be something?'

'Are you crazy? It's just a piece of paper!' I'd never yelled at Gran in my life, but I was yelling now. All my hopes and dreams for the future were tied up with Barragunyah; I'd never given university a thought. Blinded by tears, I ran from the house.

At the yards I called to Obi, the palomino gelding Gran bought me after Pebbles died. He trotted over, ears pricked, hoping for a carrot, then flinging his head up in surprise when I leapt onto his back and urged him, unbridled, through the gate.

My legs were trembling, and Obi was puffing and snorting when I slipped from his back next to the dry creek bed. Like everywhere else, the once-green glade where I used to sit and daydream about running Barragunyah was brown and desiccated – as dead as the future I'd planned. Burying my face in Obi's silver mane, I sobbed until I felt as hollow and wasted as the dying trees. When I could cry no more, I wiped my face and sat down to think.

And the more I thought, the more ashamed I became. Gran had enough to deal with without me acting like a spoilt brat. I was young enough to find new dreams, but Gran was over seventy and Barragunyah was the only place – the only life – she had ever known. What would she do if it was taken from her? I should be helping, not adding to her misery.

But university? The idea terrified me – classes filled with kids who knew what they were doing, teachers asking questions I couldn't answer, finding my way through the maze of sandstone buildings Peter had loved.

What I needed was a job so I could help Gran buy back the land she'd had to sell; a thought that raised a whole lot of other problems. A job doing what? I was qualified for nothing. I had no work experience. Who'd hire me? Nobody in their right mind. I had no idea what Gran owed the bank, no idea what sort of jobs paid well. In fact, I realised, I didn't have much idea about anything that went on in the world beyond Barragunyah.

It was time I grew up.

I rode back slowly, trying to work out how I could help Gran. I came up with zilch. The best thing I could do was get out of her way – at least it would be one less mouth to feed Two, in fact, because Miss Adams would leave too.

But where would I go? My mother was in London, Peter in Melbourne. Surely even an unskilled person like me could get a job in a big city. Maybe I could earn enough to send money back to Gran. Could I live with Peter? Would he want me to? Unlikely on both counts. The last time I'd seen my brother was when Gran and I went to Sydney for his graduation three years ago and we'd had little to say to each other then. As for my mother, I hadn't seen her since she left. She phoned occasionally, and sent interesting postcards and gifts from exotic places, but she no longer seemed real to me. I didn't know her at all.

# ANNIE

Annie stared through the window as David steered their hire car down the rutted track. 'I can't believe how awful the place looks,' she said. 'I know there's a drought, but Barragunyah's got good bores – at least some of the paddocks should have green feed. My mother loves this place. Why would she let everything get so run down?'

'Maybe she's been ill,' David said. 'Didn't you say she was in her seventies?'

'Yes, but she's as fit as a fiddle.' Annie frowned. 'Well, I guess I haven't seen her in a while, but Julia would have told me if Mum was sick.'

David glanced at her. 'I'd say the drought's been worse than she let on. The chap at the service station said everyone's doing it tough.'

'Yeah, it'd be just like her to downplay it. I think she'd die before she asked for help.'

'Not much you could have done from London, old thing.' David squeezed her knee affectionately.

'True. But I'm back now. I'll find out what's going on.' Annie smiled at him. 'I can't wait to see the look on her face when I tell her we're married. Julia too. They'll be so surprised.'

David raised one eyebrow, his brown eyes glinting with amusement. 'Surprise may be an understatement, my sweet. I still think we should have telephoned to warn them we were coming. If things are as bad as they look, two extra to feed could be the last straw.'

Annie laughed. 'Oh, stop worrying! I told you, Barragunyah can feed an army.'

Gina hugged Annie again. 'It's wonderful to see you, darling. And to meet you, David. I'm just sorry the place looks so unwelcoming at present.'

'Yeah, what's going on?' Annie asked. 'Aren't the bores working? And what's with that weird name above the fancy gate up near the north boundary?'

'It's a long story,' Gina said. 'Bring in your things and get settled. I'll explain over afternoon tea.'

David squeezed Annie's shoulder. 'I'll get our bags. You catch up with your mother.'

'Thanks, love.' Annie grinned at her mother as they watched him stride across the veranda and down the steps to where the car was parked outside the fence. 'An improvement on Rob, isn't he?'

Gina smiled, but her eyes were full of questions. 'He seems lovely, darling, but it would have been nice to meet him before the wedding.'

'You know what they say about old habits?' Annie laughed. 'I like shocking you.'

'Oh well, at least this is a pleasant shock.'

Pleasant in lots of ways, Gina thought, gazing at her daughter. Annie was almost fifty, but in her slim jeans and white t-shirt, and her copper shoulder-length hair streaked with blonde highlights, she looked ten years younger. It was more than that though – the tension in her face had gone, and the anger that had always simmered beneath the surface. 'You look happy, darling. Even better, you seem content.'

'Content? I suppose I am.' Annie smiled and slipped her arm through her mother's. 'You, on the other hand, look stressed. Let's get inside out of this awful heat and you can tell me what's going on. Where's Julia, by the way?'

'She's gone for a ride.' Gina hesitated. 'I'm sure she'll be back soon.'

Annie looked up as Agnes placed a plate of scones and a dish of jam beside the teapot. 'You've forgotten the cream,' she said, laughing. 'Shall I fetch it?'

'If you feel like a trip to Darrobine,' Agnes sniffed. 'And then you'd have to strike it lucky to get any. The milk in the jug's that powdered stuff, by the way.'

'Well, that's got to be a first.' Annie raised her eyebrows as Agnes returned to the kitchen, then turned to her mother. 'Things are that bad? What else haven't you told me?'

Gina was saved from answering as a screen door slammed shut. 'That'll be Julia.'

Annie took a deep breath. She was more nervous about introducing her daughter to David than she'd realised.

'Gran, whose car... Mum? What are you doing here?' Julia stared at Annie warily.

'My God, you've grown so tall!' Annie jumped up and hugged her, then stood back. 'Let me look at you!'

At seventeen, Julia stood eye to eye with Annie and had the same slim build, but the similarity ended there. While Annie looked fresh and stylish, Julia looked unkempt. Her boots were scuffed, her jeans and checked shirt were faded and grubby, and her long dark hair, pulled back from her face in a rough ponytail, looked like it needed a good wash. Judging by her red puffy eyes, Annie was sure she'd been crying.

'Are you okay?' Annie reached out and tentatively touched Julia's face.

Julia pulled back, scowling. 'Why wouldn't I be?'

Some things never change, Annie thought. Still the same grumpy Julia. She smiled brightly. 'I've a surprise, darling. I'd like you to meet my husband – and your stepfather, I guess – David Wiseman.'

'Give her a break, Annie, love. Don't dump the stepdad thing on her yet.' David stood up and held out his hand to Julia. 'It's good to meet you, Julia. Please, just call me David.'

Julia hesitated, shook the proffered hand briefly, then stared accusingly at her mother. 'You never said you were getting married.'

'I wanted to surprise you.' Annie's smile faltered. 'I hope you're happy for me.'

'Why? You don't usually care how I feel when you spring your surprises.'

'Julia!' Gina protested.

'Well, it's true, Gran! She just turns up after six years and expects everything to be the same. Did she even phone to see if we had enough food for them?'

Julia felt tears building behind her eyes again as she glared at her mother. 'Things change, you know. Gran might lose Barragunyah. What'll she do then? What happens to me?' She swiped away the tears with the back of her hand. 'Not that you'd care. So yes, Mum, I'm wildly happy for you. Now you can go back to your comfy city life and forget about us for another six years!'

An awkward silence fell as Julia turned and strode from the room. Gina sighed. 'I'm sorry, darling, I'm afraid you've caught the repercussions of some news I gave Julia earlier.'

'Should I go after her?' Annie's voice shook.

'No, let her be. She's a sensible girl, she'll come round. I'm sure she didn't mean it.'

'I think she did,' Annie said softly. 'And she's right about me. But that business about losing Barragunyah? That can't be true, surely?'

Gina shrugged. 'I might hold on if it rains soon. The bores have run dry, and I've had to sell most of the land to keep the bank at bay. I'm not the only one. Foreign investors have done very well out of this drought.'

'Why didn't you tell me?'

'There was nothing you could do. I didn't want you worrying.'

David cleared his throat. 'Er, none of my business, but we may be able to help out financially once we know the details.'

'Thank you, David, you're very kind. But I don't want you and Annie sending good money after bad. Barragunyah must survive or fall on its merits.'

'But Mum, where would you go if you had to sell?' Annie looked at her, appalled. 'What would you do?'

Gina looked away for a minute, staring across her land. When she turned back, her face was composed. 'I'll face that when I come to it,' she said quietly. 'Meanwhile, let's not allow these scones to go to waste or Agnes will put a curse on us.'

Annie picked up a scone and put it down again. 'What Julia said… Are you really short of food?'

'Of course not.' Gina smiled ruefully. 'Although the variety and quality may not be what you expected. We're having rabbit stew tonight, thanks to Ruby's skill with a rifle.'

'Ruby's still with you? And Gillian? Where are they?'

'They've done up the old shearers' hut for themselves. They wanted a place to call their own rather than just bedrooms in the main house. They don't usually bother coming up for afternoon tea these days, but they'll have seen the car, so I expect them any minute. Miss Adams, Julia's tutor, is probably taking a nap. She doesn't cope well with the heat.'

'Can you afford to pay them all? From what you told us, Barragunyah can't be providing any income.' Annie frowned. 'Dammit, I should be paying Julia's tutor. I never gave it a thought…'

Gina sighed. 'Do you want me to lay it all out for you now? You must be tired after your drive and I'm sure David can't be interested.'

'Ah, but I am.' He smiled and reached for a scone. 'Annie's been telling me about this place ever since we booked our flight – it certainly has an interesting history. Why don't you fill me in on the current status? The more I know, the better I can work out how we can help.'

'No, really, David. Thank you, but...'

'Mum, don't get on your high horse. David knows what he's talking about. Just tell us the way things are. Tell us everything.'

The sun was setting when Annie left Gina and David poring over the ledgers and went looking for Julia. She found her on the veranda, curled up on an old daybed, gazing miserably across the bare brown paddocks.

'I thought it got cooler once the sun went down,' Annie said, leaning against a veranda post. She pulled the fabric of her t-shirt away from her sweaty skin. 'I guess my memory's faulty.'

Julia sniffed and wiped her nose on her arm. 'It won't get cool until it rains,' she muttered. 'You'll be long gone by then.'

'Yes. We planned to stay a few weeks, but I think we might leave tomorrow.'

'No surprise there.'

Annie tilted her head as she looked at her daughter. 'Julia, I'm not going to pretend I've been a good mother. I deserved everything you said earlier.' She paused, frowning slightly. 'Look, I can't change the past, but I can make amends.'

Julia raised her eyebrows but remained silent.

'Okay, not to you, maybe, but I can help your grandmother save Barragunyah.' Noting the flicker of interest in her daughter's eyes, Annie continued. 'I can't do anything about the land she's already sold, but I might be able to help save what remains.'

'Does she owe the bank a lot?' Julia mumbled. 'She didn't tell me.'

'I think so. David's going over the details with her now. He'll come up with a plan. He's good at things like that.' Annie smiled. 'But while they were talking, I thought up a plan of my own.'

'Such as?' Julia sniffed again, but she was sitting up now, paying attention, her eyes fixed on Annie.

'Such as selling my house in Newtown.'

'Oh.' Julia seemed to deflate. 'That old place won't be worth much.'

'Actually, it's worth quite a lot. The agent who's been renting it for me since Peter left keeps pestering me to sell. Apparently, the inner city is being gentrified and there's a huge demand for Victorian terraces.'

'How much is a lot?'

'If we spruce it up a bit, over a million, I think.'

'You're kidding!' It seemed an impossible amount to Julia. 'How much of that would you give Gran? I mean, even if we get good rain it'll take ages to build up the herd again.'

'I'd give her all of it, of course. She bought that house for me when I needed help; the least I can do is give her the money back now she needs it.'

'But where would you live?'

Annie sat beside her daughter and took her hands. 'I'm not staying in Australia, Julia. My home's in London now, with David.' She smiled. 'There's a room there for you, if you want it.'

Julia pulled her hands free. 'I'm not leaving Barragunyah!' She frowned and lifted her shoulders helplessly. 'At least, that was the plan until today.'

'And now?'

'Gran reckons there's no future here. She wants me to go to university.'

'I see.' Annie nodded thoughtfully. 'Julia, I know this is not what you want to hear, but that's not a bad idea.' She held up her hand as Julia began to protest. 'Wait, hear me out. We can only save what's left of Barragunyah, so it will never be the breeding stud it once was. I'm sure you understand that better than I do.'

'I don't care. It's where I belong.' Julia looked away, tears filling her eyes again.

'Julia, there's nothing here for you now. Even if the drought ended tomorrow, it would take years to establish even a small herd. You could earn a university degree in that time.'

'What difference will a piece of paper make?'

'It will give you options, Julia. Who knows what the future holds? You can sit around doing nothing while you wait to see what happens, or you can do something productive in the meantime. The only certainty is that time will pass anyway.'

# JULIA

Life is full of irony. Leaving Barragunyah during that drought was the hardest thing I'd ever done. Now, in the middle of a flood, leaving is all I want to do. Why won't she let me go? What does she want of me?

Not knowing what time I might land in, what ghosts I might meet, I've given up trying to cross the creek. I haven't quite given up hope. Mary hasn't let me starve, so she must have something in mind for me. Whether I'll be happy about it is the big question.

Sometimes I see her at dawn, drifting with the mist like a dusky wraith. And late at night, when I can't sleep for the thundering on the roof, I've seen her dancing in the rain, her skin gleaming in rainbow colours like oil on a pool of dark water. She keeps me fed. She keeps me safe. She keeps me.

I don't know why.

I agreed to return to Sydney with my mother and David. Miss Adams came with us, barely concealing her relief at escaping Barragunyah three months earlier than she'd expected. Sitting beside my tutor in the back of the car on the way to Lurradallan airport, I stared through the window at the ravaged landscape, listening in glum silence as she chatted with Mum and David, making plans for my education as if it mattered, filling in the gaps with trivialities. I remember hating them all for their unrelenting cheerfulness.

I hated the plane too, for the swift and easy distance it put between me and everything I loved, for the cruel blue sky that was its element, and for the baked brown earth revealed in all its horror as we soared above it. I rested my head against the glass of the window, unaware that tears were rolling down my face until Miss Adams patted my arm and handed me a neatly folded handkerchief.

Sydney was noisy and alarming after the tranquillity of Barragunyah. From the hot anger of hating, I slipped into cold despair. Was this to be my life from now on?

David hailed a taxi for Miss Adams who was going to stay with her sister. As he opened the cab door for her, she shook my hand and smiled her tight little smile. 'This is all most disturbing for you, my dear, but the strangeness will pass. I shall see you in two weeks. Until then, try to keep up with your studies.'

Then I watched my last link with Barragunyah disappear into the traffic, leaving me with two strangers.

# GINA

Gina slowed her horse to a walk, allowing it to find its own way among the sand and pebbles of the dry creek bed. This place had been her saviour once, helping her to shape loss and despair into some sort of meaning after her mother died and Annie rejected her. The beauty alone was a solace then, now the desolate terrain was without a trace of consolation.

She was getting too old to fight for a decimated land that no longer responded to her love and care. Ruby and Gillian were not getting any younger either, and even in its diminished size, Barragunyah could not be properly managed by three ageing women. Without Julia, the place had no future.

Yet she'd been right to send her granddaughter away. Barragunyah might have no future without Julia, but if she'd remained, the girl's own prospects were limited. It would never be the property it once was, never be the first-class breeding stud Alice and Mac had set up, the place she, Gina, had helped build into something that fitted their grand dreams. A wistful smile flitted across Gina's face. With all its problems and demands, she could not imagine a better life, a better place to live.

Until this bloody drought.

Was this how her neighbour, Jim Collins, had felt before he pulled the trigger?

They'd attended his funeral last week, paying their respects like everyone else in the district, voicing the same platitudes to his widow and children. What real comfort could you offer someone whose home and livelihood, past and future, had been sold by the bank to offset loans? Jim's family had farmed that land for generations, and they'd lost it simply because it hadn't rained. Nobody talked about the spectre that lurked behind the tragedy – the knowledge that Jim wasn't the first and most likely wouldn't be the last. Every one of the mourners at the funeral knew it could have been them. Might yet be them.

It certainly could have been her.

David had saved Barragunyah, covering the debts until Annie sold her house in Newtown. Despite Gina's protests, Annie had been adamant, insisting the money rightfully belonged to Barragunyah. It remained to be seen if her optimistic prediction about the sale price would be realised.

Six months, they'd said. Six months to visit Peter in Melbourne, spruce up the house and put it on the market. Enough time to allow Julia to finish her HSC and decide on a university. Then, if the house sold, they would return to England.

Would she ever see her daughter again? She hoped so, but given her own advanced age, and their history of too many years passing between visits, it seemed unlikely.

Gina took off her Akubra and raked a hand through her sweat-damp hair, her thoughts drifting. David and Annie's brief visit was possibly the first time she had ever felt really comfortable with her daughter. They'd managed to laugh together, to talk without arguing, to share memories and stories. It was clearly David who made the difference. He somehow brought out the best in Annie, his calm, easy-going nature encouraging her to be softer, less confrontational.

Of course, Annie wasn't the only one who'd changed. Gina knew she was different too. She was less sure of herself these days, more questioning about why she did things, what she expected of other people, what she expected from life itself. It had taken her a long time, but she knew now that expectations usually led to disappointments, that relationships were complex, that difficulties between people were rarely one-sided.

The conversation they had avoided – she'd avoided – was about Julia's future. Gina was afraid Annie would persuade her to go with them to London and if that happened, she wasn't sure she could bear it. She already missed her granddaughter more than she'd thought possible. Imagining her living on the other side of the world made her heart physically ache. But Julia's life was her own, the choices hers to make for good or ill. Whatever she decided, Gina knew she would have to accept it.

But dear God, how she missed her!

Gina turned her horse for home.

# ANNIE

Annie opened the door to the small back bedroom off the first landing. 'This was Erica's room. Do you remember? It's the quietest room in the house, so I thought it might suit you for the next few months while you're studying.'

'Fine.' Julia shrugged, then glanced at her mother curiously. 'Where's Erica now?'

'Living in the south of France with her girlfriend.'

'Girlfriend? As in…'

'Yes. She and Lucille are lovers.'

'Seriously? But Erica always had loads of boyfriends.'

'True, but none of them were around for long before she sent them packing.' Annie grinned. 'It took her a while to work out it wasn't them, it was her.'

'Wow! Is she happy?'

'Ecstatic. They've renovated a gorgeous old manor near Carcassonne and run it as a bed-and-breakfast. David and I have stayed a couple of times. You'd love it.'

It was as if shutters had slammed shut on her daughter's curiosity. 'How would you know?' she muttered. 'You don't know anything about me.'

Annie sighed. 'So talk to me, Julia. Tell me about the things that make you happy, what pisses you off, what makes you cry. I know I've been a lousy mum, but I'm trying to do better. Help me out here.'

'What's the point? You'll be gone in six months.'

'Then come to London with us!' Annie grasped Julia's hands. 'Give me a chance to make things up to you. There's a big, beautiful world out there, darling, don't wait as long as I did to explore it.'

Julia pulled away. 'I hate cities.'

'And you know this, how? Because you've lived in so many?' Annie raised her eyebrows. 'You chose not to go to boarding school, Julia, and that's fine, but as a result you've led a very sheltered life. Think about it. You're seventeen. You have no friends your own age. I doubt you've even spoken to a boy. It's the nineties, baby, and this is not normal.'

'It's my normal,' Julia snapped.

But Annie could tell from the uncertainty in her daughter's eyes that she'd hit a nerve. She nodded. 'You're tired. We're all tired. Let's make up your bed and we'll talk tomorrow.'

When Julia came downstairs the next morning David was in the kitchen making coffee. She sniffed appreciatively. 'That smells good.'

David smiled. 'Black? Or would you prefer cream in yours?'

'Cream please. Where's Mum? Still in bed, I suppose.'

'Actually, she's gone to buy croissants. She says there used to be a little French place in King Street that made the world's best. She's hoping it's still there.'

Julia tilted her head. 'I remember that place… It had the most amazing macarons. I used to look in the window and practically drool until Mum or Erica bought me one.'

'Ah, speak of the devil.' David cupped his ear, frowning as the front gate squealed. 'I'll oil that today,' he said vaguely. 'Let's hope our shopper was successful. I'm starving.'

Annie was smiling as she strode into the kitchen. 'Julia, you'll never guess what I bought you!'

'I'll bet I can guess,' David winked at Julia.

'Ha, not a chance,' Annie shot back.

'So it's not a macaron?'

Annie's face fell. 'How did…'

Julia laughed. 'Really? You remembered? I didn't think you would.'

'You two have been talking behind my back. That's not allowed.' Annie placed a box of croissants on the table and handed Julia a paper bag. Taking the mug of coffee David handed her, she sat down and opened the box. 'Let's have breakfast while I tell you what I've planned for today.'

Annie climbed wearily to her feet as their train pulled into Newtown station. 'What a day! I'm getting too old for this walking caper.' She glanced at Julia, striding along the platform as if the day had just begun. 'So tell me, what do you think of Sydney now?'

'I had a really good day, Mum. Thanks.'

'The big city's not as bad as you thought?'

Julia shrugged. 'It was okay,' she said, reluctant to admit that her enjoyment hadn't come from exploring the city, but from spending time with her mother, seeing where she'd worked, hearing about the protests and demonstrations she'd been involved in, getting to know the person inside her mother's skin. 'I liked Circular Quay and The Rocks. Hyde Park was nice too.'

Annie raised her eyebrows. 'Okaaay, that's a start, I suppose. You'll find Melbourne a bit different.'

'Melbourne?' Julia frowned. 'You never said anything about that.'

'Didn't I? We're flying down next week to see Pete. You'll come, won't you?'

'Do I have to?'

Annie took a deep breath and counted silently to ten. Six years ago, she would have blown her stack, but David had shown her saner ways of dealing with difficult people or, as he preferred to put it, people *she* found difficult—it had taken her a while to realise there was a difference. 'You don't have to, Julia, but I hope you will.'

Julia wrinkled her nose but said nothing until they turned the corner onto Station Street. 'Mum, I've been thinking…' She glanced at Annie. 'If I do go to uni, where am I going to live? When you sell the house, I mean.'

Annie gave a wry grin. 'Any chance you could consider that question as an incentive to come to London?'

'What about Gran?'

'What do you mean? You know she won't leave Barragunyah.'

'I mean, how do you think she'll feel if you and I are both on the other side of the world? She's getting old, Mum. She needs to know one of us is around to help out if she gets sick or something.'

'Of course, I hadn't thought…' Annie reddened but rallied quickly. 'It'll only be for three or four years while you're at university. Ruby or Gill could call Pete, he's only a few hours away by plane.'

'Peter! What use would he be? He never calls. He sends Gran expensive perfume for Christmas and thinks he's done his duty. If he cared at all, he'd know she hates perfume.'

'I see. Okay, clearly that won't work.' She glanced at Julia. 'You know, just when I think I've grown up, you remind me I haven't changed at all. Still the same thoughtless old Annie, eh?'

'Mum, I wasn't trying to …'

'I know. But look, just think about London, will you? If you decide to live with us, we'll think of some way to make sure Gran has extra support.' Annie pushed the front gate, which opened silently. She smiled. 'I knew David would fix that squeak. He's brilliant at fixing things. He'll help us sort something out.'

'Did someone mention my name?' David greeted them from halfway up a ladder in the front room where he was changing a light globe. His face was speckled with white paint.

Annie laughed. 'Look at you! I thought we were going to leave the painting until after Melbourne.'

'Found some paint in the basement and couldn't help myself. The kitchen will need a second coat but it's looking good, though I say so myself. Switch that light on, will you?'

Julia flicked the switch and the room lit up.

'Terrific,' said Annie. 'Since you've been so busy, I guess I'm cooking dinner?'

'There's a casserole in the oven.'

'Really? No wonder I married you. You're beyond marvellous.'

David climbed down from the ladder and kissed Annie's forehead. 'I love it when you worship me,' he said, grinning. 'But the casserole's from the old dear next door. To welcome you back, she said.'

'That's kind of her.' Annie chewed her lip. 'Now what the hell was her name?'

'Mrs Roberts,' Julia said. 'She used to feed me whenever you were late home. She was old then, she must be ancient by now.'

'She did look as if she had a few years notched up,' David agreed.

'I'd better go check on the poor old woman's casserole then,' Annie said tersely.

David wondered at her troubled expression as she headed down the hallway.

Annie lay with her head on David's chest, breathing in the sweaty aroma of their lovemaking. His arm was curled around her shoulders, his fingers lightly stroking her breast. She loved this man so much it hurt, though she often wondered what he saw in her.

They had met when she'd arrived at his London flat to interview him for the business magazine she'd started working for the previous day. Ten embarrassing minutes later, she'd been forced to admit that she wasn't actually a journalist, that she knew nothing about stocks and finance, and that she had lied to get the job. She'd expected him to be furious, but he'd laughed and set about interviewing her instead. When she left four hours later, she had an article and a letter of resignation drafted for the magazine, and a six-month contract to write copy and design brochures for a charitable fund-raising venture David and his business partner were setting up.

Annie had never met anyone like David. Twelve years older than her, he had greying hair and a warm smile that lit up his brown eyes and melted her heart. Equally committed to fighting injustices and inequalities, they made a good team, his meticulous thought processes a perfect foil for her impetuosity. As their relationship grew from mentor to friend, from friend to lover, she found that being with David and observing the respectful way he dealt with a wide range of individuals tempered her own way of operating. He understood people and their motives in ways that she never had, and she was often brought face to face with the evidence that he also knew her far better than she knew herself. The trouble was, he only knew the person she was now, the person she'd become because of him. If he'd known her before, he probably wouldn't have liked her at all.

He turned to her now. 'You're upset. Want to talk about it?'

'I don't know.' She wriggled her shoulders and sighed. 'Okay, in a nutshell then. I thought I'd changed, but today I realised that I'm still the selfish mother and ungrateful daughter I always was. And I don't know how to fix it.'

David pulled her closer. 'You can't fix the past,' he said. 'It is what it is. You're a good person now, Annie and that's what matters. Your mother's a remarkable woman and Julia's a smart kid. They'll know you're making an effort.'

'I'm not so sure about that. You know what Julia said when I asked her to come to London with us?'

'What?'

'That if she did, her grandmother would have no family support if she became ill.' Annie's voice cracked. 'I hadn't given a thought to that possibility. I didn't even remember the name of my next-door neighbour, but Julia did, and she was a kid when she was last here. Let's face it; I'm a self-centred, selfish bitch.'

David hugged her. 'Don't talk like that about the woman I love. You're always thinking about others and fighting their battles. Maybe you need to focus your caring a bit closer to home.'

'I thought I was, but now…'

'Annie, darling.' David put a finger under her chin and tilted her head so he could see her face. 'Are you going to insist that Julia returns to London with us?'

'No, of course not.'

'Yet once you would have done exactly that, right?'

'I guess so, yes.'

'Enough said.' He kissed her on the forehead. 'The best thing we can do for Julia is help her decide which university will suit her and find her somewhere nearby to live.'

'She'll go to Sydney, of course. Like Pete did.'

'Have you asked her?'

'She won't talk about it.' Annie was silent for a moment. 'It must be on her mind though, because today she asked me where she'd live when I sold the house.'

'Hmm… I suspect the thought of living in a big city scares her. Have you considered she might find a regional university more comfortable?'

'I suppose. But do they have the same academic standards?'

'Why don't you suggest she do some research tomorrow and see what she comes up with? All these changes have been foisted upon her by circumstance—perhaps she'd like some say in planning her own future.'

# JULIA

I stumble down the dark corridors of memory, pulled and prodded by the force my heedless ancestors called *Mary*. Did they think a name would tame her? Shape her into something manageable? I am reluctant. She is relentless. Her grievances pierce my thoughts like needles: *Unearthing the history of others is easy,* she sneers. *Look to your own past...*

When I do, every twist and turn reveals moments in time where my choices shifted the pattern of things, altered trajectories, unravelled and rewove the fabric of my life and of the lives of others. Old ghosts haunt these corridors, pointing to thresholds that were crossed when they should have been avoided and side-stepped when they should have been crossed, pointing to doors that should have remained closed and to those I should have opened.

I resent being tormented by *shoulds*, yet they are all me, those judgemental phantoms with their pointing fingers. I tell myself it is what it is, but my past is crowded with Julias searching for answers, for meaning, for justification.

Memories leap like flames in the darkness, blaze a moment, then turn to ashes before I can grasp their significance. I see what she is doing. She is blaming my neglect, my absence, my choices, for Barragunyah's demise.

Fearful, hesitant, dragging my feet like a frightened child, I crossed the dreaded threshold into university and found it unexpectedly congenial. I had David to thank for that. The regional campus he helped me choose was large enough to have good staff and facilities, and small enough to allow me to find my way around without feeling overwhelmed. As soon as I received my HSC results and secured my place there, David and Mum hired a car and we drove north to the large country town where the university was situated. It was David too, who found and paid the rent on the little self-contained garden flat that was to be my home for longer than any of us expected.

To everyone's surprise, mine most of all, I loved university life. I relished the mental challenges and leaps of understanding, the after-class discussions in cafes, the friendships, the teachers. Like most people, I also took delight in excelling at something I loved, and time flew past unnoticed as I earned an Honours degree, a postgraduate scholarship, a doctorate. When I was offered a position on staff, I accepted immediately. Wasn't that exactly what I had always wanted?

Laughter echoes through these silent rooms and a cold wind scatters the remnants of older dreams as she makes me see it through her eyes, twisting my memories so that everything is about Barragunyah. I see myself drifting away from my old life as I become increasingly at home in that big country town, kayaking on the river, exploring the rainforests, relaxing with friends on nearby beaches, dabbling in romance. What I perceive as my transformation from a timid, naïve girl into a confident young woman, *she* sees as disloyalty and betrayal.

I was severing my roots, cutting myself loose. Forgetting.

The long summer breaks I spent at Barragunyah became shorter each year as I hurried back to my friends, my lover, my studies, my work. Even while I was on the property, my thoughts were often elsewhere, and I overlooked signs that should have been obvious to me.

I say overlook. She says ignore.

She insists I acknowledge now what I avoided then – that though the rains had come and the land had healed, Gran had not.

# GINA

Gina watched the car get smaller and smaller as Julia drove away. A trick of the eye, she thought, a matter of perspective and perception, because it was really she, Gina, who was diminishing, she who was leaving.

There was so little to leave it should have been easy. It was guilt that kept her bound to the earth, to this special place that had declined under her watch. She knew it was foolish, pointless, to blame herself, but who else was at fault? The decay had begun when she sold that first parcel of land to buy Annie's house. There was no going back from that.

How fragile are the plans we make, the dreams we dream, she mused. How ingenuous to believe things will go on as they always have, or that we can control anything. She had started the rot, but it was the drought that destroyed years of carefully selected bloodlines, fragmented the property, and put an end to the generations of women who had cared enough to nurture this land.

And a child who went away and came back a woman with plans of her own.

Gina grabbed the handrail and hauled herself up the three steps to the veranda, cursing the pain in her hip, the weakness in her legs. She had brushed away Julia's concerns about her frailties, but now felt a surge of resentment that her granddaughter had accepted her offhand responses so complacently. Julia, who had once been a younger version of herself, living and breathing for Barragunyah, was now more interested in talking about the teaching position she'd been offered at the university than in an old woman's ailments or the tribulations of farming. Gina sighed as she sank into the battered old settee. And why not? Her own time had passed, the girl's future was her own – she should not be held responsible for the dreams of her ancestors.

Agnes poked her head around the doorway. 'I'm about to make a cuppa. Want one?'

'That'd be lovely. Thank you.'

Agnes had aged too, Gina thought, as the housekeeper nodded and withdrew, paying for each extra year, as she did herself, with a hodgepodge of aches and pains. Sometimes, recalling the long friendship between Alice and Mac, Gina wished she and Agnes could have been closer; futile thoughts brought on by loneliness no doubt. Agnes had warmed over the years but rarely had much to say about anything outside her domestic domain.

Once Gina had been able to share her thoughts and her plans for Barragunyah with Ruby and Gillian, but though their little shearers' shack was barely twenty minutes' walk away, they seldom ventured as far as the main house these days, apparently preferring to keep to themselves. Pride kept her from inviting them. Since receiving government pensions, they were independent of Gina now. Apart from the shack, of course, which she would gladly give them if the legalities weren't so complicated.

Gina stared at her age-speckled hands. She supposed this was how it would be from now on. Barragunyah's days would end in the company of redundant old women. The two teenage girls she'd hired to check the fences and care for the diminished herd had no interest in the place beyond the money she paid them for working three days a week. There was so little for them to do anyway, Gina wondered why she bothered. She sighed again.

'Sighing won't change things,' Agnes said, placing a laden tray on the table. 'The girl's got to live her own life.'

'Julia, you mean?'

'Who else would you be mooning over?'

Gina shrugged, a slight lift of her bony old shoulders. 'I was actually thinking of young Laura and Beccy. But yes, Julia's never far from my thoughts.'

Agnes set out cups and saucers and plonked herself down in a chair. 'Ever thought of selling up and getting out? You're what, eighty-two now? Earned your retirement, I'd say.'

Gina shook her head. 'Where would I go? What would I do?'

'Do nothing. That's the point of retiring.' Agnes gave a sly grin as she poured the tea. 'You could buy yourself a pretty little cottage in Darrobine. Learn to play bridge.'

'Bridge? Me?' Gina stared at her with an expression of horror on her face.

Agnes let out a snort of laughter. 'That look says it all.' She pushed a plate of freshly made biscuits across the table. 'There's no way you'll leave this place willingly. Wouldn't want to myself, to tell the truth. I'd be a bit lost without my garden and chooks.'

Gina looked at her, surprised her usually reticent housekeeper had admitted to having personal attachments. 'Yes,' she murmured, 'that's how I'd feel if I left. Lost.'

'But why put money and effort into raising cattle? Those days are behind you, love.' Agnes tilted her head to one side. 'You could live here without farming you know.'

'Sell the herd?' Gina frowned. 'I'd feel I was betraying Alice's dream. Besides, I worked hard to save those bloodlines after the drought.'

'Things change,' Agnes said gently. 'People get old. Dreams run their course. From what you've told me about Alice, I think she'd tell you it was time to let go. Time to rest.'

Gina shifted her gaze, staring broodingly across the paddocks.

'Maybe you're right. There's not enough land left anyway to run a decent herd.' She sighed again. 'I just never imagined that I'd be the one to bring all those years of hard work to an end.'

# JULIA

If I admit I'm the one who brought Barragunyah down, will Mary let me go?

It's not as if she hates me. This morning on the kitchen bench, I found four warm brown eggs resting inside the woven raffia basket I used when I was a child to collect eggs from the henhouse – the basket that fell to pieces years ago and was thrown away. My mouth waters as I place the eggs in a saucepan to boil. My eyes are watering too, for her kindness, the caring, the knowledge that I'm not alone.

That's what she wants me to think.

What I'm actually thinking is, what does she want in return?

A new day will dawn in an hour or so, but now, when I look through the window into the darkness, I see my reflection and behind my wan face, phantoms shimmering in the candlelight. I cannot see them clearly, but I know who they are: Alice and Mac, Ellen, Gina.

Annie.

My mother's presence catches me by surprise. What is she doing at Barragunyah? I stare through her, feeling the old anger resurfacing, the sadness surging up to grab me by the throat – emotions visceral in their power. Memories of the time that produced so much pain flash through my mind like lightning, flaring bright and sharp, and I think how odd it is the way trivial things stick in your mind when something momentous occurs. I can't eat porridge now without being reminded of that September morning in 2001 when I switched on the television and saw planes spearing through a brilliant blue sky to crash into the twin towers of New York City.

But an event doesn't have to be as earth-shattering as September 11 for it to be personally momentous. When the relationship I was slowly forging with my mother came to an abrupt end I was at work, eating an apple as I marked assignments, and each detail of that moment is burned into my mind – the green tanginess of the apple, the poor structure of the essay. I can see myself writing in the margins with my red pen as I pick up the phone…

'Julia? Is that you?' A male voice, vaguely familiar.

I glanced at the caller ID. 'Pete?' The last time I'd spoken to my brother was at Christmas. 'How are you? What's up?'

He ignored my questions. 'Um, it's bad news, I'm afraid.'

'Anything I can do?' I half-expected him to say his marriage was on the rocks. I'd only met Denise once – at their wedding – but I thought then that her neediness and posturing would drive Peter nuts before long.

'Look, I don't really know how to tell you. Are you sitting down?'

'Peter, just say it!'

'Mum's dead.' His voice shook. 'There was…'

'Don't be ridiculous! I was talking to her last night.'

'Yeah, me too. It happened late afternoon London time, so early this morning here.'

'*What* happened? She sounded fine when I spoke to her.'

'I know. Sorry. I'm doing this badly.' He cleared his throat. 'I just got a call from London — their solicitor I think, or maybe it was someone from the Australian consulate – I didn't really take it in. Mum and David were in a car accident. They were… Neither of them survived, was how he put it.'

I stared at my phone, as stunned as if someone had thrown a bucket of icy water over me. What was I supposed to say? How was I meant to feel?

'Julia? Are you there?' Peter's voice sounded a long way off. 'It's a shock, I know. I'm still not thinking straight.' He paused. 'I just need to know if you want to come with me.'

'Come where?'

'To London. After David, I'm Mum's next of kin, so I have to go and… well, sort things out. And there's the funeral. I thought you'd want to…'

I tried to pull some relevant words out of the mush that was my brain. 'Of course. Yes. I should. I will. When?'

'As soon as possible. I'll try to get us on the same flight, but with me in Melbourne and you up there… I'll have to let you know.'

'Okay. Thanks.'

'Right. I'm going to organise some indefinite leave at work. You should do the same.'

'Should I? Oh, yes, I suppose I…' A sudden thought pierced through my brain fog. 'Pete? Have you told Gran?'

'Um, no. I was hoping you would.'

'Me? But…' I paused. Gran was eighty-three – if Pete told her the way he'd told me she'd have a heart attack. 'Okay,' I agreed reluctantly.

'Good. I'll call again as soon as I've got our flights sorted.'

He hung up. I sat there mindlessly holding the phone for a long time before I punched in Barragunyah's number.

When Agnes answered, I was in no mood to make small talk. 'Hi, Agnes. Can I speak to Gran please?'

There was a momentary silence. 'Been a while since your last call. Busy, I suppose?'

She caught me off balance. I felt my face grow hot. 'Yes, I…'

Agnes usually keeps her thoughts to herself, but suddenly she's Boudicca, up on her high horse and brandishing a spear. 'Too busy to make a five-minute phone call to cheer her up when she's ill?'

'Gran's sick? What's wrong with her?'

'Severe case of the flu. Not good at her age.' Another jab of the spear.

'Will she be okay?'

'The doc says she's on the mend. Can't see it myself.' Agnes's voice softened. 'She misses you, love. Don't leave it so long between calls.'

'Of course, I didn't think… I'm sorry,' I said awkwardly. 'Listen Agnes, I have some really bad news and if she's been sick…'

'How bad?'

'The worst.' I stifled a sob. 'Mum died yesterday. A car accident.'

'Oh, lovey, I'm so sorry.'

'But Gran… When I tell her I'm afraid she'll…'

'She has to be told, love. There's nothing wrong with her heart, if that's what you're thinking. Hang on a minute, I'll see if she's awake.'

The clatter of the phone being put down, the hollow sound of silence, the humming in my brain. What was I doing so far from Barragunyah when Gran was ill? How could I sleep so soundly, so dreamlessly, while my mother was dying?

How could I not know these things?

'Hello? Julia?' A croaky old woman's voice that didn't sound like anyone I knew.

'Gran? I'm sorry, I didn't know you'd been sick. I should have…'

'It's all right, darling. I'm fine.' A bout of coughing made a lie of her words. I waited until it eased, until her questions wheezed thinly across the distance.

'Agnes said you have bad news. You haven't lost your job?'

'No. Listen, Gran, there's no easy way to say this, so I'm just going to say it.' I took a deep breath. 'Mum and David were in a car accident yesterday. They both… They didn't make it.'

I heard her breath catch. 'Julia, what are you… Is Annie… Did she die?'

'Yes. Oh, Gran, I'm so sorry to tell you like this. I should be there with you.'

'Me? This is not about me. You've lost your mother and…' Her old-woman voice was suddenly thick with grief. 'Why Annie? It's not right. I'm supposed to die first.'

I could hear her crying softly and felt tears sting my own eyes. A lump wedged in my throat making speech impossible. What could I say anyway? What does anyone say at times like this when words like hope have no meaning?

Gran had nailed it – it wasn't right. When reality sank in, I knew I would miss my mother and the relationship we'd developed since she'd been with David, but for most of my life Gran had been my mother, not Annie. Fear rose inside me like a flooding river. Suddenly I couldn't breathe, couldn't swallow. What if Gran died too? What if she died while I was on the other side of the world?

Her rasping voice quelled my panic. 'We'll have to go to the… to London,' she said.

'Pete and I will go. You're not well enough to travel, Gran.'

'Annie's my daughter. I can't let strangers bury her.'

'It's a long, tiring flight, Gran. I doubt your doctor will allow you to go.'

'He prescribes my medicine, he doesn't control my life.' She sounded indignant, more like her old self. 'Besides, I'm used to aeroplanes now.'

I smiled through my tears. Gran had made her first plane trip at the age of seventy-eight when I graduated with my bachelor's degree. Since then, she'd flown to Melbourne for Peter's wedding, and here again to see me get my doctorate. She enjoyed her flights and had been slightly scornful of Mum and David's jet lag.

'I know you don't mind flying, Gran, but…' I let it rest; I doubted she had a passport anyway. We were just avoiding the other conversation, sidestepping a sorrow too raw for words. 'Talk to your doctor and see what he says.'

My heart skipped a beat as the reason for the journey wormed its way deeper into my foggy brain. My second London visit that I'd been planning for later in the year had suddenly become something to dread. I cleared my throat, focused on now. 'Is there anything you want me to do when I get there? Or take? I mean…'

'I know what you mean.' She gave a short gasp of pain and began coughing again. I waited for the spasm to ease, my guilt growing. Why hadn't I called before? How had I allowed this distance to grow between us?

When Gran spoke again, her voice was thready and faint. 'I wish I knew…' Her words stumbled and fell into the void that stretched between us. 'I don't even know what songs she liked…' The cough returned, worse this time, harsh and unrelenting.

The hacking sound faded, and I heard Agnes's voice. 'She needs to rest, lovey. Anything I can do?'

'Just look after her, Agnes.'

'That goes without saying.'

'Thanks. I'll let you know when I'm leaving.' I disconnected.

Outside my office window a group of students laughed and jostled each other as they headed towards the library. A magpie picked at a crust of bread on the lawn. A wayward breeze stirred the branches of a grevillea. A kookaburra laughed. So, this is what death does, I thought. It changes everything, yet nothing changes.

Peter and I sat beside each other on the plane and tried to build a bridge across the gulf that separated us. We spoke of the past, our conflicting recollections rubbing against each other like sandpaper, smoothing out bumps, removing discrepancies. Discussion of the present shrank to what we did each day, to Peter's work, and mine. Each time we mentioned our mother the conversation trembled and fell at our feet.

I ventured into the personal. 'I thought Denise would come with you.'

'Why? She only met Mum once, at the wedding.'

'To support you, I mean.'

'That'll be the day,' he said bitterly.

'Problems on the home front?' I glanced at him sympathetically, recalling the turmoil of emotions when my first big love affair had ended.

'You could say that.' He shot me a searching look. 'To tell you the truth, our marriage is all but over. We rarely talk, we never laugh. Shopping is the only thing that makes Denise happy, so all we seem to do when we're together is argue about money.'

I frowned. 'Surely she's entitled to spend her salary however she chooses?'

'*Her* salary? She quit her job six months after we married. It's my money she spends.' He looked away. 'It's not just that – I think she's having an affair.'

'I'm sorry, Pete. I had no idea.' I put my hand on his arm. 'My input probably isn't worth much, but shouldn't you confront her? Bring it out in the open?'

He nodded. 'As soon as I have proof. I've got a private detective on it.'

'That seems a bit drastic.'

'It's necessary. Denise is an expert at twisting things to make me the guilty one.'

'Hmm, I know how that feels.'

He stared at me. 'You too? I didn't know if I should ask about your love life.'

'If you'd asked six months ago, I'd have had something to tell you. Not anymore.' I shrugged. 'I thought it was serious, but now I wonder if he was just marking time until he found someone more willing to adore him. And like you said, every time I tried to discuss what I saw as a problem, he turned things around so it was all my fault.'

Peter rubbed his chin, which was speckled with the promise of a five o'clock shadow. 'It's probably not all that remarkable we chose the wrong partners. We didn't exactly have a good role model, did we?'

I looked at him, surprised he'd brought it up. 'True. I guess we can take comfort from the fact that Mum worked it out eventually. David is…' I winced, shook my head angrily. 'I mean *was* – perfect for her.'

'Yeah. Too bad…'

'I know.'

'Something to drink?' The flight attendant smiled at us.

And the conversation we'd been avoiding since Singapore evaporated.

It says a lot about my state of mind that part of me was expecting Mum and David to pick us up from Heathrow, as they had on my first visit. I followed Peter unthinkingly as we cleared customs and waited at the carousel to collect our bags, alert to faces in the crowd, looking for David's wide grin, Mum's cheerful wave. It wasn't until we were standing at the taxi rank it hit me. They weren't coming. Ever. For a moment, I felt as if I might fall.

'Are you okay?' Peter asked. 'You look as if you've seen a ghost.'

I took a deep breath. 'I'm fine. The weather's a bit of a shock, though.'

'Yeah, it's bloody freezing. Let's hope we don't have to wait long for a cab.'

'Where are we staying?' Until that moment, I hadn't given it a thought.

'A hotel near Victoria Station. Luke and Meredith both offered to put us up, but I thought it best not to be under any obligation.'

'Why's that?' I'd met David's offspring on my last trip and liked

Luke a lot. Meredith, not so much, though we'd managed to be polite to each other.

'Because they've got a hidden agenda. When I spoke to Meredith, she let a couple of things slip about the will.'

'What will?'

'Geez, Julia. Do I have to spell it out?'

'Yes, actually.'

A taxi pulled up, saving me from elaborating on my ignorance. Unlike Peter, who'd nodded off soon after dinner was served, I hadn't slept a wink on the plane. Now I had a headache and felt queasy and disoriented. We loaded our luggage into the boot and Peter slid into the seat beside the driver. I stood on the pavement, feeling suddenly bereft.

'What are you waiting for?' Peter asked impatiently.

I climbed into the back of the cab and sat silently while he gave the cabbie our address and made small talk.

I'd never been to a funeral, never had reason to think about grief and how people mourn, yet for some reason I believed that the service would help me come to terms with my aching loss.

I could not have been more wrong.

It might have been different if we'd had some say in how the funeral was planned. Before we met up with Meredith and Luke in a London restaurant, we'd made a list of Mum's favourite songs, jotted down some memories we could shape into a bio, decided we'd prefer a celebrant to a priest. We could have spared ourselves the effort. Meredith already had everything organised down to the smallest detail – flowers, hymns, priest, Bible readings.

When I suggested some changes, she shook her head. 'You have no idea how much time and effort I've put into this. Changing it now is out of the question.'

'If we replaced the hymns with songs they loved it would be more personal,' I said.

'Absolutely not! It's a church service, not a concert.'

I could tell Peter was becoming irritated. 'Our mother wasn't religious,' he said sharply. 'I didn't think David was either.'

'Exactly.' Luke shrugged. 'Believe me, we've had this argument. She won't budge.'

'I'm doing it for Daddy.' Meredith seemed on the verge of tears. 'A lot of important people will come, so it's got to be perfect. If you don't like what I've done, organise a separate service for Annie – if you can book a church.'

'That's a stupid idea, Merri!' Luke snapped. 'It's a joint will so Sullivan won't deal with it until they're both buried.' He turned to Peter and me. 'Look, I'm sorry if it's not what you want, but surely the most important thing is that they're together? Do a few hymns matter?'

Peter nodded swayed, I suspect, by Luke's mention of the will being delayed. He glanced at me. 'It's not ideal,' he said, 'but trying to organise a separate funeral in a city we don't know would be a nightmare.'

I wasn't happy, but it was hard to deny the truth of that.

Two days later, Peter and I sat alone on the front pew of an ancient church as it filled with people we didn't know. The matching pew on the other side of the aisle was crowded. Luke with his wife and son, Meredith with her husband and three small children. Two stylish older women. Was one of them their mother, David's ex-wife? Meredith's husband had his arm around her as she sobbed quietly.

I couldn't squeeze out a single tear. I felt like a stranger, watching the proceedings from a distance. It was all wrong, this place, these people. Mourners were filing into the pews behind us, but how many of them knew Annie? How many of them cared? As if in answer, someone sat beside me and took my hand.

Startled, I turned my head. 'Erica!'

'Hello, darling.' She put her arms around me and drew me close in a ferocious hug. And I found I could cry after all.

It was Erica who got me through the following week. If it hadn't been for her all the squabbling and angst about who deserved what would have unravelled me.

'It was awful,' I told her when we caught up for coffee after the third meeting with the solicitor. 'Meredith and Luke are threatening to contest the will. Peter's backing them.'

Erica raised her eyebrows and gave a Gallic shrug – I loved seeing how French she'd become. 'They'd be wasting their time,' she said. 'David told Anthony to make sure everything was detailed enough to be watertight.'

'That's what Sullivan said – the solicitor. How did you know?'

'Anthony Sullivan is an old friend, and I was one of the witnesses.' She looked at me curiously. 'How do you feel about it? It's an awful lot of money to leave a charity.'

'I'm glad,' I said. 'That charity was their baby, something they created together. They were proud of it. I'd hate to think of it dying because...' I shrugged, looked away. 'Well, because they did.'

'Me too.' Erica patted my hand. 'Annie told me it's the most successful organisation in the country for helping victims of domestic violence. They set up that trust fund to make sure it would never be shut down for lack of money.'

I glanced at her uncertainly. 'Do you think they knew? I mean, their will was only updated a month ago, and it's so specific...'

'Knew they were going to have that accident? Absolutely not,' Erica said firmly. 'What they knew – what David knew, anyway – is that his kids, despite being well-heeled themselves, are materialistic and acquisitive. He wanted his money to help people struggling to make ends meet, not to buy Meredith more designer clothes or Luke a new Jaguar.'

'And Mum? Did she think Pete and I would waste it too?'

'Annie never thought of that money as hers, *chèri*, though David insisted it was.' Erica smiled, remembering. 'When Annie and I first came to London, we were both pretty broke. Annie was working behind a bar before she got that job with David.'

'I know. But David told me the charity wouldn't have been nearly as successful without Mum's passion and input.' I frowned. 'Meredith and Luke are trying to make out she was some sort of gold digger.'

'*Merde!* They know damned well she wasn't.' Erica tilted her head and scrutinised me thoughtfully. 'What about the five thousand pounds they left each of you? They knew Merri and Luke would be pissed to receive so little – how do you feel?'

'Haven't given it a thought to be honest. I'm grateful to get anything. Pete's siding with the others I'm afraid.'

'Hmm. Probably could've predicted that.'

'Meredith and Luke are arguing about who gets the house too,' I said. 'They were furious when Sullivan said it was to be used as a safe house for domestic violence victims.'

'Don't worry, *chèri*, once their own lawyers look at it, they'll be forced to back off. Every detail of that will was double-checked for loopholes. The thing is, Annie and David intended to talk it through with each of you, explaining what they'd done and why, but...' She shook her head, dabbed at her eyes with a tissue, and changed the subject. 'Enough of that. How much time have you got off work?'

'They got casuals to cover all my classes so I'm off until next semester. Why?'

'Come and stay with Lucille and me for a while. You'll love Carcassonne. It's the perfect place for you to soak up some healing time.'

My heart leapt at the thought of strolling through the medieval city, breathing its atmosphere, soaking up its history. Why not? I hesitated and thought about Gran. She'd projected a stoic façade each time I'd phoned from London, but I knew her grief for my mother had opened old wounds.

'I'd love to stay with you and Lucille, but it will have to be some other time,' I said reluctantly. 'I need to return to Barragunyah as soon as possible.'

# GINA

Gina sat on an old settee on the veranda, enjoying the pale sunshine and the blush of green over the paddocks that told her spring was on its way with the promise of new life. Yet all she could think about was death, the implacable enemy that had brought her to her knees so many times.

Mac, Alice, and her mother had been old when they died – around the age she was now, in fact – and although she'd grieved deeply, their deaths were not untimely. The shocking death of little James, and losing Tom to the war, had been brutal and much harder to come to terms with. Now Annie had been taken from her just as suddenly, and all the unanswered questions she'd had then had come back to plague her. But in the end, she supposed, the only important question was this: Where does consciousness go when we take our last breath?

Where are you now, Annie?

Her mind wandered. What was it Mac had said as she neared the end of her long life? The old Scotswoman's voice slipped into her thoughts as clear as if it were yesterday; *Dying is nothing – a leap across a creek and a whole new adventure begins.* Had it been like that for Annie? Or Tom? How could it, when a life ended suddenly and a person was unprepared?

Thinking of Mac reminded her of their conversations about the lost girl. Gina smiled. Funny, she hadn't thought about that for years, although at the time it had been on her mind a lot. She had dreamed about her, even believed the girl was hunting her for some reason. *It's you she's searching for,* Mac had said.

Gina brushed a straying wisp of hair from her face and sighed. Sometimes her memories of long ago seemed sharper than what had happened this morning – a sure sign of old age – one thought leading to another, drifting away from the moment, taking her back...

Back to the day the girl had stepped from her dreams into life, the day she'd seen her in broad daylight right here on this veranda. *She was wearing my clothes.* It was impossible of course, although Mac hadn't thought it especially strange. She'd spoken of time being slippery, of how past and future sometimes got mixed up. *The girl is out of time,* she'd said. Gina repeated the words aloud, wondering suddenly if it had been an observation or a warning. She wished she could remember more clearly what Mac had said. For some reason, it seemed important now, though she couldn't imagine why.

A breeze sprang up and Gina shivered, absently tugging at the blanket Agnes had tucked around her knees. Ruby and Gillian had seen the lost girl once. Gina's brows knitted together as she tried to pinpoint when. Was it when Annie had arrived home pregnant with Peter? Yes, that was it. She, Gina, had been worried about the baby being born at Barragunyah – *what if it's a boy?* – but Annie had been scornful, called her superstitious for believing the old tales about Mary. That's when Ruby and Gillian had stepped in. *We saw her yesterday... tall and dark like the stories say, with those creepy eyes. She dropped a couple of skinned rabbits on the veranda and a woman came out of the house and took them inside.* Ah yes, and when she'd asked what the woman looked like – *a younger version of you* – she had known at once it was the lost girl.

Gina rubbed her temples. Why was she raking up the past when all she wanted to think about was Annie? Her beautiful, wild, difficult Annie who had finally found love and contentment. Why hadn't she been allowed time to enjoy it? Why was an old woman like her left to grow ever more useless while someone as vibrant as Annie was taken? Someone who could still do good in the world?

It was hard to focus on Annie when this other something kept niggling away like a worm in the back of her mind. Something about that lost girl. She closed her eyes, tried to picture her, *saw* a picture of her as colourful as the day it was taken. Just before the drought it was, the two of them together, squinting into the sun, laughing. Gina and Julia in happier times. Julia looking exactly like a younger version of her.

Gina blinked. Was Julia the lost girl? It made no sense. Julia wasn't lost, she was in London. She'd telephoned just last night to say she was coming home to Barragunyah. The news had lifted Gina's spirits, given her a reason to get out of bed where she'd been malingering – wishing her life away, if she was honest – since Annie died. The flu may have put her in bed, but it was the whirlwind of emotional turmoil that had kept her there. Grief for her daughter, mixed with anger and guilt and yes, fear. Anger at herself for being too ill to travel with Julia and Peter to the funeral, guilt because she hated the finality of funerals and was secretly relieved to be let off, and fear for... What? For Julia? She shivered again, but it wasn't the breeze this time. It was a cold, implacable fear that her granddaughter, like everyone else she'd loved deeply, would be taken from her.

*The girl is out of time*, Mac had said and now Gina thought about it, it sounded like a warning. Perhaps the question wasn't *where* the girl was lost – every dream and sighting indicated she was lost right here at Barragunyah – but *when*. Gina frowned. Whichever way she looked at it the puzzle remained. Julia knew every corner of Barragunyah, so it was unlikely she'd be lost here, which made the *when* of the conundrum all the more curious. Gina rubbed her temples again, closed her eyes against the glare. Trying to unravel all those tangled threads was giving her a headache. Julia was coming home in a few days – she would put the matter aside until they could work it out together.

# JULIA

*I was wearing her clothes.* Gran was a young woman when she saw me on the veranda wearing the long green cardigan Ellen had knitted for her. In real time – although I'm no longer sure there's such a thing – that was nearly seventy years ago. For me it was – what?— Yesterday? Last month? Next week? Time means nothing here.

I'm wearing her clothes now.

Trying to make sense of it gives me a headache. Should I forego logic and simply accept my life was interwoven with Gran's years before I was born? But there is something left of me that clings to reason even while it retreats further from my grasp with each passing day. All I know for sure is that Mary is responsible.

Who else here can loosen the threads of time?

When I returned from London after Mum's funeral, I went straight to Barragunyah. Gran was still recovering from the flu and most afternoons we sat on the veranda quietly reminiscing, sharing our memories of Annie. It was a healing time for both of us, despite the ambiguous stories we told each other.

In my old life – in that other world where a house is just a house and time flows in a linear fashion – I was a historian, and most historians agree that memory is unreliable. At the best of times, the stories we think of as real and true are dredged from a past we recreate with each remembering. And at the worst of times? Who knows what twists and turns our memories take to reshape despair into optimism and bogeymen into angels? What did it take, I wonder, to transform Barragunyah from a haven to a prison? What would it take to turn me from the lost girl to one who is found?

Only nobody knows I am here. I'm not sure I'm here myself.

When I first realised my predicament, I had hope. Now I have none. It is one thing to be lost in a place, and something quite different to be lost in time.

How can I find meaning in my imprisonment? How do I unearth what *She* wants of me? A gut feeling tells me I need to go back to the day Gran told me she was going to sell Barragunyah.

# GINA

When Julia phoned from Lurradallan to say she'd hired a car and was on her way, Gina was surprised to find herself on the verge of telling her to turn back. 'Can't wait to see you, darling,' she said. But she was trembling when she put down the phone.

She knew where her uneasiness sprang from. She'd been longing to see Julia since Annie died, knowing instinctively that they needed to talk through their shared loss together. But it wasn't that conversation which worried her. It was the other one. The one she kept pushing aside as if not thinking about it would make it disappear.

The one about leaving Barragunyah.

From the beginning, from Alice down through the generations, they'd all known they were merely custodians of a place that had a more significant caretaker, one whose purpose they would never fathom. Gina had betrayed an unspoken trust when she sold off that first parcel of land to help Annie, but she'd hoped, when Julia came to stay and loved the place as she did, that things might be mended. The drought put an end to those hopes. To survive its ravages, she had betrayed Barragunyah again, taking pieces of land she didn't truly own and exchanging the precious earth for money. The proceeds from the sale of Annie's Sydney house had come back to Barragunyah in time to save what was left of it, but it could never restore what was lost.

Gina knew now she would be the last custodian, but she was old, and time was running out. If she sold now, Barragunyah's wrath would fall on her, and rightly so. If she delayed, Julia would bear the burden, and that was unthinkable. Unfortunately, knowing what to do and putting the process into action were two separate things.

Whatever she did, there would be consequences.

They sat on the veranda steps, drinking tea and enjoying the late afternoon sun. 'Mum and I were just beginning to understand each other,' Julia said. 'I thought we'd have plenty of time to make up for those lost years then…'

'I know.' Gina rubbed her hands together, trying to ward off a chill that never quite left her these days. 'Annie was always so angry with me – I couldn't blame her, but it made for some difficult times. When she met David, I think she was happy for the first time in her life.' Tears pricked her eyes and she shook her head. 'I can't begin to tell you how hard it is to admit that, Julia. To admit that I brought a child into the world and made her miserable.'

Julia took her grandmother's cool, dry hands in hers. 'You can't blame yourself, Gran. Some personalities just don't get along. Mum and I brought out the worst in each other, too.' She smiled. 'Besides, you mustn't think she was always angry or miserable – when I was a kid, I remember Mum having lots of friends, and she was always the life of a party.'

'Yes, I can imagine.' Gina's smile didn't reach her eyes. 'I never knew that side of her, and now I never will.' She sighed. 'Don't make the mistakes I did, Julia. We think we have years ahead of us to make amends, to do better, to love more, but the truth is we never know when our time to make those reparations will run out.'

They were silent for a while, then Gina said, 'There's something else I need to tell you, darling.'

'Oh? What's that?'

'I've sold the Angus herd. I haven't the heart or the energy for it anymore.'

Julia stared at her in surprise. 'But there were cows in the top paddock when I drove past. I was thinking how fat and healthy they looked.'

'Yes, but they're no longer mine. They're on agistment here until they've calved, then the buyer will have them trucked out.'

'I see…' Julia looked at her uneasily, sensing her grandmother's sadness. 'Is it too late to change your mind? You've been ill; you might feel differently when you're better.'

'I'm eighty-five, Julia. I just can't do it anymore.'

'Are you?' Julia said, startled. 'God, I'm an idiot! I knew that, of course, it's just… Honestly, I've never given your age a second thought!'

Gina laughed softly. 'Neither did I until that flu laid me low and made me face facts.' She sat passively, watching Julia study her face, wondering if her beloved granddaughter saw the skulking spectre of death she saw herself each time she looked in the mirror.

But Julia was mentally kicking herself, her thoughts skipping wildly from one idea to another as she searched for solutions. After a while she said, 'What if I came back here to live? We could run Barragunyah together like we planned before that bloody drought hit. Maybe we…'

'Julia, love, you know there's not enough land left to make it worthwhile.' Gina hesitated, but it had to be said. 'When the cattle have gone, I'm selling Barragunyah.'

'What? No, Gran, you can't! Where would you go? What would you do?'

Gina nodded. 'Those are questions that have kept me here beyond my usefulness. And the others, of course.'

'Ruby and Gillian, you mean?'

'And Agnes. Barragunyah is their home, too. But Ruby and

Gillian are nearly my age, Agnes only ten years younger. This place is riddled with useless old women waiting to die.'

'Don't say that!' Julia looked at her in dismay. 'What about those two girls you told me about?'

'Oh, them. Laura got a job in Darrobine pub and Beccy decided it was no fun driving all the way out here alone.' Gina shrugged. 'They were never interested beyond the money I paid them anyway.'

Julia sighed. 'You've been thinking about this for a while, haven't you?'

'It was all I could think of when I was ill.' Gina gave a slight shiver and rubbed her arms. 'I realised what a mess I was leaving you to sort out when I die.'

'Oh, Gran...' Julia sidled along the step and hugged her. 'You mustn't worry about things like that. We'll work something out.'

'I hope so. I thought that while you're here, you could help me decide the best way to go about things.' Gina took a sip of tea and pulled a face. 'This is cold. Should I ask Agnes to bring us a fresh pot?'

'No, let's go inside, you don't want to catch a chill.' Julia stood up and reached out a hand to help her grandmother. 'I'm finding it hard to get my head around this, but if you're serious, we'll need to talk to your accountant and get your stock and station agent out here to value the place.'

Gina grunted as she struggled to her feet. 'We need to talk to Ruby and the others first. They're having dinner with us tonight in honour of your visit, so that's as good a time as any.' She smiled sadly at Julia. 'It may not make for the cheeriest welcome, though.'

Gina stared across the dining table at Ruby and Gillian. 'You knew I was thinking of selling?'

'No, but we knew you'd have to come to it sooner or later.' Ruby said. 'You're not getting any younger, Gina.'

'Neither are we,' Gillian added. 'We thought we'd be dead and buried by now, but when it looked like we might outlive you, we made contingency plans.'

'Contingency plans?' Julia laughed, enjoying the banter, which had been livelier than she'd expected. Despite the deeply etched lines in their faces, the age spots on their hands, and Gill's cropped white hair and bony frame, they were as sharp and teasing as ever. Ruby's halo of wiry hair, Julia had been amused to see, was dyed the same flamboyant red as the day Julia had met her, and it had been shocking even then.

'We pooled our savings and bought a cottage in Darrobine a couple of years ago.' Gillian said, darting a meaningful glance at Gina. 'We didn't want you worrying about us when the time came to sell. We knew you'd have enough on your plate.'

Gina raised her eyebrows. 'Yet you stayed?'

'Of course we did,' Ruby said. 'We love this place, but we're not blind.' She chuckled. 'Not yet, anyway. And even Blind Freddie could see that four old women – begging your pardon, young Agnes – couldn't live out here in splendid isolation indefinitely.'

'Splendid isolation?' Gina pulled a face. 'That sums it up, doesn't it? I sometimes think I've spent my life pretending changes in the world beyond Barragunyah don't affect us, but they catch up eventually.' She glanced at Agnes. 'What about you, Agnes? Where would you go if I sold Barragunyah?'

'With you, of course. You'll need somebody to look after you.'

Gina shook her head. 'That may be a luxury I can't afford, Agnes dear.'

'Luxury? Ha! Necessity, more like,' Agnes sniffed. 'When did you last boil an egg, clean a bathroom, or make your own bed? You need me.'

Gina raised her eyebrows indignantly. 'I'm grateful for all you do for me, Agnes, but I'm sure I could do those things myself if I had to.'

'That'll be a rare day,' Ruby cackled. 'Hope I live to see it.'

'Well, really…' Gina looked around tetchily at the grinning faces. Even Julia was trying hard to smother a grin. 'What? You all think I'm incapable?'

'Not incapable, Gran, just inexperienced.' Julia laughed aloud. 'Have you ever done anything even slightly domestic?'

Gina frowned, her thoughts stretching back over the years. In her mind's eye she could see herself as a child, going to Dulcie when she wanted a snack or couldn't find her socks, and later there was Vera, meals without fuss, tea and fresh scones supplied on demand, the house kept spotless while she, Gina, got on with the important work of running Barragunyah.

'Because I haven't had to doesn't mean I can't,' she said sharply. 'I appreciate your offer, Agnes,' she added more gently, 'but I really have no idea what's ahead.'

'Anyway, we don't know how long the property will take to sell,' Julia added. 'Let's wait and see what the agent says. Do you want me to phone him tomorrow?'

Gina shook her head. 'I'll do that. Jim and I are old friends. But you could telephone my accountant. Let him know what we've got in mind, ask what he needs.' She let out a long sigh. 'Thank you all for understanding. You've taken a great weight off my mind.'

Julia ventured out to the veranda as the stock and station agent drove off. 'How did it go?'

Gina shrugged and lowered herself into an old cane chair that had seen better days. 'Jim says it's hard to value as so much land has been sold off. He thinks some of the neighbouring properties might show an interest in the land, but not the house.' She gestured to Julia to pull up a matching chair. 'It's not easy trying to see Barragunyah through a buyer's eyes as just an old house and a bit of land.'

'It will always be more than that to us, Gran, and that's what matters.'

Gina grimaced. 'Maybe. There's a reprieve of sorts – Jim suggests I wait until after the cows have gone.'

'That's a few months off, isn't it?'

'Yes, it'll be almost Christmas by then. You don't suppose…?'

'We could put off the sale until the new year? Absolutely! If it's to be our last Christmas here, let's make it special.'

'You'd come back? So soon?'

'Wouldn't miss it for the world.'

Gina gave a fleeting smile. 'Let's ask Ruby and Gillian to come over again tonight so we can let them know what we're planning. I'll tell Agnes there'll be five for dinner again.'

# JULIA

Four years down the track everyone who sat around the dining table that night, talking about Christmas and making plans to move on, is dead except me.

And as the child I carry is unlikely to see daylight, it seems I am the last descendant of John Larsen, the man who believed he could force Barragunyah to serve him, who possibly murdered her previous caretakers, who thought his desires could prevail over an ancient and incomprehensible power.

John had no idea what he was dealing with.

Gran and I didn't have that excuse. We both knew what Barragunyah was capable of. What made us think she would let us go before we paid our dues?

Leaving Barragunyah was never going to be easy.

Not then. Not now.

I crossed the causeway and found myself standing on the veranda in the faint light of dawn. Our last Christmas at Barragunyah had come and gone. The paddocks were lush and green with no cattle to keep the grass down, and a fresh breeze carried the scent of damp earth and eucalyptus.

Ruby and Gillian had moved into their cottage in Darrobine, and I had been helping Agnes and Gran spruce up the house before it was placed on the market. Not that Gran could do much. In the few months I'd been away, she had grown more fragile and although it galled her to be dependent on anyone, I knew she was glad Agnes chose to stay with her.

I was feeling agitated and crabby after tossing and turning all night wondering how to present my idea so that it sounded appealing, rather than the wrench I knew it would be. It was bad enough that they had to leave here, but asking them to come and live with me in a town they didn't know seemed insensitive, no matter how much I told myself it was for the best.

I heard the door open and turned, unsurprised to see Gran in her dressing gown, padding out on bare feet to join me.

'You couldn't sleep either?'

'Not a wink.' Her white hair was loose around her shoulders, her eyes misty as she looked past me to the land she loved. 'I will miss this.' We stood in silence for a while, watching the changing colours as the light grew stronger, then she shivered in the morning chill, pulled her robe closer. 'Do you want tea? The kettle's on.'

'Okay.' I followed her down the hall to the kitchen and the warmth of the Aga, to the kettle already hissing and spitting on the hotplate. 'You sit down; I'll make it,' I said.

Gran nodded absently and settled herself in a chair, gazing vacantly into space as I scooped tea into the pot and added hot water. She jumped slightly, startled out of her reverie when I placed a steaming mug in front of her. I sat opposite and wrapped my hands around my own mug, absorbing the heat.

'Are you having second thoughts?' I asked.

Her bony shoulders lifted slightly. 'Of course. But no matter how I look at it, I can't see any other way out. I don't want you having to deal with the repercussions when I'm gone.'

I remember thinking that was a strange word to use – *repercussions* – but I let it pass.

'I don't suppose you'd consider living with me?' I said tentatively. 'You and Agnes, I mean. You don't have to decide right away, but will you think about it? I'd love to have you.'

She glared at me, and I silently cursed myself – dumping it on her like that was exactly what I meant to avoid. 'I'm sorry, I should have...'

The glare became a snarl. 'You don't understand! You never have!'

She was yelling. I was speechless; Gran never yelled.

'She won't let me, Annie... She won't... Can't fight her...'

'Gran?' I jumped to my feet as the mug slipped from her hand, spilling hot tea on her dressing gown before shattering on the floor. I raced around the table in time to catch her as she fell. Her eyes were wide and staring, her mouth sagging to one side as she muttered incoherently. I held her tight and shouted for Agnes.

A stroke, the doctor told me the next day when tests confirmed our fears. He suggested we move her from the tiny Darrobine Hospital to the larger one at Lurradallan, which has a rehabilitation unit.

I took that as a positive sign. 'How long will it take her to fully recover?'

He considered me over the top of his spectacles. 'Hard to say. Gina's as tough as an old boot, but she wasn't really over that flu when her daughter died. Then planning to move on top of all that... It all adds up.' He paused. 'She may never fully recover.'

'But surely... the rehabilitation...'

'Will certainly help. That's all I can promise at this stage.' He looked at me guardedly. 'That's if she doesn't have another stroke.'

'Is that likely?'

'It's possible. She'll be on preventative medication, but given her age there's no guarantee.'

I looked past him to the bed where Gran was sleeping. Her lined skin was pale and waxy, her drooping mouth all wrong. She looked as if someone made a mask of her face then crumpled it into a different shape. The hands that could gentle a frightened horse, mend a fence, or deliver a calf, were veined and mottled with liver spots and lay still and useless on the white hospital sheets. I couldn't bear to see her like this. I wanted her to wake up and talk to me, tell me what to do, but the doctor had warned me that her speech might be impaired.

'I'll sit with her a while,' I said.

He nodded and told me he'll check in again later. I sat in the chair beside the bed and took one of her hands in both of mine. 'What now, Gran?' The simple question encompassed everything – her future, my future, Barragunyah's future. But even if she could speak, I doubted she'd have any answers.

Something else held that power.

# GINA

Shadows flitting around her like crows waiting to pick at a carcase. An eerie silence. A grim twilight world where nothing was as it seemed.

It *seemed* to be Barragunyah. Through the gloomy half-light, Gina could make out familiar landmarks that should have guided her home. But no matter which direction she took she finished up here, at the flooded causeway. It made no sense, because even if she could have crossed, she didn't want to. She wanted to go the other way, back to the house where Alice and Mac and her mother were waiting.

Retreating from the murky creek waters surging at her feet, she gazed across the darkened landscape, trying to recall what had brought her here. The last thing she remembered was the warmth of the Aga and somebody making tea. Was it her mother? No, it was that lost girl. Just thinking about her made Gina uneasy. She asked too many questions. Questions she, Gina, was afraid to answer because... Why?

Was it because Mary wouldn't like her answers?

Gina shivered, grasping at a memory as it whirled past like a leaf in a storm. They'd been making plans, she and the lost girl, when Mary appeared out of nowhere, her anger crackling like lightning, making a tempest of Gina's words, her voice slicing into the spaces between her thoughts. *You will not leave until you make things right,* she hissed. *What was lost must be found, what was imposed must be purged*. And with no warning at all, Gina had found herself here, drifting amid layers of mist and shadows.

Gina had lost many things in her long life. Images loomed out of the twilight and vanished before she could properly name them; a baby, a beloved, a mother, a grandmother, a daughter, dear friends. And now, unable to find her way home, it seemed likely that she had also lost her memory. Confused and unsettled, she turned and trudged back to the house, hoping she could find her way this time, yet somehow knowing that she wouldn't.

The thick mist was settling, concealing the rise and fall of the land, making her journey more difficult. The darkness shifted and Gina cried out in pain as something sharp probed her thoughts, sending them scattering like mice in a grain bin. She stopped, frightened. Where was she? What was she doing out here alone in the dark?

Something reached out of the shadows and grasped her hand. Frightened, she pulled away and tried to run, but her feet were rooted to the earth. She could feel the blood in her veins slowing, replaced by the slow pulse of sap and rich dark soil. Leaves began to sprout from her fingers and vines writhed from her ears, twisting into a tight band around her head. *Not yet,* Gran, the lost girl whispered, clinging to her burgeoning fingers, drawing her back. Trying to change the unchangeable.

# JULIA

I watch them. The old woman clinging to life by a thread as she stumbles through shadowlands, the young woman asleep in a chair beside her, dreaming of death. I know what awaits them, for their future is my past.

Let me tell you how it unfolds.

The plan to sell Barragunyah will be put on hold. Gran will begin her rehabilitation at Lurradallan, and I will return to work. Six months later, Gran and Agnes will come to live with me. The move will not be easy for them. They will miss Barragunyah, miss their independence, talk about returning when Gran recovers. We will muddle along as well as we can for a year until Agnes is diagnosed with cancer. In four months, she will be gone. A week after her funeral, Gran will have a second stroke.

Putting Gran in a nursing home was the hardest decision I've ever had to make, but I didn't know what else to do. She was ninety. She couldn't walk or feed or bathe herself. She could barely speak. This was the person I loved more than anyone in the world, but I had neither the time nor the skills to provide the attention she required.

Stuart said a nursing home was the only choice. But he would say that, wouldn't he?

Yes, him. The accidental father of the little alien growing inside me.

When Gran and Agnes came to live with me, I expected my social life, narrow though it was, to shrink even more. I certainly gave no thought to romance. Yet somehow this recently divorced man I had known as a colleague for two years, wormed his way into my heart and my bed.

To be honest, I didn't resist too hard. Much as I loved Gran and Agnes, it was a relief to occasionally escape the medical schedules and dietary requirements of old women. I got into the habit of staying at his place a couple of nights a week, enjoying a glass of wine, letting him cook for me. I liked Stuart, liked his lovemaking, his sense of humour, his intellect. In fact, I was well on the way to falling in love with him when Agnes became ill.

It was all downhill from there.

Gran and Agnes looked after each other while I was at work, but I couldn't leave them alone at night. Instead of understanding, Stuart sulked, became more demanding, then disappeared off my radar for a while. To give him credit, he came to Agnes's funeral, and he was at my side when Gran was taken to hospital, but within days, before I even knew the prognosis, he was urging me to put her in a nursing home.

He wasn't the only one. Peter flew up from Melbourne, visited Gran once, then said the same. As did her doctors. I knew it was the sensible thing to do, but what does sense have to do with love? They didn't know Gran like I did, didn't know her strength and wisdom, the trials she'd overcome, the independent life she had lived. In the end, when I made the choice, it felt like a betrayal.

Gran lingered in that place for over a year. Sometimes when I visited, she knew who I was. Sometimes she called me Annie, sometimes recognition escaped her altogether. Conversation was difficult, but she seemed to find the sound of my voice soothing when I read to her or told her about my day. Mostly I just sat with her, brushed her hair, smoothed lotion into her work-worn hands. Each time, after I left her, I sat in my car and cried.

Then I went home to Stuart.

You know the rest.

Except for this. The day before Gran died, she told me she wanted to go home. Her words were hard to understand, but there was no doubting what she meant.

# GINA

The darkness fell suddenly, as if a violent storm was on the way. In the distance, Gina could see lights from the house shining through the gloom, showing her the way home. She smiled, picturing their surprise when she walked in; she had been away so long they'd probably given up on her. She stopped for a minute, puzzled. How long, exactly? It seemed like years, but when she tried to put a time to it, she felt confused. And when she thought about it, she wasn't even sure where she'd been. Or why. Why would she leave Barragunyah? She sighed and the unanswered questions drifted away, forgotten in an instant.

The lights were closer now, yet as she trudged towards them Gina wondered if she would make it. She couldn't recall ever being so tired, each step an effort, as if she were slogging through thick mud. She thought about calling for help, but something told her the darkness would swallow her voice and spit her words back at her. Keep going, she told herself, you'll soon be home.

The word made her feel better. *Home.* How she'd missed it. She hadn't liked that other place although she knew they'd done their best to make her comfortable. She frowned, trying to remember who *they* were and where that other place was. But it didn't matter now. She was almost there.

She climbed the steps to the veranda and crossed the worn boards, peering through the glass in the French doors, taking a moment alone to prepare herself.

Ellen was in the kitchen and she turned, smiling, as Alice came in. Gina was pleased to see her mother looking so well; there was a lightness about her that Gina hadn't seen for years. As for Alice – well, wasn't it odd that Alice and Ellen looked to be around the same age? Not much older than she, Gina, in fact, and she was, what? Forty? Fifty? She couldn't remember. It was becoming harder to shake free of the fog clouding her thoughts.

Mac was standing by the Aga warming her hands, waiting for the kettle to boil. Gina felt a little shock at how suddenly she'd appeared but was no longer surprised she looked the same age as Alice and Ellen. Despite Mac's taller stature, and the wiry ginger hair that contrasted with Ellen's blonde and Alice's brunette, the three might have been sisters. And I'm the fourth sister, she thought, the one they're waiting for.

Gina pulled at the door, astonished to find it locked. Since when did doors get locked at Barragunyah? She tapped the glass, and when that drew no response, banged on the timber frame. Why were they ignoring her? Surely they could hear the racket she was making?

She watched Mac bring the teapot to the table while Ellen got cups and saucers from the cupboard. Alice opened the biscuit tin, offering it around as they sat talking and laughing.

Gina rattled the door. She was close to tears. This was her home – why wouldn't they let her in? She shivered. It was darker now, and cold, making the warmth and light of the kitchen look more inviting. *Why are you surprised?* She turned to see Mary's silver eyes staring at her from the place where shadows were deepest. *You failed the task I set. It is up to the other one now, the last one. If she succeeds, the door will open for you.*

# JULIA

So here I am. The last of the Barragunyah women, diluted, watered down until I am nothing but a smudged afterword in the stories of my foremothers. And I'm tired of it. Tired of living between the lines of Barragunyah's narrative, tired of being her cipher, her prisoner, her plaything. Tired of rabbit stew.

I'm angry too. Angry enough to hit back, to make a statement of my own. Angry enough to bring the whole sorry shambles to an end.

And now, finally, I know how to do it.

It must be close to two weeks since the rain stopped. Most days have been warm and sunny, with a scent of spring in the air. The water in the creeks has receded, the muddy yard between house and woodshed has dried and hardened, the paddocks are flushed with green. I still cannot cross the causeway without finishing up in someone else's story, but I have better things to occupy the time I have left.

Instead of gathering chronicles, I'm gathering kindling.

I assemble all the remaining newspapers from the baskets beside the Aga and bring in what is left of the old dry wood from the shed. With these materials, I build a bonfire on the living room floor, layering it with old magazines I found in a cupboard. Then I carefully tuck all my other gatherings through the pyre – journals, albums, cardboard boxes of letters and photographs, magazine cuttings, tissue paper. Right at the top, like a star on a Christmas tree, I place Gina's wedding dress.

I hunt through the shed and find some half-empty fuel cans. The two large ones are labelled diesel, another smells like petrol, and I'm fairly sure the three small rusty cans contain kerosene. I make several trips with a wheelbarrow to transport everything back to the house. By then it's almost dark.

Perfect.

I can't lift the drums of diesel, so I just tip them, pouring the syrupy liquid through the paper and firewood on the lowest layer of my construct, where it spreads to form oily patches on the wooden floor. The petrol and kerosene I splash even-handedly over the rest, saving the last of it for the wedding dress. I hear someone sobbing as fuel soaks into the cream silk and antique lace.

I think it might be me.

All I need now is a match and a rag-wrapped stick soaked in kerosene.

The vapours from the petrol might explode, but I'm ready for that. Before my flaming torch hits the pile, I'm running from the house as if the hounds of hell are after me. Perhaps they are.

My hands are empty. I have taken nothing, not the tiniest memento. I'm wearing the clothes I came in – jeans, t-shirt, parka, sneakers. Without looking back, I race into the night until I judge that I'm safe to enjoy my handiwork. Then I turn to bear witness.

The blaze is magnificent.

I've left the French doors to the living room open to let in the breeze, and flames are already licking at the veranda. The windows in my bedroom are glowing red and orange and yellow. I hear glass shattering and see flames leap free from several other windows. Within the inferno, I glimpse the shadowy shapes of Barragunyah's trapped phantoms.

The fire is roaring now, leaping high into the night sky—even at this safe distance I can feel the heat on my face. I'm pretty sure that my handiwork will be visible to people on surrounding properties. Perhaps someone will come to inspect the damage.

I settle down on the grass and lean back on my elbows. It is a large house, old and stubborn; it will take a while to turn to ashes.

But I can wait.

By dawn, the house that John Larson built is nothing but buckled sheets of roofing iron, a mangled Aga, and a few smouldering beams. I walk the perimeter of scorched earth, checking to make sure that nothing has escaped.

Mary is doing her own assessment. Her silver eyes meet mine and this time I don't look away. *Is it done?*

The ghost of a smile crosses her face. Then she is gone.

As I turn my back on Barragunyah and head for the causeway, the golden silence of early morning is shattered by a clattering, mechanical sound and in the distance, I see a helicopter coming over the horizon. A little late to put out the fire, but just in time for me.

Deep inside my body I feel a flutter of butterfly wings. *Hang in there, baby,* I whisper. *We're home free.*

# ACKNOWLEDGEMENTS

As this is a book about family generations, I want to start by acknowledging the contributions of my own family. First, to my mother whose stories permeated my childhood, and to my father who made me dig deep for his. Special thanks to my daughter, Diana Kidd, whose sharp intellect and blunt tongue challenge me to do my best work, and to my son, Scott Linden Jones, whose encouragement never fails to spur me on when I falter. Thanks too, to my grandsons – Josh Kidd, for his excellent techie help, and Ben Kidd, for interesting conversations about cover designs. And not forgetting Norm, who always supported my desire to write even though he thought I was crazy.

To my friend and fellow writer, Marie Matthews, always my first go-to reader, thanks once again for an honest and thoughtful critique on a (very) rough draft. Thanks too, to my friends in Tamborine Mountain Library's Last Thursday Book Club, Lorraine Slater, Susan Lochran, and Gisela Meehl, whose insightful comments helped me rethink some awkward storylines and helped make this a better book.

Shawline Publishing Group Pty Ltd
www.shawlinepublishing.com.au

More great Shawline titles can be found here:

New titles also available through Books@Home Pty Ltd.
Subscribe today - www.booksathome.com.au